Saros Cowasjee teaches English at the University of Regina. Before going to Canada in 1963, he was for two years an Assistant Editor with the Times of India Press, Bombay. Educated in India and England, he has published several critical studies, three novels and has edited two collections of short stories.

By the same author

Novels

Goodbye to Elsa
Nude Therapy
Suffer Little Children

Criticism

Sean O'Casey: the Man Behind the Plays
O'Casey
*So Many Freedoms: A Study of the Major Fiction of Mulk
Raj Anand*

Collection

More Stories from the Raj and After (editor)

Stories from the Raj

from Kipling to Independence

*Selected and Introduced by Saros Cowasjee
with a Preface by Paul Theroux*

**TRIAD
GRAFTON BOOKS**

LONDON GLASGOW
TORONTO SYDNEY AUCKLAND

Triad
Grafton Books
8 Grafton Street, London W1X 3LA

Published by Triad Grafton 1983
Reprinted 1985, 1987

Triad Paperbacks Ltd is an imprint of
Chatto, Bodley Head & Jonathan Cape Ltd and
Grafton Books, A Division of the Collins Publishing Group

This edition first published in Great Britain by
The Bodley Head 1982
This selection, introduction and preface copyright ©
The Bodley Head 1982

ISBN 0-586-05625-4

Printed and bound in Great Britain by
Collins, Glasgow

Set in Plantin

To the memory of my Father

CONTENTS

ACKNOWLEDGEMENTS

Thanks are due to the following copyright-holders for permission
to reprint the stories listed:
'Lispeth' and 'The Head of the District' by Rudyard Kipling (The
National Trust and Macmillan London Ltd.); 'The Honour of Daud
Khan' by Lionel James (William Blackwood and Sons Ltd.); 'Pearls
and Swine' by Leonard Woolf (Mrs. M. T. Parsons and The Hogarth
Press Ltd.); 'The Widow' by Katherine Mayo (the Estate of the late
Katherine Mayo and Jonathan Cape Ltd.); 'Shooting an Elephant'
and 'A Hanging' by George Orwell (the Estate of the late George
Orwell and Martin Secker and Warburg Ltd.); 'The Fearless Will
Always Have It' by Joseph Hitrec (William Morris Agency, Inc.);
'A Game of Halma' by Christine Weston (the author); 'Karma' by
Khushwant Singh (the author).
Every effort has been made to trace the owners of copyright material
but in some cases we have not been successful. We apologise to
anyone our enquiries did not reach and invite them to apply to
The Bodley Head for proper acknowledgement, if it is due.

EDITOR'S NOTE

The editor thanks the Public Services Division of the University of
Regina Library for help received.

The date of first publication, as far as it has been ascertainable,
appears in parentheses at the end of each story.

PREFACE

Paul Theroux

Even the plainest tale from the hills is full of local colour. But the colour in these stories is not the pink princely India — silks, incense, temples and ceremonials. This is the India of demons and civil servants, burdened white men and frenzied natives (and frenzied white men and burdened natives). Many of the authors show a marked preference for fakirs and Pathans, blood feuds and fatal misunderstandings. Life is hard for their characters, and death is usually sudden and violent — the hacked-off head, the sting of the poisonous centipede. Even when the theme is Duty the deaths are awful: in 'The Rise of Ram Din' a man is starved to death in a go-down, and in 'The Crime of Narsingji' there is mass murder. This is to say nothing of the hangings (two), beheadings (two), or the many instances of madness. Culturally speaking, the twain seldom meet here, and when they do the result is often disastrous. Almost every story contains a cruel irony.

That, I think, is the effect of Kipling. He is the poet of colonial ironies and cruelties. He was not a reformer, but a witness. He has every right to come first in this collection, because each of the stories that follow his were written in his shadow: he began the short story tradition in India. Flora Annie Steel was so keenly aware of Kipling, her biographer Violet Powell tells us, that she 'rarely mentioned him'. (Yet Kipling's father illustrated Mrs Steel's first book of stories.) There are Kiplingesque touches in many of the other stories. Orwell said that Kipling was his favourite poet. The only story that is not in the Kipling mode is Katherine Mayo's 'The Widow', but this is a tendentious anti-Gandhi story, written in the 1920s. Its sarcasm and slant will surprise anyone who has the usual regard for Gandhi's piety and code of *satyagraha*:

> In the very streets of the capital secret plotters and killers vied with open assassins to terrorise all who opposed the will of the new-made saint, Gandhi, then at the zenith of his power. And though the saint himself continued to preach 'non-violence' his speech, day by day, was the speech that breeds hatred and destruction and drives simple folk to the spilling of blood.

The blame for the nastiness (humiliation, assault, suicide) is laid at Gandhi's door and is a kind of preparation for the chuckling Burmese magistrate in 'A Hanging' and Orwell's confiding in 'Shooting an Elephant':

> . . . I was stuck between my hatred of the empire I served and my rage against the evil-spirited little beasts who tried to make my job impossible. With one part of my mind I thought of the British Raj as an unbreakable tyranny . . . with another part I thought that the greatest joy in the world would be to drive a bayonet in a Buddhist priest's guts.

Reformers, nationalists and boxwallahs get a rough ride in these stories. No one is ridiculed more heartily than Grish Chunder Dé, M.A., the educated Bengali in Kipling's 'The Head of the District'. He talks of Oxford and 'Home' and the bump-suppers, cricket matches and hunting-runs he has read about in books. This poor man is an easy mark, of course, but what is more interesting is the way Kipling finds fault with him. 'We must get these fellows in hand,' the nervous Indian says; 'get them well in hand, and drive them on a tight rein. No use, you know, being slack with your District.' Englishmen who say this sort of thing in Kipling stories are stout-hearted leaders; Indians who say it are cowards and mimics. But Kipling was reflecting a common prejudice: the educated Tamil, the bespectacled Bengali, the nationalistic Gujerati – they were laughable; but the dauntless Pathan with his trusty Lee-Enfield and his code of 'death before dishonour' was a fully admirable figure, even when he was leading a charge against you.

It is perhaps not so astonishing that English-speaking Indians, the Empire's children (or rather orphans), were despised and the inflexible Pathans and tribal warriors on the frontier praised; there is lip-service but there are few illusions here about the wisdom of colonial rule. Look at little Lispeth, baptised and anglicised, and fiendishly deceived by the chaplain's wife. In other stories, colonial civilisation means that when the Reformer's wife is unveiled her pockmarks will be evident; that at the school prize-giving the 15-year-old (and married) Mussumât Kirpo will be handed a doll; that the English parents in 'The Centipede' are responsible for the death of their infant because they don't believe in the native mumbo-jumbo, and that Ram Din will become a powerful servant because his English sahib is a bully and a moral coward. In Orwell's eyes, the Raj made him a collaborator in a brutal hanging and a spineless elephant-killer. No wonder British writers in India respected the unvanquished Pathans! In Leonard Woolf's story, the British sahibs are the dregs of the earth, and in 'The Dancing Fakir' by John Eyton the transformation is complete: the Englishman has turned into a sponging and facile native.

One of the most surprising stories in this collection shares none of these characteristics. There is no violence in 'A Mother in India', no crime, no blood, not much local colour, not even any Indians – the 'big fat spider of a money-lender' in the first paragraph has no name. And yet this is as vivid a tale of the Raj as any in the book. What a wonderful story of mother and daughter, and how thoroughly colonial the estrangements of their situation. The mother's values are those of the Raj; she is downright and practical and bold – a soldier's wife. The daughter, who has been raised in England, is inexperienced, and a little timid and insipid – a born spinster. Sara Jeannette Duncan's story is full of subtleties, and completely sensible. It is one of the best stories here – it is also the only truly humorous one.

Apart from Kipling and Orwell, the authors here are not household names. Flora Annie Steel's best-selling novel of the Mutiny, *On the Face of the Waters* (1896), is no longer obtainable and is probably unread. Katherine Mayo is known for *Mother India* not *Slaves of the Gods*, and Leonard Woolf's talent as a novelist (*The Village in the Jungle*, a powerful portrait of Ceylonese life, is a disturbing masterpiece) has been overshadowed – unfairly, I think – by that of his wife.

Saros Cowasjee has rendered us a great service by disinterring these stories and bringing so many of these writers out of an undeserved obscurity. Amazingly, half of them are women. These are more than documents of a dead past, and colourful stories of a half-forgotten time; they are part of the romance and terror of India, which was also an English adventure, made accessible and lighted by the imagination.

INTRODUCTION

Saros Cowasjee

This anthology of short stories has been put together to question the oft-repeated assertions by critics that Anglo-Indian* fiction has little of literary value outside Kipling, Forster and Orwell. Since Forster's fiction on the subject is confined to *A Passage to India* and Orwell's to *Burmese Days* and a couple of short stories, the field might seem to belong to Kipling alone. But this is far from being the case. Anglo-India produced a large body of work, perhaps the largest of any community in relation to its size. Granted that the bulk is mediocre (a truism for literature anywhere in the world), there still remains much that is good by any standard of excellence. This selection by no means exhausts what is good; in my choice of stories I have restricted myself largely to fiction which shows interaction between the British and the Indian people. Such interaction is not so frequent as one might suppose, for Anglo-Indian writers were less interested in portraying Indians than in portraying their own lives and the physical India which they loved and hated in turn. Sara Jeannette Duncan brilliantly captures the tragedy of the English woman in 'A Mother in India', and Edmund Candler in 'Mecca' beautifully evokes the smell, the colour, and the vegetation of India. The Indians, with few exceptions, rarely appear as fully realised characters. Though in life they may have filled more varied roles, in much of early fiction they appear as cooks, bearers, ayahs, fakirs, and too frequently as

*The term 'Anglo-Indian' was applied originally to the British in India, and only later to people of mixed British and Indian descent. Here it is used in its original meaning. A good study of Anglo-Indian literature can be found in Allen J. Greenberger's *The British Image of India* (1969).

thugs and thieves. No wonder Edward Thompson felt that the Indians have been abused in Anglo-Indian fiction – an opinion with which many Indians, especially Hindus, would agree.

Although there are works of fiction that date back to the 1820s and even earlier, Anglo-Indian fiction began in earnest with Kipling. It came to an end with the dissolution of the Raj in 1947 – which brought independence to India, Burma and Ceylon. The stories in this anthology span some seventy years and are all set in India, save for the two Orwell stories which have Burma for their setting (Burma was very much a part of the British Raj and was for long administered from Calcutta). All the writers of the stories are British with the exception of Katherine Mayo, Joseph Hitrec and Khushwant Singh. Mayo and Hitrec, though not British, are in their attitude and approach to India completely un-Indian and their inclusion in this anthology poses no problems. But Khushwant Singh needs special pleading. He is an Indian and his story 'Karma' – though conceived and written in 1943 – was first published in 1948, one year after my cutting off date. Both these factors should have led to his exclusion, but I decided otherwise. I felt that a story about the Raj by an Indian might offer the British reader a contrasting view, and Khushwant Singh's was the only one that met my literary criteria of selection. The story deals with a legacy the British gave to India: the Westernised Indian, the 'brown Sahibs' as they are comically known today. The joke is, however, not at the cost of Sir Mohan Lal alone and his attempts to go British. The two tommies, representatives of the King who find the King's English befuddling, are equally ridiculous.

This anthology, among other things, reveals the British attitudes towards India and how they went through a radical change over the years. But the stories have been selected primarily for their literary qualities and only secondarily for their social importance. This explains why certain features of British life in India are totally absent: we have no picture of British club life, no summers in Simla, no polo matches, no tiger hunts, no princes, no pigsticking. The insistence on literary merit explains to some extent the omission of three of Anglo-India's most prolific writers: Bithia Mary Croker, F.E.F. Penny and Ethel W. Savi. These three women together turned out close to a hundred and fifty novels, but they lacked the style and craftsmanship of the two major women writers of the period – Flora Annie Steel and Alice Perrin. I hope that their stories in this volume will lead to a renewed interest in their works, for both writers have something of Kipling's genius without his pungency.

A systematic study of Anglo-Indian fiction shows a movement from confidence in the Raj to a mood of doubt and despair. This is borne out by the stories in this selection. At one end of the spectrum we have Kipling's 'The Head of the District'. Its message is clear: the British are brave, resourceful and ordained to rule. They have no choice in the matter – they must rule India even if they don't want to. Who else should rule India? Certainly not the Indians – the Indian people themselves won't accept one of their own to govern them. Says a Pathan to an English officer when a Bengali is put in charge of the district: 'But, O Sahib, has the Government gone mad to send a black Bengali dog to us? And am I to pay service to such an one? And are you to work under him? What does it mean?'

At the other end of the spectrum is George Orwell. He questions the very ethics of one nation governing another and describes the British Raj as an 'unbreakable tyranny'. The white man's life in the East, he concludes, is one long attempt not to be laughed at. In 'Shooting an Elephant', the narrator is forced into killing an animal he no longer regards as dangerous, simply because this is what the crowd watching expects him to do. The story shows the cumulative effect of the 'native' will pitted against a ruling white minority. In a ceaseless effort to impress those whom he governs, the white man begins to wear a mask, 'and his face grows to fit it'. The ruler, thus, becomes the ruled. In ruling others, it is his own freedom he destroys.

Though sharply opposed in their views, the pro-Raj and the anti-Raj writers had this in common: they drew their conclusions from what effect the British rule had on the rulers themselves. Kipling felt that the Empire was valuable chiefly in that it provided the British with an opportunity for self-development. Orwell felt that the Empire was evil, for among other things it debased the British character. Ironically, neither group seriously concerned itself with what British rule did to India − neither was interested in the Indians for their own sake. It is therefore not surprising that those who opposed the Raj did not necessarily show the Indians in a more favourable light than those who supported the Raj. However, with the emergence of the anti-Raj writers, the British themselves began to be less flatteringly portrayed. This can be seen in Christine Weston's 'A Game of Halma', where the domiciled Englishman is portrayed as a bully. But the most scathing portrayal of an Englishman appears in Leonard Woolf's 'Pearls and Swine' − a story very closely modelled, both in the manner of its narration and in the depiction of its central character, on Conrad's *Heart of Darkness*.

A good many of the stories in this anthology do not deal overtly with the question of the Raj. Even Kipling's 'The Head of the District' transcends its political purpose to show the hardships of life on the Frontier and the British admiration for its warlike tribesmen. It also shows the Indians as irresponsible children (a common British view) who are, with a few exceptions, most acceptable when supervised by their British nurse. Leonard Woolf's 'Pearls and Swine' goes beyond the portrayal of a detribalised Englishman to show the love-hate relationship that some Englishmen felt for India. It also gives a vivid account of how death and disease stalked the sub-continent. And Orwell in his 'Shooting an Elephant' does not stop with his criticism of imperialism, but goes on to plead for the sanctity of life – a major theme in his writing. His 'A Hanging' is perhaps the most powerful indictment of capital punishment in English literature.

What of some of the other stories in this volume? In 'A Mother in India', Sara Jeannette Duncan presents, in a quiet tone and with biting irony, the heart-rending plight of a mother forced by circumstances to send her child to England. More painful than the initial separation is the alienation that follows. Helena is on a visit to England to see her daughter after a separation of five years. She is led to her child sleeping in a crib. 'Won't you kiss her?' one of the child's well-meaning guardians asks the visiting mother. 'I don't think I could take such an advantage of her,' says the mother.

Just as Sara Jeannette Duncan gives us a glimpse into the hard life of English women in India, Flora Annie Steel, Katherine Mayo and Maud Diver give us an insight into the tragic lot of Indian women. Both Steel and Mayo write from knowledge and both claim authenticity for their respective sketches, 'The Reformer's Wife' and 'The Widow', but the venom shines through Mayo's portrayal, while Steel's is laced with sympathy and understanding. Maud Diver's 'The Gods of the East' touches on the problems of Indian women only obliquely. Its aim is to show, in the author's own words, 'the Hindu's innate love of the horrible and the grim'. Despite this, the principal character – a Brahman priest – is portrayed with considerable dignity, and the story moves to its conclusion with the inevitability of a Greek tragedy.

Though the Indian National Congress was founded in 1885, the Indian nationalists did not appear in Anglo-Indian fiction until Edmund Candler's *Siri Ram, Revolutionist* (1912). Since then they have generally been portrayed in an unfriendly light − even by the anti-Raj writers. John Eyton in 'The Dancing Fakir' and Joseph Hitrec in 'The Fearless Will Always Have It' show them as cowards who are motivated by self-interest. They are quick to flee in the face of danger. The main thrust of Eyton's story, however, is not to belittle the nationalists, but to show what happens when an Englishman goes 'native'. Eyton is quick to point out that even in a detribalised Englishman like Jackson there remains a residue of goodness, and that in a crisis he will, like any true Englishman, stand up for his own people. Otto Rothfeld's 'The Crime of Narsingji' demonstrates the respect the British had for the martial races − in this case the Rajputs. What if Narsingji had killed five people? Weren't those he killed cowardly and 'base-born' Indians? And isn't Narsingji loyal and obedient to the Raj? We are not told what sentence was handed down to Narsingji, but in this particular case it is just as well we do not know.

Among the authors represented in this anthology, the neglect of Alice Perrin is the most difficult to understand. Her stories are cleverly crafted; Indian idioms are translated, not literally, but with a feel for the English language. A brilliant satirist, she portrays the English and the Indians with a fine eye for the comic and the eccentric. Without revealing any of her own biases, she shows the mutual contempt the two races often had for each other. In 'The Rise of Ram Din' when the son asks his father what he should do when a sahib beats him for no fault of his own, the father advises:

'Take thy beating and say nothing. Above all things, do not run away. The Feringhees themselves are brave, though they are dogs and sons of dogs, and when they behold courage in others do they respect it. A beating does little harm. I lived once with a colonel-sahib who gave medicine as a punishment, and that was bad.'

In 'The Centipede' when the ayah is told that her Indian cure for fever (a centipede fried in clarified butter and applied to the forehead) has contributed to the death of her ward, she dismisses the charge with assured self-confidence and sublime haughtiness:

'The babba died? Yes. But had the mem-sahib not screamed and clutched her when she beheld the evil one, the child would have slept on and awakened cured. The centipede that had issued forth from her ear would have crawled away doing no harm. Whereas the mem-sahib endeavoured to pluck it away, and so, as is the custom of its kind, the creature clung with its poison feet, which are as red-hot wires. Thus it all happened through the foolishness and ignorance of the white people, who think they know all and that the dark people know nothing – '

With its dead-pan humour, its incisive irony, and the splendid audacity of its narrator who is aware of how much she has been censured, this story would be an ornament to any anthology.

Giving reasons why Anglo-Indian novelists seldom obtained a wide hearing in England, Edward F. Oaten wrote:

A concomitant cause of their ill-success in England was their disregard of the well-known, if lamentable, fact, that in things Indian, *qua* India, English people are, or were, profoundly uninterested.

This was in 1908, when the Raj was at its peak. Since then the Raj has vanished. What is being offered here is not 'things Indian' or things English, but the literature that came from the meeting of the two races — sometimes happily, sometimes unhappily.

University of Regina
Regina, Canada, 1982

RUDYARD KIPLING

Lispeth

Look, you have cast out Love! What Gods are these
    You bid me please?
The Three in One, the One in Three? Not so!
To my own Gods I go.
It may be they shall give me greater ease
Than your cold Christ and tangled Trinities.

She was the daughter of Sonoo, a Hill-man of the Himalayas,
and Jadéh his wife. One year their maize failed, and two bears
spent the night in their only opium poppy-field just above the
Sutlej Valley on the Kotgarh side; so, next season, they
turned Christian, and brought their baby to the Mission to be
baptised. The Kotgarh Chaplain christened her Elizabeth,
and 'Lispeth' is the Hill or *pahari* pronunciation.

Later cholera came into the Kotgarh Valley and carried off
Sonoo and Jadéh, and Lispeth became half servant, half
companion, to the wife of the then Chaplain of Kotgarh. This
was after the reign of the Moravian missionaries in that place,
but before Kotgarh had quite forgotten her title of 'Mistress
of the Northern Hills'.

Whether Christianity improved Lispeth, or whether the
gods of her own people would have done as much for her
under any circumstances, I do not know; but she grew very
lovely. When a Hill-girl grows lovely, she is worth travelling
fifty miles over bad ground to look upon. Lispeth had a
Greek face — one of those faces people paint so often, and see
so seldom. She was of a pale, ivory colour, and, for her race,

extremely tall. Also, she possessed eyes that were wonderful; and, had she not been dressed in the abominable print-cloths affected by Missions, you would, meeting her on the hillside unexpectedly, have thought her the original Diana of the Romans going out to slay.

Lispeth took to Christianity readily, and did not abandon it when she realized womanhood, as do some Hill-girls. Her own people hated her because she had, they said, become a white woman and washed herself daily; and the Chaplain's wife did not know what to do with her. One cannot ask a stately goddess, five foot ten in her shoes, to clean plates and dishes. She played with the Chaplain's children and took classes in the Sunday School, and read all the books in the house, and grew more and more beautiful, like the Princess in fairy tales. The Chaplain's wife said that the girl ought to take service in Simla as a nurse or something 'genteel'. But Lispeth did not want to take service. She was very happy where she was.

When travellers — there were not many in those years — came in to Kotgarh, Lispeth used to lock herself into her own room for fear they might take her away to Simla, or out into the unknown world.

One day, a few months after she was seventeen years old, Lispeth went out for a walk. She did not walk in the manner of English ladies — a mile and a half out, with a carriage-ride back again. She covered between twenty and thirty miles in her little constitutionals, all about and about, between Kotgarh and Narkunda. This time she came back at full dusk, stepping down the breakneck descent into Kotgarh with something heavy in her arms. The Chaplain's wife was dozing in the drawing-room when Lispeth came in breathing heavily and very exhausted with her burden. Lispeth put it down on the sofa, and said simply, 'This is my husband. I found him on the Bagi Road. He has hurt himself. We will nurse him, and when he is well, your husband shall marry him to me.'

This was the first mention Lispeth had ever made of her matrimonial views, and the Chaplain's wife shrieked with horror. However, the man on the sofa needed attention first. He was a young Englishman, and his head had been cut to the bone by something jagged. Lispeth said she had found him down the hillside, and had brought him in. He was breathing queerly and was unconscious.

He was put to bed and tended by the Chaplain, who knew something of medicine; and Lispeth waited outside the door in case she could be useful. She explained to the Chaplain that this was the man she meant to marry; and the Chaplain and his wife lectured her severely on the impropriety of her conduct. Lispeth listened quietly, and repeated her first proposition. It takes a great deal of Christianity to wipe out uncivilised Eastern instincts, such as falling in love at first sight. Lispeth, having found the man she worshipped, did not see why she should keep silent as to her choice. She had no intention of being sent away, either. She was going to nurse that Englishman until he was well enough to marry her. This was her programme.

After a fortnight of slight fever and inflammation, the Englishman recovered coherence and thanked the Chaplain and his wife, and Lispeth – especially Lispeth – for their kindness. He was a traveller in the East, he said – they never talked about 'globe-trotters' in those days, when the P. & O. fleet was young and small – and had come from Dehra Dun to hunt for plants and butterflies among the Simla hills. No one at Simla, therefore, knew anything about him. He fancied that he must have fallen over the cliff while reaching out for a fern on a rotten tree-trunk, and that his coolies must have stolen his baggage and fled. He thought he would go back to Simla when he was a little stronger. He desired no more mountaineering.

He made small haste to go away, and recovered his strength slowly. Lispeth objected to being advised either by the Chaplain or his wife; therefore the latter spoke to the Englishman, and told him how matters stood in Lispeth's heart. He laughed a good deal and said it was very pretty and romantic, but, as he was engaged to a girl at Home, he fancied that nothing would happen. Certainly he would behave with discretion. He did that. Still he found it very pleasant to talk to Lispeth, and walk with Lispeth and say nice things to her, and call her pet names, while he was getting strong enough to go away. It meant nothing at all to him, and everything in the world to Lispeth. She was very happy while the fortnight lasted, because she had found a man to love.

Being a savage by birth, she took no trouble to hide her feelings, and the Englishman was amused. When he went away, Lispeth walked with him up the Hill as far as Narkunda, very troubled and very miserable. The Chaplain's wife, being a good Christian and disliking anything in the shape of fuss or scandal — Lispeth was beyond her management entirely — had told the Englishman to tell Lispeth that he was coming back to marry her. 'She is but a child, you know, and, I fear, at heart a heathen,' said the Chaplain's wife. So all the twelve miles up the Hill the Englishman, with his arm round Lispeth's waist, was assuring the girl that he would come back to marry her; and Lispeth made him promise over and over again. She wept on the Narkunda Ridge till he had passed out of sight along the Muttiani path.

Then she dried her tears and went in to Kotgarh again, and said to the Chaplain's wife, 'He will come back and marry me. He has gone to his own people to tell them so.' And the Chaplain's wife soothed Lispeth and said, 'He will come back.' At the end of two months, Lispeth grew impatient, and was told that the Englishman had gone over the seas to England. She knew where England was, because she had read little geography primers; but, of course, she had no conception of the nature of the sea, being a Hill-girl. There was an old puzzle-map of the World in the house. Lispeth had played with it when she was a child. She unearthed it again, and put it together of evenings, and cried to herself, and tried to imagine where her Englishman was. As she had no ideas of distance or steamboats, her notions were some-what wild. It would not have made the least difference had she been perfectly correct; for the Englishman had no inten-tion of coming back to marry a Hill-girl. He forgot all about her by the time he was butterfly-hunting in Assam. He wrote a book on the East afterwards. Lispeth's name did not appear there.

At the end of three months, Lispeth made daily pilgrimage to Narkunda to see if her Englishman was coming along the road. It gave her comfort, and the Chaplain's wife finding her happier thought that she was getting over her 'barbarous and most indelicate folly'. A little later, the walks ceased to help Lispeth and her temper grew very bad. The Chaplain's wife thought this a profitable time to let her know the real state of affairs — that the Englishman had only promised his love to keep her quiet — that he had never meant anything, and that it was wrong and improper of Lispeth to think of marriage with an Englishman, who was of a superior clay, besides being promised in marriage to a girl of his own people. Lispeth said that all this was clearly impossible because he had said he loved her, and the Chaplain's wife had, with her own lips, asserted that the Englishman was coming back.

'How can what he and you said be untrue?' asked Lispeth.

'We said it as an excuse to keep you quiet, child,' said the Chaplain's wife.

'Then you have lied to me,' said Lispeth, 'you and he?'

The Chaplain's wife bowed her head, and said nothing. Lispeth was silent, too, for a little time; then she went out down the valley, and returned in the dress of a Hill-girl – infamously dirty, but without the nose-stud and ear-rings. She had her hair braided into the long pigtail, helped out with black thread, that Hill-women wear.

'I am going back to my own people,' said she. 'You have killed Lispeth. There is only left old Jadéh's daughter – the daughter of a *pahari* and the servant of Tarka Devi. You are all liars, you English.'

By the time the Chaplain's wife had recovered from the shock of the announcement that Lispeth had 'verted to her mother's gods, the girl had gone; and she never came back.

She took to her own unclean people savagely, as if to make up the arrears of the life she had stepped out of; and, in a little time, she married a woodcutter who beat her after the manner of *paharis*, and her beauty faded soon.

'There is no law whereby you can account for the vagaries of the heathen,' said the Chaplain's wife, 'and I believe that Lispeth was always at heart an infidel.' Seeing she had been taken into the Church of England at the mature age of five weeks, this statement does not do credit to the Chaplain's wife.

Lispeth was a very old woman when she died. She had always a perfect command of English, and when she was sufficiently drunk, could sometimes be induced to tell the story of her first love-affair.

It was hard then to realise that the bleared, wrinkled creature, exactly like a wisp of charred rag, could ever have been 'Lispeth of the Kotgarh Mission'.

(1888)

RUDYARD KIPLING
The Head of the District

There's a convict more in the Central Jail,
Behind the old mud wall;
There's a lifter less on the Border trail,
And the Queen's Peace over all,
Dear boys,
The Queen's Peace over all!

For we must bear our leader's blame,
On us the shame will fall,
If we lift our hand from a fettered land
And the Queen's Peace over all,
Dear boys,
The Queen's Peace over all!

The Indus had risen in flood without warning. Last night it was a fordable shallow; to-night five miles of raving muddy water parted bank and caving bank, and the river was still rising under the moon. A litter borne by six bearded men, all unused to the work, stopped in the white sand that bordered the whiter plain.

'It's God's will,' they said. 'We dare not cross to-night, even in a boat. Let us light a fire and cook food. We be tired men.'

They looked at the litter inquiringly. Within, the Deputy-Commissioner of the Kot-Kumharsen District lay dying of fever. They had brought him across country, six fighting men of a Frontier clan that he had won over to the paths of a moderate righteousness, when he had broken down at the foot of their inhospitable hills. And Tallantire, his Assistant, rode with them, heavy-hearted as heavy-eyed with sorrow and lack of sleep. He had served under the sick man for three years, and had learned to love him as men associated in toil of the hardest learn to love — or hate. Dropping from his horse he parted the curtains of the litter and peered inside.

'Orde — Orde, old man, can you hear? We have to wait till the river goes down, worse luck.'

'I hear,' returned a dry whisper. 'Wait till the river goes down. I thought we should reach camp before the dawn. Polly knows. She'll meet me.'

One of the litter-men stared across the river and caught a faint twinkle of light on the far side. He whispered to Tallantire, 'There are his camp-fires, and his wife. They will cross in the morning, for they have better boats. Can he live so long?'

Tallantire shook his head. Yardley-Orde was very near to death. What need to vex his soul with hopes of a meeting that could not be? The river gulped at the banks, brought down a cliff of sand, and snarled the more hungrily. The litter-men sought for fuel in the waste — dried camel-thorn and refuse of the camps that had waited at the ford. Their swordbelts clinked as they moved softly in the haze of the moonlight, and Tallantire's horse coughed to explain that he would like a blanket.

'I'm cold too,' said the voice from the litter. 'I fancy this is the end. Poor Polly!'

Tallantire rearranged the blankets; Khoda Dad Khan, seeing this, stripped off his own heavy-wadded sheepskin coat and added it to the pile. 'I shall be warm by the fire presently,' said he. Tallantire took the wasted body of his chief into his arms and held it against his breast. Perhaps if they kept him very warm Orde might live to see his wife once more. If only blind Providence would send a three-foot fall in the river!

'That's better,' said Orde faintly. 'Sorry to be a nuisance, but is — is there anything to drink?'

They gave him milk and whisky, and Tallantire felt a little warmth against his own breast. Orde began to mutter.

'It isn't that I mind dying,' he said. 'It's leaving Polly and the District. Thank God! we have no children. Dick, you know, I'm dipped — awfully dipped — debts in my first five years' service. It isn't much of a pension, but enough for her. She has her mother at home. Getting there is a difficulty. And — and — you see, not being a soldier's wife — '

'We'll arrange the passage home, of course,' said Tallantire quietly.

'It's not nice to think of sending round the hat; but, good Lord! how many men I lie here and remember that had to do it! Morten's dead — he was of my year. Shaughnessy is dead, and he had children; I remember he used to read us their school-letters; what a bore we thought him! Evans is dead — Kot-Kumharsen killed him! Ricketts of Myndonie is dead — and I'm going too. "Man that is born of a woman is small potatoes and few in the hill." That reminds me, Dick; the four Khusru Kheyl villages in our border want a one-third remittance this spring. That's fair; their crops are bad. See that they get it, and speak to Ferris about the canal. I should like to have lived till that was finished; it means so much for the North-Indus villages — but Ferris is an idle beggar — wake him up. You'll have charge of the District till my successor comes. I wish they would appoint you permanently; you know the folk. I suppose it will be Bullows, though. Good man, but too weak for Frontier work; and he doesn't understand the priests. The blind priest at Jagai will bear watching. You'll find it in my papers — in the uniform-case, I think. Call the Khusru Kheyl men up; I'll hold my last public audience. Khoda Dad Khan!'

The leader of the men sprang to the side of the litter, his companions following.

'Men, I'm dying,' said Orde quickly, in the vernacular; 'and soon there will be no more Orde Sahib to twist your tails and prevent you from raiding cattle.'

'God forbid this thing!' broke out the deep bass chorus. 'The Sahib is not going to die.'

'Yes, he is; and then he will know whether Mohammed speaks truth, or Moses. But you must be good men when I am not here. Such of you as live in our borders must pay your taxes quietly as before. I have spoken of the villages to be gently treated this year. Such of you as live in the hills must refrain from cattle-lifting, and burn no more thatch, and turn a deaf ear to the voice of the priests, who, not knowing the strength of the Government, would lead you into foolish wars, wherein you will surely die and your crops be eaten by strangers. And you must not sack any caravans, and must leave your arms at the Police post when you come in; as has been your custom, and my order. And Tallantire Sahib will be with you, but I do not know who takes my place. I speak now true talk, for I am as it were already dead, my children — for though ye be strong men, ye are children.'

'And thou art our father and our mother,' broke in Khoda Dad Khan with an oath. 'What shall we do, now there is no one to speak for us, or to teach us to go wisely?'

'There remains Tallantire Sahib. Go to him; he knows your talk and your heart. Keep the young men quiet, listen to the old men, and obey. Khoda Dad Khan, take my ring. The watch and chain go to thy brother. Keep those things for my sake, and I will speak to whatever God I may encounter and tell him that the Khusru Kheyl are good men. Ye have my leave to go.'

Khoda Dad Khan, the ring upon his finger, choked audibly as he caught the well-known formula that closed an interview. His brother turned to look across the river. The dawn was breaking, and a speck of white showed on the dull silver of the stream. 'She comes,' said the man under his breath. 'Can he live for another two hours?' And he pulled the newly-acquired watch out of his belt and looked uncomprehendingly at the dial as he had seen Englishmen do.

For two hours the bellying sail tacked and blundered up and down the river, Tallantire still clasping Orde in his arms, and Khoda Dad Khan chafing his feet. He spoke now and again of the District and his wife, but, as the end neared, more frequently of the latter. They hoped he did not know that she was even then risking her life in a crazy native boat to regain him. But the awful foreknowledge of the dying deceived them. Wrenching himself forward, Orde looked through the curtains and saw how near was the sail. 'That's Polly,' he said simply, though his mouth was wried with agony. 'Polly and − the grimmest practical joke ever played on a man. Dick − you'll − have − to − explain.'

And an hour later Tallantire met on the bank a woman in a gingham riding-habit and sun-hat who cried out to him for her husband − her boy and her darling − while Khoda Dad Khan threw himself face-down on the sand and covered his eyes.

II

The very simplicity of the notion was its charm. What more easy to win a reputation for far-seeing statesmanship, originality, and, above all, deference to the desires of the people, than by appointing a child of the country to the rule of that country? Two hundred millions of the most loving and grateful folk under Her Majesty's dominion would laud the fact, and their praise would endure for ever. Yet he was indifferent

to praise or blame, as befitted the Very Greatest of All the
Viceroys. His administration was based upon principle, and
the principle must be enforced in season and out of season.
His pen and tongue had created the New India, teeming with
possibilities – loud-voiced, insistent, a nation among nations
– all his very own. Wherefore the Very Greatest of All the
Viceroys took another step in advance, and with it counsel of
those who should have advised him on the appointment of a
successor to Yardley-Orde. There was a gentleman and a
member of the Bengal Civil Service who had won his place
and a university degree to boot in fair and open competition
with the sons of the English. He was cultured, of the world,
and, if report spoke truly, had wisely and, above all, sym-
pathetically ruled a crowded District in South-Eastern
Bengal. He had been to England and charmed many
drawing-rooms there. His name, if the Viceroy recollected
aright, was Mr Grish Chunder Dé, M.A. In short, did anybody see any objection to the appointment, always on principle, of a man of the people to rule the people? The District
in South-Eastern Bengal might with advantage, he appre-
hended, pass over to a younger civilian of Mr G.C. Dé's
nationality (who had written a remarkably clever pamphlet on
the political value of sympathy in administration); and Mr
G.C. Dé could be transferred northward to Kot-Kumharsen.
The Viceroy was averse, on principle, to interfering with
appointments under control of the Provincial Governments.
He wished it to be understood that he merely recommended
and advised in this instance. As regarded the mere question
of race, Mr Grish Chunder Dé was more English than the
English, and yet possessed of that peculiar sympathy and
insight which the best among the best Service in the world
could only win to at the end of their service.

The stern, black-bearded kings who sit about the Council-
board of India divided on the step, with the inevitable result

of driving the Very Greatest of All the Viceroys into the borders of hysteria, and a bewildered obstinacy pathetic as that of a child.

'The principle is sound enough,' said the weary-eyed Head of the Red Provinces in which Kot-Kumharsen lay, for he too held theories. 'The only difficulty is – '

'Put the screw on the District officials; brigade Dé with a very strong Deputy-commissioner on each side of him; give him the best Assistant in the Province; rub the fear of God into the people beforehand; and if anything goes wrong, say that his colleagues didn't back him up. All these lovely little experiments recoil on the District Officer in the end,' said the Knight of the Drawn Sword with a truthful brutality that made the Head of the Red Provinces shudder. And on a tacit understanding of this kind the transfer was accomplished, as quietly as might be for many reasons.

It is sad to think that what goes for public opinion in India did not generally see the wisdom of the Viceroy's appointment. There were not lacking indeed hireling organs, notoriously in the pay of a tyrannous bureaucracy, who more than hinted that His Excellency was a fool, a dreamer of dreams, a doctrinaire, and, worst of all, a trifler with the lives of men. The *Viceroy's Excellence Gazette*, published in Calcutta, was at pains to thank 'our beloved Viceroy for once more and again thus gloriously vindicating the potentialities of the Bengali nations for extended executive and administrative duties in foreign parts beyond our ken. We do not at all doubt that our excellent fellow-townsman, Mr Grish Chunder Dé, Esq., M.A., will uphold the prestige of the Bengali, notwithstanding what underhand intrigue and *peshbundi* may be set on foot to insidiously nip his fame and blast his prospects among the proud civilians, some of which will now have to serve under a despised native and take orders too. How will you like that, Misters? We entreat our beloved

Viceroy still to substantiate himself superiorly to race-prejudice and colour-blindness, and to allow the flower of his now *our* Civil Service all the full pays and allowances granted to his more fortunate brethren.'

III

'When does this man take over charge? I'm alone just now, and I gather that I'm to stand fast under him.'

'Would you have cared for a transfer?' said Bullows keenly. Then, laying his hand on Tallantire's shoulder: 'We're all in the same boat; don't desert us. And yet, why the devil should you stay, if you can get another charge?'

'It was Orde's,' said Tallantire simply.

'Well, it's Dé's now. He's a Bengali of the Bengalis, crammed with code and case law; a beautiful man so far as routine and desk-work go, and pleasant to talk to. They naturally have always kept him in his own home District, where all his sisters and his cousins and his aunts lived, somewhere south of Dacca. He did no more than turn the place into a pleasant little family preserve, allowed his subordinates to do what they liked, and let everybody have a chance at the shekels. Consequently he's immensely popular down there.'

'I've nothing to do with that. How on earth am I to explain to the District that they are going to be governed by a Bengali? Do you — does the Government, I mean — suppose that the Khusru Kheyl will sit quiet when they once know? What will the Mohammedan heads of villages say? How will the Police — Muzbi Sikhs and Pathans — how will *they* work under him? We couldn't say anything if the Government appointed a sweeper; but my people will say a good deal, you know that. It's a piece of cruel folly!'

'My dear boy, I know all that, and more. I've represented

it, and have been told that I am exhibiting "culpable and puerile prejudice". By Jove, if the Khusru Kheyl don't exhibit something worse than that I don't know the Border! The chances are that you will have the District alight on your hands, and I shall have to leave my work and help you pull through. I needn't ask you to stand by the Bengali man in every possible way. You'll do that for your own sake.'

'For Orde's. I can't say that I care twopence personally.'

'Don't be an ass. It's grievous enough, God knows, and the Government will know later on; but that's no reason for your sulking. *You* must try to run the District; *you* must stand between him and as much insult as possible; *you* must show him the ropes; *you* must pacify the Khusru Kheyl, and just warn Curbar of the Police to look out for trouble, by the way. I'm always at the end of a telegraph-wire, and willing to peril my reputation to hold the District together. You'll lose yours, of course. If you keep things straight, and he isn't actually beaten with a stick when he's on tour, he'll get all the credit. If anything goes wrong, you'll be told that you didn't support him loyally.'

'I know what I've got to do,' said Tallantire wearily, 'and I'm going to do it. But it's hard.'

'The work is with us, the event is with Allah — as Orde used to say when he was more than usually in hot water.' And Bullows rode away.

That two gentlemen in Her Majesty's Bengal Civil Service should thus discuss a third, also in that Service, and a cultured and affable man withal, seems strange and saddening. Yet listen to the artless babble of the Blind Mullah of Jagai, the priest of the Khusru Kheyl, sitting upon a rock overlooking the Border. Five years before, a chance-hurled shell from a screw-gun battery had dashed earth in the face of the Mullah, then urging a rush of Ghazis against half-a-dozen British bayonets. So he became blind, and hated the English none the less for the little accident. Yardley-Orde knew his failing, and had many times laughed at him therefor.

'Dogs, you are,' said the blind Mullah to the listening tribesmen round the fire. 'Whipped dogs! Because you listened to Orde Sahib and called him father and behaved as his children, the British Government have proven how they regard you. Orde Sahib ye know is dead.'

'Ai! ai! ai!' said half-a-dozen voices.

'He was a man. Comes now in his stead, whom think ye? A Bengali of Bengal — an eater of fish from the South.'

'A lie!' said Khoda Dad Khan. 'And but for the small matter of thy priesthood, I'd drive my gun butt-first down thy throat.'

'Oho, art thou there, lickspittle of the English? Go in tomorrow across the Border to pay service to Orde Sahib's successor, and thou shalt slip thy shoes at the tent-door of a Bengali, as thou shalt hand thy offering to a Bengali's black fist. This I know; and in my youth, when a young man spoke evil to a Mullah holding the doors of Heaven and Hell, the gun-butt was not rammed down the Mullah's gullet. No!'

The Blind Mullah hated Khoda Dad Khan with Afghan hatred, both being rivals for the headship of the tribe; but the latter was feared for bodily as the other for spiritual gifts. Khoda Dad Khan looked at Orde's ring and grunted. 'I go in to-morrow because I am not an old fool, preaching war against the English. If the Government, smitten with madness, have done this, the . . . '

'Then,' croaked the Mullah, 'thou wilt take out the young men and strike at the four villages within the Border?'

'Or wring thy neck, black raven of Jehannum, for a bearer of ill tidings.'

Khoda Dad Khan oiled his long locks with great care, put on his best Bokhara belt, a new turban-cap, and fine green shoes, and accompanied by a few friends came down from the hills to pay a visit to the new Deputy-Commissioner of Kot-Kumharsen. Also he bore tribute — four or five priceless gold mohurs of Akbar's time in a white handkerchief. These the Deputy-Commissioner would touch and remit. The little ceremony used to be a sign that, so far as Khoda Dad Khan's personal influence went, the Khusru Kheyl would be good boys — till the next time; especially if Khoda Dad Khan happened to like the new Deputy-Commissioner. In Yardley-Orde's consulship his visit concluded with a sumptuous dinner and perhaps forbidden liquors; certainly with some wonderful tales and great good-fellowship. Then Khoda Dad Khan would swagger back to his hold, vowing that Orde Sahib was one prince and Tallantire Sahib another, and that whosoever went a-raiding into British territory would be flayed alive. On this occasion he found the Deputy-Commissioner's tents looking much as usual. Regarding himself as privileged, he strode through the open door to confront a suave, portly Bengali in English costume writing at a table. Unversed in the elevating influence of education, and not in the least caring for university degrees, Khoda Dad Khan promptly set the man down for a Babu — the native clerk of the Deputy-Commissioner — a hated and despised animal.

'Ugh!' said he cheerfully. 'Where's your master, Babujee?'

'I am the Deputy-Commissioner,' said the gentleman in English.

Now, he overvalued the effects of university degrees, and stared Khoda Dad Khan in the face. But if from your earliest infancy you have been accustomed to look on battle, murder, and sudden death, if spilt blood affects your nerves as much as red paint, and, above all, if you have faithfully believed that the Bengali was the servant of all Hindustan, and that all Hindustan was vastly inferior to your own large, lustful self, you can endure, even though uneducated, a very

large amount of looking over. You can even stare down a
graduate of an Oxford college if the latter has been born in a
hothouse, of stock bred in a hothouse, and fearing physical
pain as some men fear sin; especially if your opponent's
mother has frightened him to sleep in his youth with horrible
stories of devils inhabiting Afghanistan, and dismal legends
of the black North. The eyes behind the gold spectacles
sought the floor. Khoda Dad Khan chuckled, and swung out
to find Tallantire hard by. 'Here,' said he roughly, thrusting
the coins before him, 'touch and remit. That answers for *my*
good behaviour. But, O Sahib, has the Government gone
mad to send a black Bengali dog to us? And am I to pay
service to such an one? And are you to work under him?
What does it mean?'

'It is an order,' said Tallantire. He had expected something
of this kind. 'He is a very clever S-sahib.'

'He a Sahib! He's a *kala admi* – a black man – unfit to run
at the tail of a potter's donkey. All the peoples of the earth
have harried Bengal. It is written. Thou knowest when we of
the North wanted women or plunder, whither went we? To
Bengal – where else? What child's talk is this of Sahibdom –
after Orde Sahib too! Of a truth the Blind Mullah was right.'

'What of him?' asked Tallantire uneasily. He mistrusted
that old man with his dead eyes and his deadly tongue.

'Nay, now, because of the oath that I sware to Orde Sahib
when we watched him die by the river yonder, I will tell. In
the first place, is it true that the English have set the heel of
the Bengali on their own neck, and that there is no more
English rule in the land?'

'I am here,' said Tallantire, 'and I serve the Maharanee of
England.'

'The Mullah said otherwise, and further that because we
loved Orde Sahib the Government sent us a pig to show that
we were dogs, who till now have been held by the strong

hand. Also that they were taking away the white soldiers, that more Hindustanis might come, and that all was changing.'

This is the worst of ill-considered handling of a very large country. What looks so feasible in Calcutta, so right in Bombay, so unassailable in Madras, is misunderstood by the North, and entirely changes its complexion on the banks of the Indus. Khoda Dad Khan explained as clearly as he could that, though he himself intended to be good, he really could not answer for the more reckless members of his tribe under the leadership of the Blind Mullah. They might or they might not give trouble, but they certainly had no intention whatever of obeying the new Deputy-Commissioner. Was Tallantire perfectly sure that in the event of any systematic Border-raiding the force in the District could put it down promptly?

'Tell the Mullah if he talks any more fool's talk,' said Tallantire curtly, 'that he takes his men on to certain death, and his tribe to blockade, trespass-fine, and blood-money. But why do I talk to one who no longer carries ..ight in the counsels of the tribe?'

Khoda Dad Khan pocketed that insult. He had learned something that he much wanted to know, and returned to his hills to be sarcastically complimented by the Mullah, whose tongue raging round the camp-fires was deadlier flame than ever dung-cake fed.

IV

Be pleased to consider here for a moment the unknown District of Kot-Kumharsen. It lay cut lengthwise by the Indus under the line of the Khusru hills – ramparts of useless earth and tumbled stone. It was seventy miles long by fifty broad, maintained a population of something less than two hundred thousand, and paid taxes to the extent of forty thousand pounds a year on an area that was by rather more than half sheer, hopeless waste. The cultivators were not gentle people, the miners for salt were less gentle still, and the cattle-breeders least gentle of all. A Police post in the top right-hand corner and a tiny mud fort in the top left-hand corner prevented as much salt-smuggling and cattle-lifting as the influence of the Civilians could not put down; and in the bottom right-hand corner lay Jumala, the District head-quarters − a pitiful knot of lime-washed barns facetiously rented as houses, reeking with Frontier fever, leaking in the rain, and ovens in the summer.

It was to this place that Grish Chunder Dé was travelling, there formally to take over charge of the District. But the news of his coming had gone before. Bengalis were as scarce as poodles among the simple Borderers, who cut each other's heads open with their long spades and worshipped impartially at Hindu and Mohammedan shrines. They crowded to see him, pointing at him, and diversely comparing him to a gravid milch-buffalo, or a broken-down horse, as their limited range of metaphor prompted. They laughed at his police guard, and wished to know how long the burly Sikhs were going to lead Bengali apes. They inquired whether he had brought his women with him, and advised him explicitly not to tamper with theirs. It remained for a wrinkled hag by the roadside to slap her lean breasts as he passed, crying, 'I have suckled six that could have eaten six thousand of *him*. The Government shot them, and made this That a King!' Whereat a blue-turbaned, huge-boned plough-mender shouted, 'Have hope, mother o' mine! He may yet go the way of thy wastrels.' And the children, the little brown puff-balls, regarded curiously. It was generally a good thing for infancy to stray into Orde Sahib's tent, where copper coins were to be won for the mere wishing, the tales of the most authentic, such as even their mothers knew but the first half of. No!

This fat black man could never tell them how Pir Prith hauled the eye-teeth out of ten devils; how the big stones came to lie all in a row on the top of the Khusru hills, and what happened if you shouted through the village-gate to the grey wolf at even, 'Badl Khas is dead.' Meantime Grish Chunder Dé talked hastily and much to Tallantire, after the manner of those who are 'more English than the English' – of Oxford and 'Home,' with much curious book-knowledge of bump-suppers, cricket-matches, hunting-runs, and other unholy sports of the alien. 'We must get these fellows in hand,' he said once or twice uneasily; 'get them well in hand, and drive them on a tight rein. No use, you know, being slack with your District.'

And a moment later Tallantire heard Debendra Nath Dé, who brotherly-wise had followed his kinsman's fortune and hoped for the shadow of his protection as a pleader, whisper in Bengali, 'Better are dried fish at Dacca than drawn swords at Delhi. Brother of mine, these men are devils, as our mother said. And you will always have to ride upon a horse!'

That night there was a public audience in a broken-down little town thirty miles from Jumala, when the new Deputy-Commissioner, in reply to the greetings of the subordinate native officials, delivered a speech. It was a carefully thought-out speech, which would have been very valuable had not his third sentence begun with three innocent words, '*Hamara hookum hai* – It is my order.' Then there was a laugh, clear and bell-like, from the back of the big tent, where a few Border land-holders sat, and the laugh grew and scorn mingled with it, and the lean, keen face of Debendra Nath Dé paled, and Grish Chunder turning to Tallantire spake: '*You* – you put up this arrangement.' Upon that instant the noise of hoofs rang without, and there entered Curbar, the District Superintendent of Police, sweating and dusty. The state had tossed him into a corner of the Province for seventeen weary years, there to check smuggling of salt, and to hope for promotion that never came. He had forgotten how to keep his white uniform clean, and screwed rusty spurs into patent-leather shoes, and clothed his head indifferently with a helmet or a turban. Soured, old, worn with heat and cold, he waited till he should be entitled to sufficient pension to keep him from starving.

'Tallantire,' said he, disregarding Grish Chunder Dé, 'come outside. I want to speak to you.' They withdrew. 'It's this,' continued Curbar. 'The Khusru Kheyl have rushed and cut up half-a-dozen of the coolies on Ferris's new canal-embankment; killed a couple of men and carried off a woman. I wouldn't trouble you about that − Ferris is after them and Hugonin, my assistant, with ten mounted police. But that's only the beginning, I fancy. Their fires are out on the Hassan Ardeb heights, and unless we're pretty quick there'll be a flare-up all along our Border. They are sure to raid the four Khusru villages on our side of the line: there's been bad blood between them for years; and you know the Blind Mullah has been preaching a holy war since Orde went out. What's your notion?'

'Damn!' said Tallantire thoughtfully. 'They've begun quick. Well, it seems to me I'd better ride off to Fort Ziar and get what men I can there to picket among the lowland villages, if it's not too late. Tommy Dodd commands at Fort Ziar, I think. Ferris and Hugonin ought to teach the canal thieves a lesson, and − No, we can't have the Head of the Police ostentatiously guarding the Treasury. You go back to the canal. I'll wire Bullows to come in to Jumala with a strong Police guard, and sit on the Treasury. They won't touch the place, but it looks well.'

'I − I − I insist upon knowing what this means,' said the voice of the Deputy-Commissioner, who had followed the speakers.

'Oh!' said Curbar, who being in the Police could not understand that fifteen years of education must, on principle, change the Bengali into a Briton. 'There has been a fight on the Border, and heaps of men are killed. There's going to be another fight, and heaps more will be killed.'

'What for?'

'Because the teeming millions of this District don't exactly approve of you, and think that under your benign rule they are going to have a good time. It strikes me that you had better make arrangements. I act, as you know, by your orders. What do you advise?'

'I — I take you all to witness that I have not yet assumed charge of the District,' stammered the Deputy-Commissioner, not in the tones of the 'more English'.

'Ah, I thought so. Well, as I was saying, Tallantire, your plan is sound. Carry it out. Do you want an escort?'

'No; only a decent horse. But how about wiring to headquarters?'

'I fancy, from the colour of his cheeks, that your superior officer will send some wonderful telegrams before the night's over. Let him do that, and we shall have half the troops of the Province coming up to see what's the trouble. Well, run along, and take care of yourself — the Khusru Kheyl jab upwards from below, remember. Ho! Mir Khan, give Tallantire Sahib the best of the horses, and tell five men to ride to Jumala with the Deputy-Commissioner Sahib Bahadur. There is a hurry toward.'

There was; and it was not in the least bettered by Debendra Nath Dé clinging to a policeman's bridle and demanding the shortest, the very shortest, way to Jumala. Now originality is fatal to the Bengali. Debendra Nath should have stayed with his brother, who rode steadfastly for Jumala on the railway-line, thanking Gods entirely unknown to the most catholic of universities that he had not taken charge of the District, and could still — happy resource of a fertile race! — fall sick.

And I grieve to say that when he reached his goal two policemen, not devoid of rude wit, who had been conferring together as they bumped in their saddles, arranged an entertainment for his behoof. It consisted of first one and then the other entering his room with prodigious details of war, the massing of bloodthirsty and devilish tribes, and the burning of towns. It was almost as good, said these scamps, as riding with Curbar after evasive Afghans. Each invention kept the hearer at work for half an hour on telegrams which the sack of Delhi would hardly have justified. To every power that could move a bayonet or transfer a terrified man, Grish Chunder Dé appealed telegraphically. He was alone, his assistants had fled, and in truth he had not taken over charge of the District. Had the telegrams been despatched many things would have occurred; but since the only signaller in Jumala had gone to bed, and the stationmaster, after one look at the tremendous pile of paper, discovered that railway regulations forbade the forwarding of Imperial messages, Policemen Ram Singh and Nihal Singh were fain to turn the stuff into a pillow and slept on it very comfortably.

Tallantire drove his spurs into a rampant skewbald stallion with china-blue eyes, and settled himself for the forty-mile ride to Fort Ziar. Knowing his District blindfold, he wasted no time hunting for short cuts, but headed across the richer grazing-ground to the ford where Orde had died and been buried. The dusty ground deadened the noise of his horse's hoofs, the moon threw his shadow, a restless goblin, before him, and the heavy dew drenched him to the skin. Hillock scrub that brushed against the horse's belly, unmetalled road where the whip-like foliage of the tamarisks lashed his forehead, illimitable levels of lowland furred with bent and speckled with drowsing cattle, waste, and hillock anew, dragged themselves past, and the skewbald was labouring in the deep sand of the Indus ford. Tallantire was conscious of no distinct thought till the nose of the dawdling ferry-boat grounded on the farther side, and his horse shied snorting at the white headstone of Orde's grave. Then he uncovered, and shouted that the dead might hear, 'They're out, old man! Wish me luck.' In the chill of the dawn he was hammering with a stirrup-iron at the gate of the Fort Ziar, where fifty sabres of that tattered regiment, the Baluch Beshaklis, were supposed to guard Her Majesty's interest along a few hundred miles of Border. This particular fort was commanded by a subaltern, who, born of the ancient family of the Derouletts, naturally answered to the name of Tommy Dodd. Him Tallantire found robed in a sheepskin coat, shaking with fever like an aspen, and trying to read the native apothecary's list of invalids.

'So you've come, too,' said he. 'Well, we're all sick here, and I don't think I can horse thirty men; but we're bub – bub – bub – blessed willing. Stop, does this impress you as a trap or a lie?' He tossed a scrap of paper to Tallantire, on which was written painfully in crabbed Gurmukhi: 'We cannot hold young horses. They will feed after the moon goes down in the four Border villages issuing from the Jagai Pass on the next night.' Then in English roundhand: 'Your sincere friend.'

'Good man!' said Tallantire. 'That's Khoda Dad Khan's work, I know. It's the only piece of English he could ever keep in his head, and he is immensely proud of it. He is playing against the Blind Mullah for his own hand – the treacherous young ruffian!'

'Don't know the politics of the Khusru Kheyl, but if you're satisfied, I am. That was pitched in over the gatehead last night, and I thought we might pull ourselves together and see what was on. Oh, but we're sick with fever here and no mistake! Is this going to be a big business, think you?' said

Tommy Dodd.

Tallantire gave him briefly the outlines of the case, and
Tommy Dodd whistled and shook with fever alternately.
That day he devoted to strategy, the art of war, and the
enlivenment of the invalids, till at dusk there stood ready
forty-two troopers, lean, worn, and dishevelled, whom
Tommy Dodd surveyed with pride and addressed thus: 'Oh
men! If you die you will go to hell. Therefore endeavour to
keep alive. But if you go to hell that place cannot be hotter
than this place, and we are not told that we shall there suffer
from fever. Consequently be not afraid of dying. File out
there!' They grinned, and went.

V

It will be long ere the Khusru Kheyl forget their night attack
on the lowland villages. The Mullah had promised an easy
victory and unlimited plunder; but behold, armed troopers
of the Queen had risen out of the very earth, cutting, slashing, and riding down under the stars, so that no man knew
where to turn, and all feared that they had brought an army
about their ears, and ran back to the hills. In the panic of that
flight more men were seen to drop from wounds inflicted by
an Afghan knife jabbed upwards, and yet more from long-
range carbine-fire. Then there rose a cry of treachery, and
when they reached their own guarded heights, they had left,
with some forty dead and sixty wounded, all their confidence
in the Blind Mullah on the plains below. They clamoured,
swore, and argued round the fires; the women wailing for the
lost, and the Mullah shrieking curses on the returned.

Then Khoda Dad Khan, eloquent and unbreathed, for he
had taken no part in the fight, rose to improve the occasion.
He pointed out that the tribe owed every item of its present
misfortune to the Blind Mullah, who had lied in every pos-

sible particular and talked them into a trap. It was undoubtedly an insult that the Bengali, the son of a Bengali, should presume to administer the Border, but that fact did not, as the Mullah pretended, herald a general time of licence and lifting; and the inexplicable madness of the English had not in the least impaired their power of guarding their marches. On the contrary, the baffled and out-generalled tribe would now, just when their food-stock was lowest, be blockaded from any trade with Hindustan until they had sent hostages for good behaviour, paid compensation for disturbance, and blood-money at the rate of thirty-six English pounds per head for every villager that they might have slain. 'And ye know that those lowland dogs will make oath that we have slain scores. Will the Mullah pay the fines or must we sell our guns?' A low growl ran round the fires. 'Now, seeing that all this is the Mullah's work, and that we have gained nothing but promises of Paradise thereby, it is in my heart that we of the Khusru Kheyl lack a shrine whereat to pray. We are weakened, and henceforth how shall we dare to cross into the Madar Kheyl border, as has been our custom, to kneel to Pir Sajji's tomb? The Madar men will fall upon us, and rightly. But our Mullah is a holy man. He has helped two score of us into Paradise this night. Let him therefore accompany his flock, and we will build over his body a dome of the blue tiles of Mooltan, and burn lamps at his feet every Friday night. He shall be a saint: we shall have a shrine; and there our women shall pray for fresh seed to fill the gaps in our fighting tale. How think you?'

A grim chuckle followed the suggestion, and the soft *wheep, wheep* of unscabbarded knives followed the chuckle. It was an excellent notion, and met a long-felt want of the tribe. The Mullah sprang to his feet, glaring with withered eyeballs at the drawn death he could not see, and calling down the curses of God and Mohammed on the tribe. Then

began a game of blind-man's-buff round and between the
fires, whereof Khuruk Shah, the tribal poet, has sung in
verse that will not die.

They tickled him gently under the armpit with the knife-
point. He leaped aside screaming, only to feel a cold blade
drawn lightly over the back of his neck, or a rifle-muzzle
rubbing his beard. He called on his adherents to aid him, but
most of these lay dead on the plains, for Khoda Dad Khan
had been at some pains to arrange their decease. Men described to him the glories of the shrine they would build, and
the little children clapping their hands cried, 'Run, Mullah,
run! There's a man behind you!' In the end, when the sport
wearied, Khoda Dad Khan's brother sent a knife home
between his ribs. 'Wherefore,' said Khoda Dad Khan with
charming simplicity, 'I am now Chief of the Khusru Kheyl!'
No man gainsaid him; and they all went to sleep very stiff and
sore.

On the plain below Tommy Dodd was lecturing on the
beauties of a cavalry charge by night, and Tallantire, bowed
on his saddle, was gasping hysterically because there was a
sword dangling from his wrist flecked with the blood of the
Khusru Kheyl, the tribe that Orde had kept in leash so well.
When a Rajput trooper pointed out that the skewbald's right
ear had been taken off at the root by some blind slash of its
unskilled rider, Tallantire broke down altogether, and
laughed and sobbed till Tommy Dodd made him lie down
and rest.

'We must wait about till the morning,' said he. 'I wired to
the Colonel just before we left, to send a wing of the Beshaklis
after us. He'll be furious with me for monopolising the fun,
though. Those beggars in the hills won't give us any more
trouble.'

'Then tell the Beshaklis to go on and see what has happened to Curbar on the canal. We must patrol the whole line

of the Border. You're quite sure, Tommy, that – that stuff was – was only the skewbald's ear?'

'Oh, quite,' said Tommy. 'You just missed cutting off his head. *I* saw you when we went into the mess. Sleep, old man.'

Noon brought two squadrons of Beshaklis and a knot of furious brother officers demanding the court-martial of Tommy Dodd for 'spoiling the picnic', and a gallop across country to the canal-works where Ferris, Curbar, and Hugonin were haranguing the terror-stricken coolies on the enormity of abandoning good work and high pay, merely because half-a-dozen of their fellows had been cut down. The sight of a troop of the Beshaklis restored wavering confidence, and the Police-hunted section of the Khusru Kheyl had the joy of watching the canal-bank humming with life as usual, while such of their men as had taken refuge in the watercourses and ravines were being driven out by the troopers. By sundown began the remorseless patrol of the Border by Police and trooper, most like the cowboys' eternal ride round restless cattle.

'Now,' said Khoda Dad Khan to his fellows, pointing out a line of twinkling fires below, 'ye may see how far the old order changes. After their horse will come the little devil-guns that they can drag up to the tops of the hills, and, for aught I know, to the clouds when we crown the hills. If the tribe-council thinks good, I will go to Tallantire Sahib – who loves me – and see if I can stave off at least the blockade. Do I speak for the tribe?'

'Aye, speak for the tribe in God's name. How those accursed fires wink! Do the English send their troops on the wire – or is this the work of the Bengali?'

As Khoda Dad Khan went down the hill he was delayed by an interview with a hard-pressed tribesman, which caused him to return hastily for something he had forgotten. Then, handing himself over to the troopers who had been chasing his friend, he claimed escort to Tallantire Sahib, then with Bullows at Jumala. The Border was safe, and the time for reasons in writing had begun.

'Thank Heaven,' said Bullows, 'that the trouble came at once. Of course we can never put down the reason in black and white, but all India will understand. And it is better to have a sharp short outbreak than five years of impotent administration inside the Border. It costs less. Grish Chunder Dé has reported himself sick, and has been transferred to his own Province without any sort of reprimand. He was strong on not having taken over the District.'

'Of course,' said Tallantire bitterly. 'Well, what am I supposed to have done that was wrong?'

'Oh, you will be told that you exceeded all your powers, and should have reported, and written, and advised for three weeks until the Khusru Kheyl could really come down in force. But I don't think the authorities will dare to make a fuss about it. They've had their lesson. Have you seen Curbar's version of the affair? He can't write a report, but he can speak the truth.'

'What's the use of the truth? He'd much better tear up the report. I'm sick and heartbroken over it all. It was so utterly unnecessary — except in that it rid us of the Babu.'

Entered unabashed Khoda Dad Khan, a stuffed forage-net in his hand, and the troopers behind him.

'May you never be tired!' said he cheerily. 'Well, Sahibs, that was a good fight, and Naim Shah's mother is in debt to you, Tallantire Sahib. A clean cut, they tell me, through jaw, wadded coat, and deep into the collarbone. Well done! But I speak for the tribe. There has been a fault — a great fault. Thou knowest that I and mine, Tallantire Sahib, kept the oath we sware to Orde Sahib on the banks of the Indus.'

'As an Afghan keeps his knife — sharp on one side, blunt on the other,' said Tallantire.

'The better swing in the blow, then. But I speak God's truth. Only the Blind Mullah carried the young men on the tip of his tongue, and said that there was no more Border-law because a Bengali had been sent, and we need not fear the English at all. So they came down to avenge that insult and get plunder. Ye know what befell, and how far I helped. Now five score of us are dead or wounded, and we are all shamed and sorry, and desire no further war. Moreover, that ye may better listen to us, we have taken off the head of the Blind Mullah, whose evil counsels have led us to folly. I bring it for proof' — and he heaved on the floor the head. 'He will give no more trouble, for *I* am Chief now, and so I sit in a higher place at all audiences. Yet there is an offset to this head. That was another fault. One of the men found that black Bengali beast, through whom this trouble arose, wandering on horseback and weeping. Reflecting that he had caused loss of much good life, Alla Dad Khan, whom, if you choose, I will to-morrow shoot, whipped off his head, and I bring it to you to cover your shame, that ye may bury it. See, no man kept the spectacles, though they were of gold.'

Slowly rolled to Tallantire's feet the crop-haired head of a spectacled Bengali gentleman, open-eyed, open-mouthed — the head of Terror incarnate. Bullows bent down. 'Yet another blood-fine and a heavy one, Khoda Dad Khan, for this is the head of Debendra Nath, the man's brother. The Babu is safe long since. All but the fools of the Khusru Kheyl know that.'

'Well, I care not for carrion. Quick meat for me. The thing was under our hills asking the road to Jumala, and Alla Dad Khan showed him the road to Jehannum, being, as thou sayest, but a fool. Remains now what the Government will do to us. As the Blockade — '

'Who art thou, seller of dog's flesh,' thundered Tallantire, 'to speak of terms and treaties? Get hence to the hills — go, and wait there starving, till it shall please the Government to call thy people out for punishment — children and fools that ye be! Count your dead, and be still. Rest assured that the Government will send you a *man*!'

'Ay,' returned Khoda Dad Khan, 'for we also be men.'

As he looked Tallantire between the eyes, he added, 'And by God, Sahib, mayest thou be that man!'

(1891)

FLORA ANNIE STEEL
Mussumât Kirpo's Doll

They had gathered all the schools into the Mission House compound, and set them out in companies on the bare ground like seedlings in a bed — a perfect garden of girls, from five to fifteen, arrayed in rainbow hues; some of them in their wedding dresses of scarlet, most of them bedecked with the family jewellery, and even the shabbiest boasting a row or two of tinsel on bodice or veil.

And down the walks, drawn with mathematical accuracy between these hotbeds of learning, a few English ladies with eager, kindly faces, trotting up and down, conferring excitedly with portly Indian Christian Bible-women, and pausing occasionally to encourage some young offshoot of the Tree of Knowledge — uncertain either of its own roots or of the soil it grew in — by directing its attention to the tables set out with toys which stood under a group of date-palms and oranges. Behind these tables sat in a semi-circle more of those eager, kindly foreign faces, not confined here to one sex, but in fair proportion male and female; yet all with the same expression, the same universal kindly benevolence towards the horticultural exhibition spread out before their eyes.

At the table, pale or flushed with sheer good feeling, two or three of the chief Mission ladies, and between them, with a mundane, married look about her, contrasting strongly with her surroundings, the Commissioner's wife, about to give away the prizes. A kindly face also, despite its half-bewildered look, as one after another of the seedlings comes up to receive the reward of merit. One after another solemnly, for dotted here and there behind the screen of walls and bushes squats many a critical mother, determined that her particular plant shall receive its fair share of watering, or cease to be part of the harvest necessary for a good report. The Commissioner's wife has half a dozen children of her own, and prides herself on understanding them; but these bairns are a race apart. She neither comprehends them, nor the fluent, scholastic Hindustani with which her flushed, excited countrywomen introduce each claimant to her notice. Still she smiles, and says, '*Bobut uchcha*' (very good), and nods as if she did. In a vague way she is relieved when the books are finished and she begins upon the dolls. There is something familiar and cosmopolitan in the gloating desire of the large dark eyes, and the possessive clutch of the small hands over the treasure.

'Standard I. Mussumât Kirpo,' reads out the secretary, and a tall girl of about fifteen comes forward. A sort of annoyed surprise passes among the ladies in quick whispers. Clearly, a Japanese baby-doll with a large bald head is not the correct thing here; but it is so difficult, so almost impossible with hundreds of girls who attend school so irregularly, and really, Julia Smith might have explained! This the lady in question proceeds to do almost tearfully, until she is cut short by superior decision.

'Well, we must give it her now as there isn't anything else for her. So, dear Mrs Gordon, if you please! Of course, as a rule, we always draw the line about dolls when a girl is married. Sometimes it seems a little hard, for they are so small, you know; still, it is best to have a rule; all these tiny trifles help to emphasise our views on the child-marriage question. But if you will be kind enough in this case — just to avoid confusion — we will rectify the mistake to-morrow.'

Mussumât Kirpo took her doll stolidly — a sickly, stupid-looking girl, limping as she walked dully, stolidly back to her place.

'*Ari!*' giggled the women behind the bushes. 'That's all she is likely to get in that way. Lo! they made a bad bargain in brides in Gungo's house, and no mistake. But 'twas ill luck, not ill management; for they tell me Kirpo was straight and sound when she was betrothed. May the gods keep my daughters-in-law healthy and handsome.'

Then they forgot the joke in tender delight over more suitable gifts to the others; and so the great day passed to its ending.

'I do believe poor Kirpo's getting that doll was the only *contretemps*,' said the superintendent triumphantly, 'and that, dear Julia, you can easily remedy to-morrow, so don't fret about it.'

With this intention Julia Smith went down at the first opportunity to her school in the slums of the city. A general air of slackness pervaded the upstairs room, where only a row of little mites sat whispering to each other, while their mistress, full of yawns and stretchings, talked over the events of yesterday with her monitor. Briefly, if the Miss-*sahib* thought she was going to slave as she had done for the past year for a paltry eight yards of cotton trousering, which would not be enough to cut into the 'fassen' — why, the Miss-*sahib* was mistaken. And then with the well-known footfall on the stairs came smiles and flattery. But Kirpo was not at school. Why should she be, seeing that she was a paper-pupil and the prize-giving was over? If the Miss-*sahib* wanted to see her, she had better go round to Gungo's house in the heart of the Hindu quarter. So Julia Smith set off again to thread her way through the by-ways, till she reached the mud steps and closed door which belonged to Kuniya, the head-man of the comb-makers. This ownership has much to do with the English lady's patience in regard to Kirpo who, to tell truth, had been learning the alphabet for five years. But the girl's father-in-law was a man of influence, and Julia's gentle, proselytising eyes cast glances of longing on every house where she had not as yet found entrance. Hence her reluctance to quarrel definitely with her pupil, or rather her pupil's belongings, since poor Kirpo did not count for much in that bustling Hindu household. But for the fact that she was useful at the trade and as a general drudge, *Mai* Gungo would long ago have found some excuse for sending the girl, who had so woefully disappointed all expectations, back to her people — those people who had taken the wedding gifts and given a half-crippled, half-silly bride in exchange. Unparalleled effrontery and wickedness, to be avenged on the only head within reach.

'She wants none of your dolls or your books,' shrilled *Mai* Gungo, who was in a bad temper; 'they aren't worth anything, and I expected nothing less than a suit of clothes, or a new veil at least, else would I never have sent her from the comb-making to waste her time. Lo! Miss-*sahib*' — here the voice changed to a whine — 'we are poor folk, and she costs to feed — she who will never do her duty as a wife. Yet must not Kuniya's son remain sonless; thus is there the expense of another wife in the future.'

So the complaints went on, while Kirpo, in full hearing, sat filing away at the combs without a flicker of expression on her face.

But when Julia had settled the business with eight annas from her private pocket, and was once more picking her way through the drain-like alley, she heard limping steps behind her. It was Kirpo and the Japanese doll.

'The Miss-*sahib* has forgotten it,' she said stolidly. Julia Smith stood in the sunlight, utterly unmindful of a turgid stream of concentrated filth which at that moment came sweeping along the gutter. Her gentle, womanly eyes saw something she recognised in the child-like, yet unchild-like face looking into hers.

'Would you like to keep it, dear?' she asked gently. Kirpo nodded her head.

'She needn't know,' she explained. 'I could keep it in the cow-shed, and they will sell the book you left for me. They would sell this too. That is why I brought it back.'

This admixture of cunning rather dashed poor Julia's pity; but in the end Kirpo went back to her work with the Japanese doll carefully concealed in her veil, and for the next year Julia Smith never caught sight of it again. Things went on as if it had not been in that straggling Hindu house, with its big courtyard and dark slips of rooms. Perhaps Kirpo got up at night to play with it; perhaps she never played with it at all, but, having wrapped it in a napkin and buried it away somewhere, was content in its possession like the man with his one talent; for this miserliness belongs, as a rule, to those who have few things, not many. Once or twice, when Julia Smith found the opportunity, she would ask after the doll's welfare. Then Kirpo would nod her head mysteriously; but this was not often, for, by degrees, Julia's visits to the house and Kirpo's to the school became less frequent. The former, because *Mai* Gungo's claims grew intolerable, and the Mission lady had found firm footing in less rapacious houses. The latter, because to *Mai* Gungo's somewhat grudging relief her daughter-in-law, after nearly four years of married life, seemed disposed to save the family from the expense of another bride by presenting it with a child. Nothing, of course, could alter the fact of the girl's ugliness and stupidity and lameness; still, if she did her duty in this one point *Mai* Gungo could put up with her, especially as she really did very well at the combs. She was not worked quite so hard now, since that might affect the future promise. Perhaps this gave Kirpo more time to play with the Japanese doll, perhaps it did not. Outwardly, at any rate, life went on in the courtyard as though no such thing existed.

'She may die, the crippled ones often do,' said the gossips, scarcely lowering their voices; 'but it will be a great saving,

Mai Gungo, if the grandson comes without another daughter-in-law; they quarrel so. Besides, it is in God's hands. May He preserve both to you.' *Mai* Gungo echoed the wish, with the reservation that if the whole wish was impossible, the child at least might not suffer. Kirpo herself understood the position perfectly, and felt dimly that if she could do her duty she would be quite content to give up the comb-making once and for all. It was niggly, cramping work to sit with your crippled legs tucked under you, filing away at the hard wood all day long, while mother-in-law bustled about, scolding away in her shrill voice. It had been much greater fun at the school; and as for the prize-giving days! Kirpo had four of those red-letter glimpses of the world to recollect, but she always gave the palm of pleasure to the last, when they had laughed at her and the Japanese doll. Perhaps because she remembered it best; for, as has been said, poor Kirpo's was not a brilliant intellect.

So just about the time when the Mission House was once more buying large consignments of dolls and books, and laying in yards on yards of cotton trousering and Manchester veiling against another prize-giving, the mistress of the little school-room up two pairs of stairs said to Julia Smith:

'Kirpo had a son last week. *Mai* Gungo hath given many offerings in thanksgiving.'

'And Kirpo herself?'

'She ails, they say; but that is likely. The hour of danger is over.'

That same afternoon Julia Smith once more picked her way along the gutters to the mud steps and closed door of Kuniya's house. Kirpo was lying alone on a bed in the shadow of a grass thatch.

'And where is the baby?' asked Julia, cheerfully.

'Mother-in-law hath it. 'Tis a son — doubtless the Miss hath heard so.' There was the oddest mixture of pride and regret in the girl's dull face.

'She will let thee have it when thou art stronger,' said her visitor quickly. 'Thou must give me back the dolly, Kirpo, now thou hast a live one of thine own.'

The girl's head shifted uneasily on the hard pillow.

'Ay! and the prize-giving day must be close, I have been thinking. If the Miss-*sahib* will look behind the straw yonder she will find the doll. It is not hurt. And the Miss can give it to someone else. I don't want it any more. She might give it to a little girl this time. She could play with it.'

'*Mai* Gungo,' said Julia severely, as, on her way out, she found the mother-in-law surrounded by her gossips, exhibiting the baby to them with great pride, 'you must look to Kirpo; she thrives not. And give her the baby — she pines after it.'

'The Miss doth not understand,' flounced Gungo. 'What can Kirpo do with a baby? She is a fool; besides, a mother like that hath evil influences till the time of purification hath passed.'

Ten days afterwards the mistress of the school told Julia that Kirpo had the fever, and they did not think she would recover. It was never safe for such as she to have sons, and nothing else was to be expected.

Perhaps it was not; for Julia found her on the bare ground of the courtyard where she had been set to die. The oil lamps flared smokily at her head and her feet, and *Mai* Gungo, with the fortnight-old baby in her arms, cried '*Râm! Râm!*' lustily. But the girl lingered in life, turning her head restlessly from side to side on Mother Earth's bosom.

'Give her the baby — only for a minute,' pleaded Julia, with tears in her eyes. *Mai* Gungo frowned; but a neighbour broke in hastily:

'Ay! give it to her, gossip, lest in her evil ways she returns for it when she is dead.'

So they laid the baby beside her; but the restless head went on turning restlessly from side to side.

'My doll! my doll! I like my doll best.'

Before they could fetch it from the Mission House, Kirpo was dead.   (1894)

FLORA ANNIE STEEL
The Fakeer's Drum

'O! most almighty Wictoria, V.R., reg. britannicorum (V.I., Kaiser-i-Hind), please admit bearer to privileges of praising God on the little drum as occasion befitteth, and your petitioner will ever pray,' etc.

It was written on a scrap of foreign paper duly stamped as a petition, and it did not need the interpolation of imperial titles to prove that this was not by any means its first appearance in court. To be plain, it had an 'ancient and a fishlike smell', suggestive of many years' acquaintance with dirty humanity. I looked at the man who had presented it — a very ordinary *fakeer*, standing with hands folded humbly — and was struck by the wistful expectancy in his face. It was at once hopeful yet hopeless. Turning to the court-reader for explanation, I found a decorous smile flowing round the circle of squatting clerks. It was evidently an old-established joke.

'He is damnably noiseful man, Sir,' remarked my *sarishtidar*, cheerfully, 'and his place of sitting close to Deputy-Commissioner's bungalow. Thus European officers object; so it is always *na-munzoor*' (refused).

The sound of the familiar formula drove the hope from the old man's face; his thin shoulders seemed to droop, but he said nothing.

'How long has this been going on?' I asked.

'Fourteen years, Sir. Always on transference of officers, and it is always *na-munzoor*.' He dipped his pen in the ink, gave it the premonitory flick.

'*Munzoor*' (granted), said I, in a sudden decision. '*Munzoor* during the term of my office.'

That was but a month. I was only a *locum tenens* during leave. Only a month, and the poor old beggar had waited fourteen years to praise God on the little drum! The pathos and bathos of it hit *me* hard; but a stare of infinite surprise had replaced the circumambient smile. The *fakeer* himself seemed flabbergasted. I think he felt lost without his petition, for I saw him fumbling in his pocket as the janissaries hustled him out of court, as janissaries love to do, east or west.

That night, as I was wondering if I had smoked enough and yawned enough to make sleep possible in a hundred degrees of heat, and a hundred million mosquitoes, I was suddenly reminded of the proverb 'Charity begins at home.' It had, with a vengeance. I had thought my *sarishtidar's* language a trifle too picturesque; now I recognised its supreme accuracy. The *fakeer* was 'a damnably noiseful man'. It is useless trying to add one iota to this description, especially to those unacquainted with the torture of an Indian drum. By dawn I was in the saddle, glad to escape from my own house and the ceaseless '*Rumpa-tum-tum*', which was driving me crazy.

When I returned, the old man was awaiting me in the verandah, his face full of a great content; and the desire to murder him, which rose up in me with the thought of the twenty-nine nights yet to come, faded before it. Perfect happiness is not the lot of many, but apparently it was his. He salaamed down to the ground. '*Huzoor*,' he said, 'the great joy in me created a disturbance last night. It will not occur again. The Protector of the Poor shall sleep in peace, even though his slave praises God for him all night long. The Almighty does not require a loud drum.'

I said I was glad to hear it, and my self-complacency grew until I laid my head on the pillow somewhat earlier than usual. Then I became aware of a faint throbbing in the air, like that which follows a deep organ note — a throbbing which found its way into the drum of my ear and remained there — so faint that it kept me on the rack to know if it had stopped or was still going on. '*Rumpa-tum-tum-tum, rumpa-tum-tum-tum, rumpa* — ' Even now the impulse to make the hateful rhythm interminable seizes on me. I have to lay aside my pen and take a new one before going on.

I draw a veil over the mental struggle which followed. It would have been quite easy to rescind my permission, but the thought of one month versus fourteen years roused my pride. As representative of the '*almighty wictoria, reg. britannicorum,*' etc., I had admitted this man to the privileges of praising God on the little drum, and there was an end of it. But the effort left my nerves shattered with the strain put on them. It was the middle of the hot weather — that awful fortnight before the rains break — I was young — absolutely alone. Every morning as I rode, a perfect wreck, past the *fakeer*'s hovel by the gate, he used to ask me if I had slept well, and I lied to him. What was the use of suffering if no one was the happier for it?

At last, one evening — it was the twenty-first, I remember, for I ticked them off on a calendar like any schoolboy — I sat out among the oleanders, knowing that sleep was mine. The rains had broken, a cool wind stirred the dripping trees, the fever of unrest was over. Clouds of winged white ants besieged the lamp: what wonder, when the rafters of the old bungalow were riddled almost beyond the limits of safety by their galleries? But what did I care? I was going to sleep. And so I did, like a child, until close on the dawn. And then — by heavens, it was too bad! In the verandah surely, not faint, but loudly imperative: 'RUMPA-TUM-TUM-TUM!'

I was out of bed in an instant full of fury. The fiend incarnate must be walking round the house. I was after him

in the moonlight. Not a sign; the white oleanders were shining in the dark foliage; a firefly or two — nothing more.

'*Rumpa-tum-tum-tum*!' Fainter this time round the corner.
Not there!

'*Rumpa-tum-tum-tum!*' A mere whisper now, but loud
enough to be traced. So on the track, I was round the house to
the verandah whence I had started.

No sign — no sound!

Gracious! What was that? A crash, a thud, a roar and rattle
of earth! The house! the roof!

When by the growing light of dawn we inspected the
damage, we found the biggest rafter of all lying right across
the pillow where my head had been two minutes before. The
first sunbeams were on the still sparkling trees when, full of
curiosity, I strolled over to the *fakeer*'s hut. It also was a heap
of ruins, and when we dug the old man out from among the
ant-riddled rafters the doctor said he had been dead for many
hours.

This story may seem strange to some; others will agree
with my *sarishtidar*, who, after spending the morning over a
Johnson's dictionary and a revenue report, informed me that
'such catastrophes are but too common in this unhappy land
after heavy rain following on long-continued drought'.

(1897)

FLORA ANNIE STEEL
The Reformer's Wife

He was a dreamer of dreams, with the look in his large dark eyes which Botticelli put into the eyes of his Moses; that Moses in doublet and hose, whose figure, isolated from its surroundings, reminds one irresistibly of Christopher Columbus, or Vasco da Gama — of those, in fact, who dream of a Promised Land.

And this man dreamt as wild a dream as any. He hoped, before he died, to change the social customs of India.

He used to sit in my drawing-room, talking to me by the hour of the Prophet and his blessed Fátma — for he was a Mahommedan — and bewailing the sad degeneracy of these present days, when caste had crept into and defiled the Faith. I shall never forget the face of martyred enthusiasm with which he received my first invitation to dinner. He accepted it, as he would have accepted the stake, with fervour, and indeed to his ignorance the ordeal was supreme. However, he appeared punctual to the moment on the appointed day, and greatly relieved my mind by partaking twice of plum-pudding, which he declared to be a surpassingly cool and most digestible form of nourishment, calculated to soothe both body and mind. Though this is hardly the character usually assigned to it, I did not contradict him, for not even his eager self-sacrifice had sufficed for the soup, the fish, or the joint, and he might otherwise have left the table in a starving condition. As it was, he firmly set aside my invitation to drink water after the meal was over, with the modest remark that he had not eaten enough to warrant the indulgence.

The event caused quite a stir in that far-away little town,

set out among the ruins of a great city, on the high bank of one of the Punjab rivers; for the scene of this sketch lay out of the beaten track, beyond the reach of *babus* and barristers, patent-leather shoes and progress. Beyond the pale of civilisation altogether, among a quaint little colony of fighting Pathans who still pointed with pride to an old gate or two which had withstood siege after siege, in those old fighting days when the river had flowed beneath the walls of the city. Since then the water had ebbed seven miles to the south-east, taking with it the prestige of the stronghold, which only remained a picturesque survival; a cluster of four-storied purple-brick houses surrounded by an intermittent purple-brick wall, bastioned and loop-holed. A formidable defence, while it lasted. But it had a trick of dissolving meekly into a sort of mud hedge, in order to gain the next stately fragment, or maybe to effect an alliance with one of the frowning gateways which had defied assault. This condition of things was a source of sincere delight to my Reformer Futteh Deen (Victory of Faith) who revelled in similes. It was typical of the irrational, illogical position of the inhabitants in regard to a thousand religious and social questions, and just as one brave man could break through these sham fortifications, so one resolute example would suffice to capture the citadel of prejudice, and plant the banner of abstract Truth on its topmost pinnacle.

For he dreamt excellently well, and as he sat declaiming his Persian and Arabic periods in the drawing-room with his eyes half-shut, like one in presence of some dazzling light, I used to feel as if something might indeed be done to make the Mill of God grind a little faster.

In the matter of dining out, indeed, it seemed as if he was right. For within a week of his desperate plunge, I received an invitation to break bread with the municipal committee in the upper story of the Vice-President's house. The request, which was emblazoned in gold, engrossed on silk paper in red and black, and enclosed in a brocade envelope, was signed by the eleven members and the Reformer, who, by the way, edited a ridiculous little magazine to which the committee subscribed a few rupees a month. Solely for the purpose of being able to send copies to their friends at Court, and show that they were in the van of progress. For a man must be that, who is patron of a 'Society for the General Good of All Men in All Countries'. I was, I confess it, surprised, even though a remark that now perhaps his Honour the Lieutenant-Governor would no longer suspect his slaves of disloyalty, showed me that philanthropy had begun at home. For the little colony bore a doubtful character, being largely leavened by the new Puritanism, which Government, for reasons best known to itself, chooses to confound with Wahabeeism.

The entertainment given on the roof amid starshine and catherine-wheels proved a magnificent success, its great feature being an enormous plum-pudding which I was gravely told had been prepared by my own cook. At what cost, I shudder to think; but the rascal's grinning face as he placed it on the table convinced me that he had seized the opportunity for some almost inconceivable extortion. But there was no regret in those twelve grave, bearded faces, as one by one they tasted and approved. All this happened long before a miserable, exotic imitation of an English vestry replaced the old patrician committees, and these men were representatives of the bluest blood in the neighbourhood, many of them descendants of those who in past times had held high offices of state, and had transmitted courtly manners to their children. So the epithets bestowed on the plum-pudding were many-syllabled; but the consensus of opinion was indubitably towards its coolness, its digestibility, and its evident property of soothing the body and the mind. Again I did not deny it. How could I, out on the roof under the eternal stars, with those twelve foreign faces showing, for once, a common bond of union with the Feringhee? I should have felt like Judas Iscariot if I had struck the thirteenth chord of denial.

The Reformer made a speech afterwards, I remember, in which, being wonderfully well read, he alluded to love-feasts and sacraments, and a coming millennium, when all nations of the world should meet at one table, and — well! not exactly eat plum-pudding together, but something very like it. Then we all shook hands, and a native musician played something on the *siringhi* which they informed me was 'God Save the Queen'. It may have been. I only know that the Reformer's thin face beamed with almost pitiful delight, as he told me triumphantly that this was only the beginning.

He was right. From that time forth the plum-pudding feast became a recognised function. Not a week passed without one. Generally — for my gorge rose at the idea of my cook's extortion — in the summer-house in my garden, where I could have an excuse for providing the delicacy at my own expense. And I am bound to say that this increased intimacy bore other fruits than that contained in the pudding. For the matter of that it has continued to bear fruit, since I can truthfully date the beginning of my friendship for the people of India from the days when we ate plum-pudding together under the starshine.

The Reformer was radiant. He formed himself and his eleven into committees and sub-committees for every philanthropical object under the sun, and many an afternoon have I spent under the trees with my work watching one deputation after another retire behind the oleander hedge in order to permutate itself by deft rearrangement of members, secretaries, and vice-presidents into some fresh body bent on the regeneration of mankind. For life was leisureful, lingering and lagging along in the little town where there was neither doctor nor parson, policeman nor canal officer, nor in fact any white face save my own and my husband's. Still we went far and fast in a cheerful, unreal sort of way. We started schools and debating societies, public libraries and technical art classes. Finally we met enthusiastically over an extra-sized plum-pudding, and bound ourselves over to reduce the marriage expenditure of our daughters.

The Reformer grew more radiant than ever, and began in the drawing-room – where it appeared to me he hatched all his most daring schemes – to talk big about infant marriage, enforced widowhood, and the seclusion of women. The latter I considered to be the key to the whole position, and there-fore I felt surprised at the evident reluctance with which he met my suggestion, that he should begin his struggle by bringing his wife to visit me. He had but one, although she was childless. This was partly, no doubt, in deference to his advanced theories; but also, at least so I judged from his conversation, because of his unbounded admiration for one who by his description was a pearl among women. In fact this unseen partner had from the first been held up to me as a refutation of all my strictures on the degradation of seclusion. So, to tell truth, I was quite anxious to see this paragon, and vexed at the constant ailments and absences which prevented our becoming acquainted. The more so because this shadow of hidden virtue fettered me in argument, for Futteh Deen was an eager patriot, full of enthusiasms for India and the Indians. Once the sham fortifications were scaled, he assured me that Hindustan, and above all its women, would come to the front and put their universe to shame. Yet, despite his successes, he looked haggard and anxious; at the time I thought it was too much progress and plum-pudding com-bined, but afterwards I came to the conclusion that his conscience was ill at ease, even then.

So the heat grew apace. The fly-catchers came to dart

among the *sirus* flowers and skim round the massive dome of the old tomb in which we lived. The melons began to ripen, first by ones and twos, then in thousands — gold, and green, and russet. The corners of the streets were piled with them, and every man, woman, and child carried a crescent moon of melon at which they munched contentedly all day long. Now, even with the future good of humanity in view, I could not believe in the safety of a mixed diet of melon and plum-pudding, especially when cholera was flying about. There-fore, on the next committee-day I had a light and wholesome refection of sponge-cakes and jelly prepared for the philan-thropists. They partook of it courteously, but sparingly. It was, they said, super-excellent, but of too heating and stimu-lating a nature to be consumed in quantities. In vain I assured them that it could be digested by the most delicate stomach; that it was, in short, a recognised food for convalescents. This only confirmed them in their view, for, according to the Yunâni system, an invalid diet must be heating, strengthen-ing, stimulating. Somehow in the middle of their upside-down arguments I caught myself looking pitifully at the Reformer, and wondering at his temerity in tilting at the great mysterious mass of Eastern wisdom.

And that day, in deference to my Western zeal, he was to tilt wildly at the *zenâna* system.

His address fell flat, and for the first time I noticed a distinctly personal flavour in the discussion. Hitherto we had resolved and recorded gaily, as if we ourselves were disin-terested spectators. However, the Vice-President apologised for the general tone, with a side slash at exciting causes in the jelly and sponge-cake, whereat the other ten wagged their heads sagely, remarking that it was marvellous, stupendous, to feel the blood running riot in their veins after those few mouthfuls. Verily such food partook of magic. Only the Reformer dissented, and ate a whole sponge-cake defiantly.

Even so the final Resolution ran thus: 'That this committee views with alarm any attempt to force the natural growth of female freedom, which it holds to be strictly a matter for the individual wishes of the man.' Indeed it was with difficulty that I, as secretary, avoided the disgrace of having to record the spiteful rider, 'And that if any member wanted to unveil the ladies he could begin on his own wife.'

I was young then in knowledge of Eastern ways, and consequently indignant. The Reformer, on the other hand, was strangely humble, and tried afterwards to evade the major point by eating another sponge-cake, and making a facetious remark about experiments and vile bodies; for he was a mine of quotations, especially from the Bible, which he used to wield to my great discomfiture.

But on the point at issue I knew he could scarcely go against his own convictions, so I pressed home his duty of taking the initiative. He agreed, gently. By and by, perhaps, when his wife was more fit for the ordeal. And it was natural, even the *mem-sahiba* must allow, for unaccustomed modesty to shrink. She was to the full as devoted as he to the good cause, but at the same time – Finally, the *mem-sahiba* must remember that women were women all over the world – even though occasionally one was to be found like the *mem-sahiba* capable of acting as secretary to innumerable committees without a blush. There was something so wistful in his eager blending of flattery and excuse that I yielded for the time, though determined in the end to carry my point.

With this purpose I reverted to plum-puddings once more, and, I fear, to gross bribery of all kinds in the shape of private interviews and soft words. Finally I succeeded in getting half the members to consent to sending their wives to an after-dark at-home in my drawing-room, provided always that Mir Futteh Deen, the Reformer, would set a good example.

He looked troubled when I told him, and pointed out that

the responsibility for success or failure now lay virtually with him, yet he did not deny it.

I took elaborate precautions to ensure the most modest seclusion on the appointed evening, even to sending my husband up·a ladder to the gallery at the very top of the dome to smoke his after-dinner cigar. I remember thinking how odd it must have looked to him perched up there to see the twinkling lights of the distant city over the soft shadows of the *ferash* trees, and at his feet the glimmer of the white screens set up to form a conventional *zenán-khâna*. But I waited in vain − in my best dress, by the way. No one came, though my *ayah* assured me that several jealously guarded *dhoolies* arrived at the garden-gate and went away again when Mrs Futteh Deen never turned up.

I was virtuously indignant with the offender, and the next time he came to see me sent out a message that I was otherwise engaged. I felt a little remorseful at having done so, however, when, committee-day coming round, the Reformer was reported on the sick-list. And there he remained until after the first rain had fallen, bringing with it the real Indian spring − the spring full of roses and jasmines, of which the poets and the bul-buls sing. By this time the novelty had worn off philanthropy and plum-pudding, so that often we had a difficulty in getting a quorum together to resolve anything; and I, personally, had begun to weary for the dazzled eyes and the eager voice so full of sanguine hope.

Therefore it gave me a pang to learn from the Vice-President, who, being a Government official, was a model of punctuality, that in all probability I should never hear or see either one or the other again. Futteh Deen was dying of the rapid decline which comes so often to the Indian student.

A recurrence of a vague remorse made me put my pride in my pocket and go unasked to the Reformer's house, but my decision came too late. He had died the morning of my visit, and I think I was glad of it.

For the paragon of beauty and virtue, of education and refinement, was a very ordinary woman, years older than my poor Reformer, marked with the small-pox, and blind of one eye. Then I understood.

(1903)

SARA JEANNETTE DUNCAN
A Mother in India

I

There were times when we had to go without puddings to pay
John's uniform bills, and always I did the facings myself with
a cloth-ball to save getting new ones. I would have polished
his sword, too, if I had been allowed; I adored his sword. And
once, I remember, we painted and varnished our own dog-
cart, and very smart it looked, to save fifty rupees. We had
nothing but our pay — John had his company when we were
married, but what is that? — and life was made up of small
knowing economies, much more amusing in recollection
than in practice. We were sodden poor, and that is a fact, poor
and conscientious, which was worse. A big fat spider of a
money-lender came one day into the veranda and tempted
us — we lived in a hut, but it had a veranda — and John
threatened to report him to the police. Poor when everybody
else had enough to live in the open-handed Indian fashion,
that was what made it so hard; we were alone in our sordid
little ways. When the expectation of Cecily came to us we
made out to be delighted, knowing that the whole station
pitied us, and when Cecily came herself, with a swamping
burst of expense, we kept up the pretence splendidly. She
was peevish, poor little thing, and she threatened convulsions from the beginning, but we both knew that it was
abnormal not to love her a great deal, more than life, immediately and increasingly; and we applied ourselves
honestly to do it, with the thermometer at a hundred and
two, and the nurse leaving at the end of a fortnight because

she discovered that I had only six of everything for the table. To find out a husband's virtues, you must marry a poor man. The regiment was under-officered as usual, and John had to take parade at daylight quite three times a week; but he walked up and down the veranda with Cecily constantly till two in the morning, when a little coolness came. I usually lay awake the rest of the night in fear that a scorpion would drop from the ceiling on her. Nevertheless, we were of excellent mind toward Cecily; we were in such terror, not so much of failing in our duty towards her as towards the ideal standard of mankind. We were very anxious indeed not to come short. To be found too small for one's place in nature would have been odious. We would talk about her for an hour at a time, even when John's charger was threatening glanders and I could see his mind perpetually wandering to the stable. I would say to John that she had brought a new element into our lives – she had indeed! – and John would reply, 'I know what you mean,' and go on to prophesy that she would 'bind us together'. We didn't need binding together; we were more to each other, there in the desolation of that arid frontier outpost, than most husbands and wives; but it seemed a proper and hopeful thing to believe, so we believed it. Of course, the real experience would have come, we weren't monsters; but fate curtailed the opportunity. She was just five weeks old when the doctor told us that we must either pack her home immediately or lose her, and the very next day John went down with enteric. So Cecily was sent to England with a sergeant's wife who had lost her twins, and I settled down under the direction of a native doctor, to fight for my husband's life, without ice or proper food, or sick-room comforts of any sort. Ah! Fort Samila, with the sun glaring up from the sand! – however, it is a long time ago now. I trusted the baby willingly to Mrs Berry and to Providence, and did not fret; my capacity for worry, I suppose, was

completely absorbed. Mrs Berry's letter, describing the
child's improvement on the voyage and safe arrival came, I
remember, the day on which John was allowed his first solid
mouthful; it had been a long siege. 'Poor little wretch!' he
said when I read it aloud; and after that Cecily became an
episode.

She had gone to my husband's people; it was the best
arrangement. We were lucky that it was possible; so many
children had to be sent to strangers and hirelings. Since an
unfortunate infant must be brought into the world and set
adrift, the haven of its grandmother and its Aunt Emma and
its Aunt Alice certainly seemed providential. I had absolutely
no cause for anxiety, as I often told people, wondering that I
did not feel a little all the same. Nothing, I knew, could
exceed the conscientious devotion of all three Farnham ladies
to the child. She would appear upon their somewhat barren
horizon as a new and interesting duty, and the small addi-
tional income she also represented would be almost nominal
compensation for the care she would receive. They were
excellent persons of the kind that talk about matins and
vespers, and attend both. They helped little charities and
gave little teas, and wrote little notes, and made deprecating
allowance for the eccentricities of their titled or moneyed
acquaintances. They were the subdued, smiling, unimagina-
tively dressed women on a small definite income that you
meet at every rectory garden-party in the country, a little
snobbish, a little priggish, wholly conventional, but apart
from these weaknesses, sound and simple and dignified,
managing their two small servants with a display of the most
exact traditions, and keeping a somewhat vague and belated
but constant eye upon the doings of their country as
chronicled in a biweekly paper. They were all immensely
interested in royalty, and would read paragraphs aloud to
each other about how the Princess Beatrice or the Princess

Maud had opened a fancy bazaar, looking remarkably well in plain grey poplin trimmed with Irish lace − an industry which, as is well known, the Royal Family has set its heart on rehabilitating. Upon which Mrs Farnham's comment invariably would be, 'How thoughtful of them, dear!' and Alice would usually say, 'Well, if I were a princess, I should like something nicer than plain grey poplin.' Alice, being the youngest, was not always expected to think before she spoke. Alice painted in water-colours, but Emma was supposed to have the most common sense.

They took turns in writing to us with the greatest regularity about Cecily; only once, I think, did they miss the weekly mail, and that was when she threatened diphtheria and they thought we had better be kept in ignorance. The kind and affectionate terms of these letters never altered except with the facts they described − teething, creeping, measles, cheeks growing round and rosy, all were conveyed in the same smooth, pat, and proper phrases, so absolutely empty of any glimpse of the child's personality that after the first few months it was like reading about a somewhat uninteresting infant in a book. I was sure Cecily was not uninteresting, but her chroniclers were. We used to wade through the long, thin sheets and saw how much more satisfactory it would be when Cecily could write to us herself. Meanwhile we noted her weekly progress with much the feeling one would have about a far-away little bit of property that was giving no trouble and coming on exceedingly well. We would take possession of Cecily at our convenience; till then, it was gratifying to hear of our earned increment in dear little dimples and sweet little curls.

She was nearly four when I saw her again. We were home on three months' leave; John had just got his first brevet for doing something which he does not allow me to talk about in the Black Mountain country; and we were fearfully pleased with ourselves. I remember that excitement lasted well up to Port Said. As far as the Canal, Cecily was only one of the pleasures and interests we were going home to: John's majority was the thing that really gave savour to life. But the first faint line of Europe brought my child to my horizon; and all the rest of the way she kept her place, holding out her little arms to me, beckoning me on. Her four motherless years brought compunction to my heart and tears to my eyes; she should have all the compensation that could be. I suddenly realised how ready I was − how ready! − to have her back. I rebelled fiercely against John's decision that we must not take her with us on our return to the frontier; privately, I resolved to dispute it, and, if necessary, I saw myself abducting the child − my own child. My days and nights as the ship crept on were full of a long ache to possess her; the defrauded tenderness of the last four years rose up in me and sometimes caught at my throat. I could think and talk and dream of nothing else. John indulged me as much as was reasonable, and only once betrayed by a yawn that the subject was not for him endlessly absorbing. Then I cried and he apologised. 'You know,' he said, 'it isn't exactly the same thing. I'm not her mother.' At which I dried my tears and expanded, proud and pacified. I was her mother!

Then the rainy little station and Alice, all-embracing in a damp waterproof, and the drive in the fly, and John's mother at the gate and a necessary pause while I kissed John's mother. Dear thing, she wanted to hold our hands and look into our faces and tell us how little we had changed for all our hardships; and on the way to the house she actually stopped to point out some alterations in the flower-borders. At last the drawing-room door and the smiling housemaid turning the handle and the unforgettable picture of a little girl, a little girl unlike anything we had imagined, starting bravely to trot across the room with the little speech that had been taught her. Half-way she came; I suppose our regards were too fixed, too absorbed, for there she stopped with a wail of terror at the strange faces, and ran straight back to the outstretched arms of her Aunt Emma. The most natural thing in the world, no doubt. I walked over to a chair opposite with my hand-bag and umbrella and sat down — a spectator, aloof and silent. Aunt Emma fondled and quieted the child, apologising for her to me, coaxing her to look up, but the little figure still shook with sobs, hiding its face in the bosom that it knew. I smiled politely, like any other stranger, at Emma's deprecations, and sat impassive, looking at my alleged baby breaking her heart at the sight of her mother. It is not amusing even now to remember the anger that I felt. I did not touch her or speak to her; I simply sat observing my alien possession, in the frock I had not made and the sash I had not chosen, being coaxed and kissed and protected and petted by its Aunt Emma. Presently I asked to be taken to my room, and there I locked myself in for two atrocious hours. Just once my heart beat high, when a tiny knock came and a timid, docile little voice said that tea was ready. But I heard the rustle of a skirt, and guessed the directing angel in Aunt Emma, and responded, 'Thank you, dear, run away and say that I am coming,' with a pleasant visitor's inflection which I was able to sustain for the rest of the afternoon.

'She goes to bed at seven,' said Emma.

'Oh, does she?' said I. 'A very good hour, I should think.'

'She sleeps in my room,' said Mrs Farnham.

'We give her mutton broth very often, but seldom stock soup,' said Aunt Emma. 'Mamma thinks it is too stimulating.'

'Indeed?' said I, to all of it.

They took me up to see her in her crib, and pointed out, as she lay asleep, that though she had 'a general look' of me, her features were distinctively Farnham.

'Won't you kiss her?' asked Alice. 'You haven't kissed her yet, and she is used to so much affection.'

'I don't think I could take such an advantage of her,' I said.

They looked at each other, and Mrs Farnham said that I was plainly worn out. I mustn't sit up to prayers.

If I had been given anything like reasonable time I might have made a fight for it, but four weeks − it took a month each way in those days − was too absurdly little; I could do nothing. But I would not stay at mamma's. It was more than I would ask of myself, that daily disappointment under the mask of gratified discovery, for long.

I spent an approving, unnatural week, in my farcical character, bridling my resentment and hiding my mortification with pretty phrases; and then I went up to town and drowned my sorrows in the summer sales. I took John with me. I may have been Cecily's mother in theory, but I was John's wife in fact.

We went back to the frontier, and the regiment saw a lot of service. That meant medals and fun for my husband, but economy and anxiety for me, though I managed to be allowed as close to the firing line as any woman.

Once the Colonel's wife and I, sitting in Fort Samila, actually heard the rifles of a punitive expedition cracking on the other side of the river − that was a bad moment. My man came in after fifteen hours' fighting, and went sound asleep, sitting before his food with his knife and fork in his hands. But service makes heavy demands besides those on your wife's nerves. We had saved two thousand rupees, I remember, against another run home, and it all went like powder, in the Mirzai expedition; and the run home diminished to a month in a boarding-house in the hills.

Meanwhile, however, we had begun to correspond with our daughter, in large round words of one syllable, behind which, of course, was plain the patient guiding hand of Aunt

Emma. One could hear Aunt Emma suggesting what would be nice to say, trying to instil a little pale affection for the far-off papa and mamma. There was so little Cecily and so much Emma — of course, it could not be otherwise — that I used to take, I fear, but a perfunctory joy in these letters. When we went home again I stipulated absolutely that she was to write to us without any sort of supervision — the child was ten.

'But the spelling!' cried Aunt Emma, with lifted eyebrows.

'Her letters aren't exercises,' I was obliged to retort; 'she will do the best she can.'

We found her a docile little girl, with nice manners, a thoroughly unobjectionable child. I saw quite clearly that I could not have brought her up so well; indeed, there were moments when I fancied that Cecily, contrasting me with her aunts, wondered a little what my bringing up could have been like. With this reserve of criticism on Cecily's part, however, we got on very tolerably, largely because I found it impossible to assume any responsibility towards her, and in moments of doubt or discipline referred her to her aunts. We spent a pleasant summer with a little girl in the house whose interest in us was amusing, and whose outings it was gratifying to arrange; but when we went back, I had no desire to take her with us. I thought her very much better where she was.

Then came the period which is filled, in a subordinate degree, with Cecily's letters. I do not wish to claim more than I ought; they were not my only or even my principal interest in life. It was a long period; it lasted till she was twenty-one. John had had promotion in the meantime, and there was rather more money, but he had earned his second brevet with a bullet through one lung, and the doctors ordered our leave to be spent in South Africa. We had photographs, we knew she had grown tall and athletic and comely, and the letters were always very creditable. I had the unusual and qualified privilege of watching my daughter's development from ten to twenty-one, at a distance of four thousand miles, by means of the written word. I wrote myself as provocatively as possible; I sought for every string, but the vibration that came back across the seas to me was always other than the one I looked for, and sometimes there was none. Nevertheless, Mrs Farnham wrote me that Cecily very much valued my communications. Once when I had described an unusual excursion in a native state, I learned that she had read my letter aloud to the sewing circle. After that I abandoned description, and confined myself to such intimate personal details as no sewing circle could find amusing. The child's own letters were simply a mirror of the ideas of the Farnham ladies; that must have been so, it was not altogether my jaundiced eye. Alice and Emma and grandmamma paraded the pages in turn. I very early gave up hope of discoveries in my daughter, though as much of the original as I could detect was satisfactorily simple and sturdy. I found little things to criticise, of course, tendencies to correct; and by return post I criticised and corrected, but the distance and the deliberation seemed to touch my maxims with a kind of arid frivolity, and sometimes I tore them up. One quick, warm-blooded scolding would have been worth a sheaf of them. My studied little phrases could only inoculate her with a dislike for me without protecting her from anything under the sun.

However, I found she didn't dislike me, when John and I went home at last to bring her out. She received me with just a hint of kindness, perhaps, but on the whole very well.

II

John was recalled, of course, before the end of our furlough, which knocked various things on the head; but that is the sort

of thing one learned to take with philosophy in any length-
ened term of Her Majesty's service. Besides, there is usually
sugar for the pill; and in this case it was a Staff command
bigger than anything we expected for at least five years to
come. The excitement of it when it was explained to her gave
Cecily a charming colour. She took a good deal of interest in
the General, her papa; I think she had an idea that his
distinction would alleviate the situation in India, however it
might present itself. She accepted that prospective situation
calmly; it had been placed before her all her life. There would
always be a time when she should go and live with papa and
mamma in India, and so long as she was of an age to receive
the idea with rebel tears she was assured that papa and
mamma would give her a pony. The pony was no longer
added to the prospect; it was absorbed no doubt in the
general list of attractions calculated to reconcile a young lady
to a roof with which she had no practical acquaintance. At all
events, when I feared the embarrassment and dismay of a
pathetic parting with darling grandmamma and the aunties,
and the sweet cat and the dear vicar and all the other objects
of affection, I found an agreeable unexpected philosophy.

I may add that while I anticipated such broken-hearted
farewells I was quite prepared to take them easily. Time, I
imagined, had brought philosophy to me also, equally agreeable and equally unexpected.

It was a Bombay ship, full of returning Anglo-Indians. I
looked up and down the long saloon tables with a sense of
relief and a solace; I was again among my own people. They
belonged to Bengal and to Burma, to Madras and to the
Punjab, but they were all my people. I could pick out a score
that I knew in fact, and there were none that in imagination I
didn't know. The look of wider seas and skies, the casual
experienced glance, the touch of irony and of tolerance, how
well I knew it and how well I liked it! Dear old England,

sitting in our wake, seemed to hold by comparison a great many soft, unsophisticated people, immensely occupied about very particular trifles. How difficult it had been, all the summer, to be interested! These of my long acquaintance belonged to my country's Executive, acute, alert, with the marks of travail on them. Gladly I went in and out of the women's cabins and listened to the argot of the men; my own ruling, administering, soldiering little lot.

Cecily looked at them askance. To her the atmosphere was alien, and I perceived that gently and privately she registered objections. She cast a disapproving eye upon the wife of a Conservator of Forests, who scanned with interest a distant funnel and laid a small wager that it belonged to the Messageries Maritimes. She looked with a straightened lip at the crisply stepping women who walked the deck in short and rather shabby skirts with their hands in their jacket-pockets talking transfers and promotions; and having got up at six to make a water-colour sketch of the sunrise, she came to me in profound indignation to say that she had met a man in his pyjamas; no doubt, poor wretch, on his way to be shaved. I was unable to convince her that he was not expected to visit the barber in all his clothes.

At the end of the third day she told me that she wished these people wouldn't talk to her; she didn't like them. I had turned in the hour we left the Channel and had not left my berth since, so possibly I was not in the most amiable mood to receive a douche of cold water. 'I must try to remember, dear,' I said, 'that you have been brought up altogether in the society of pussies and vicars and elderly ladies, and of course you miss them. But you must have a little patience. I shall be up to-morrow, if this beastly sea continues to go down; and then we will try to find somebody suitable to introduce to you.'

'Thank you, mamma,' said my daughter, without a ray of

suspicion. Then she added consideringly, 'Aunt Emma and Aunt Alice do seem quite elderly ladies beside you, and yet you are older than either of them, aren't you? I wonder how that is.'

It was so innocent, so admirable, that I laughed at my own expense; while Cecily, doing her hair, considered me gravely. 'I wish you would tell me why you laugh, mamma,' quoth she; 'you laugh so often.'

We had not to wait after all for my good offices of the next morning. Cecily came down at ten o'clock that night quite happy and excited; she had been talking to a bishop, such a dear bishop. The bishop had been showing her his collection of photographs, and she had promised to play the harmonium for him at the eleven-o'clock service in the morning. 'Bless me!' said I, 'is it Sunday?' It seemed she had got on very well indeed with the bishop, who knew the married sister, at Tunbridge, of her very greatest friend. Cecily herself did not know the married sister, but that didn't matter – it was a link. The bishop was charming. 'Well, my love,' said I–I was teaching myself to use these forms of address for fear she would feel an unkind lack of them, but it was difficult – 'I am glad that somebody from my part of the world has impressed you favourably at last. I wish we had more bishops.'

'Oh, but the bishop doesn't belong to your part of the world,' responded my daughter sleepily. 'He is travelling for his health.'

It was the most unexpected and delightful thing to be packed into one's chair next morning by Dacres Tottenham. As I emerged from the music saloon after breakfast – Cecily had stayed below to look over her hymns and consider with her bishop the possibility of the anthem – Dacres's face was the first I saw; it simply illuminated, for me, that portion of the deck. I noticed with pleasure the quick toss of the cigar

overboard as he recognised and bore down upon me. We
were immense friends; John liked him too. He was one of
those people who make a tremendous difference; in all our
three hundred passengers there could be no one like him,
certainly no one whom I could be more glad to see. We
plunged at once into immediate personal affairs, we would
get at the heart of them later. He gave his vivid word to
everything he had seen and done; we laughed and exclaimed
and were silent in a concert of admirable understanding. We
were still unravelling, still demanding and explaining when
the ship's bell began to ring for church, and almost simultaneously Cecily advanced towards us. She had a proper
Sunday hat on, with flowers under the brim, and a church-
going frock; she wore gloves and clasped a prayer-book.
Most of the women who filed past to the summons of the bell
were going down as they were, in cotton blouses and serge
skirts, in tweed caps or anything, as to a kind of family
prayers. I knew exactly how they would lean against the
pillars of the saloon during the psalms. This young lady
would be little less than a rebuke to them. I surveyed her
approach; she positively walked as if it were Sunday.

'My dear,' I said, 'how *endimanchée* you look! The bishop
will be very pleased with you. This gentleman is Mr Tottenham, who administers Her Majesty's pleasure in parts of
India about Allahabad. My daughter, Dacres.' She was certainly looking very fresh, and her calm grey eyes had the
repose in them that has never known itself to be disturbed
about anything. I wondered whether she bowed so distantly
also because it was Sunday, and then I remembered that
Dacres was a young man, and that the Farnham ladies had
probably taught her that it was right to be very distant with
young men.

'It is almost eleven, mamma.'

'Yes, dear. I see you are going to church.'

'Are you not coming, mamma?'

I was well wrapped up in an extremely comfortable corner. I had *La Duchesse Bleue* uncut in my lap, and an agreeable person to talk to. I fear that in any case I should not have been inclined to attend the service, but there was something in my daughter's intonation that made me distinctly hostile to the idea. I am putting things down as they were, extenuating nothing.

'I think not, dear.'

'I've turned up two such nice seats.'

'Stay, Miss Farnham, and keep us in countenance,' said Dacres, with his charming smile. The smile displaced a look of discreet and amused observation. Dacres had an eye always for a situation, and this one was even newer to him than to me.

'No, no. She must run away and not bully her mamma,' I said. 'When she comes back we will see how much she remembers of the sermon'; and as the flat tinkle from the companion began to show signs of diminishing, Cecily, with one grieved glance, hastened down.

'You amazing lady!' said Dacres. 'A daughter — and such a tall daughter! I somehow never —'

'You knew we had one?'

'There was theory of that kind, I remember, about ten years ago. Since then — excuse me — I don't think you've mentioned her.'

'You talk as if she were a skeleton in the closet!'

'You *didn't* talk — as if she were.'

'I think she was, in a way, poor child. But the resurrection day hasn't confounded me as I deserved. She's a very good girl.'

'If you had asked me to pick out your daughter —'

'She would have been the last you would indicate! Quite so,' I said. 'She is like her father's people. I can't help that.'

'I shouldn't think you would if you could,' Dacres re-marked absently; but the sea air, perhaps, enabled me to digest his thoughtlessness with a smile.

'No,' I said, 'I am just as well pleased. I think a resemblance to me would confuse me, often.'

There was a trace of scrutiny in Dacres's glance. 'Don't you find yourself in sympathy with her?' he asked.

'My dear boy, I have seen her just twice in twenty-one years! You see, I've always stuck to John.'

'But between mother and daughter — I may be old-fashioned, but I had an idea that there was an instinct that might be depended on.'

'I am depending on it,' I said, and let my eyes follow the little blue waves that chased past the handrail. 'We are making very good speed, aren't we? Thirty-five knots since last night at ten. Are you in the sweep?'

'I never bet on the way out — can't afford it. Am I old-fashioned?' he insisted.

'Probably. Men are very slow in changing their philosophy about women. I fancy their idea of the maternal relation is firmest fixed of all.'

'We see it a beatitude!' he cried.

'I know,' I said wearily, 'and you never modify the view.'

Dacres contemplated the portion of the deck that lay between us. His eyes were discreetly lowered, but I saw embarrassment and speculation and a hint of criticism in them.

'Tell me more about it,' said he.

'Oh, for heaven's sake don't be sympathetic!' I exclaimed. 'Lend me a little philosophy instead. There is nothing to tell. There she is and there I am, in the most intimate relation in the world, constituted when she is twenty-one and I am forty.' Dacres started slightly at the ominous word; so little do men realise that the women they like can ever pass out of the constated years of attraction. 'I find the young lady very tolerable, very creditable, very nice. I find the relation atrocious. There you have it. I would like to break the relation into pieces,' I went on recklessly, 'and throw it into the sea. Such things should be tempered to one. I should feel it much less if she occupied another cabin, and would consent to call me Elizabeth or Jane. It is not as if I had been her mother always. One grows fastidious at forty — new intimacies are only possible then on a basis of temperament — '

I paused; it seemed to me that I was making excuses, and I had not the least desire in the world to do that.

'How awfully rough on the girl!' said Dacres Tottenham.

'That consideration has also occurred to me,' I said candidly, 'though I have perhaps been even more struck by its converse.'

'You had no earthly business to be her mother,' said my friend, with irritation.

I shrugged my shoulders — what would you have done? — and opened *La Duchesse Bleue*.

III

Mrs Morgan, wife of a judge of the High Court of Bombay, and I sat amidships on the cool side in the Suez Canal. She was outlining 'Soiled Linen' in chain-stitch on a green canvas bag; I was admiring the Egyptian sands. 'How charming,' said I, 'is this solitary desert in the endless oasis we are compelled to cross!'

'Oasis in the desert, you mean,' said Mrs Morgan; 'I haven't noticed any, but I happened to look up this morning as I was putting on my stockings, and I saw through my port-hole the most lovely mirage.'

I had been at school with Mrs Morgan more than twenty years agone, but she had come to the special enjoyment of the dignities of life while I still liked doing things. Mrs Morgan was the kind of person to make one realise how distressing a medium is middle age. Contemplating her precipitous lap, to which conventional attitudes were certainly more becoming, I crossed my own knees with energy, and once more resolved to be young until I was old.

'How perfectly delightful for you to be taking Cecily out!' said Mrs Morgan placidly.

'Isn't it?' I responded, watching the gliding sands.

'But she was born in sixty-nine – that makes her twenty-one. Quite time, I should say.'

'Oh, we couldn't put it off any longer. I mean – her father has such a horror of early débuts. He simply would not hear of her coming before.'

'Doesn't want her to marry in India, I dare say – the only one,' purred Mrs Morgan.

'Oh, I don't know. It isn't such a bad place. I was brought out there to marry, and I married. I've found it very satisfactory.'

'You always did say exactly what you thought, Helena,' said Mrs Morgan excusingly.

'I haven't much patience with people who bring their daughters out to give them the chance they never would have in England, and then go about devoutly hoping they won't marry in India,' I said. 'I shall be very pleased if Cecily does as well as your girls have done.'

'Mary in the Indian Civil and Jessie in the Imperial Service Troops,' sighed Mrs Morgan complacently. 'And both, my dear, within a year. It *was* a blow.'

'Oh, it must have been!' I said civilly.

There was no use in bandying words with Emily Morgan.

'There is nothing in the world like the satisfaction and pleasure one takes in one's daughters,' Mrs Morgan went on limpidly. 'And one can be in such *close* sympathy with one's girls. I have never regretted having no sons.'

'Dear me, yes. To watch oneself growing up again — call back the lovely April of one's prime, etcetera — to read every thought and anticipate every wish — there is no more golden privilege in life, dear Emily. Such a direct and natural avenue for affection, such a wide field for interest!'

I paused, lost in the volume of my admirable sentiments.

'How beautifully you talk, Helena! I wish I had the gift.'

'It doesn't mean very much,' I said truthfully.

'Oh, I think it's everything! And how companionable a girl is! I quite envy you, this season, having Cecily constantly with you and taking her about everywhere. Something quite new for you, isn't it?'

'Absolutely,' said I; 'I am looking forward to it immensely. But it is likely she will make her own friends, don't you think?' I added anxiously.

'Hardly the first season. My girls didn't. I was practically their only intimate for months. Don't be afraid; you won't be obliged to go shares in Cecily with anybody for a good long while,' added Mrs Morgan kindly. 'I know just how you feel about *that*.'

The muddy water of the Ditch chafed up from under us against its banks with a smell that enabled me to hide the emotions Mrs Morgan evoked behind my handkerchief. The pale desert was pictorial with the drifting, deepening purple shadows of clouds, and in the midst a blue glimmer of the Bitter Lakes, with a white sail on them. A little frantic Arab boy ran alongside keeping pace with the ship. Except for the smell, it was like a dream, we moved so quietly; on, gently on and on between the ridgy clay banks and the rows of piles. Peace was on the ship; you could hear what the Fourth in his white ducks said to the quartermaster in his blue denims; you could count the strokes of the electric bell in the wheelhouse; peace was on the ship as she pushed on, an ever-venturing, double-funnelled impertinence, through the sands of the ages. My eyes wandered along a plank-line in the deck till they were arrested by a petticoat I knew, when they returned of their own accord. I seemed to be always seeing that petticoat.

'I think,' resumed Mrs Morgan, whose glance had wandered in the same direction, 'that Cecily is a very fine type of our English girls. With those dark grey eyes, a *little* prominent possibly, and that good colour — it's rather high now perhaps, but she will lose quite enough of it in India — and those regular features, she would make a splendid Britannia. Do you know, I fancy she must have a great deal of character. Has she?'

'Any amount. And all of it good,' I responded, with private dejection.

'No faults at all?' chaffed Mrs Morgan.

I shook my head. 'Nothing,' I said sadly, 'that I can put my finger on. But I hope to discover a few later. The sun may bring them out.'

'Like freckles. Well, you are a lucky woman. Mine had plenty, I assure you. Untidiness was no name for Jessie, and Mary — I'm *sorry* to say that Mary sometimes fibbed.'

'How lovable of her! Cecily's neatness is a painful example to me, and I don't believe she would tell a fib to save my life.'

'Tell me,' said Mrs Morgan, as the lunch-bell rang and she gathered her occupation into her work-basket, 'who is that talking to her?'

'Oh, an old friend,' I replied easily; 'Dacres Tottenham, a dear fellow, and most benevolent. He is trying on my behalf to reconcile her to the life she'll have to lead in India.'

'She won't need much reconciling, if she's like most girls,' observed Mrs Morgan, 'but he seems to be trying very hard.'

That was quite the way I took it — on my behalf — for several days. When people have understood you very adequately for ten years you do not expect them to boggle at any problem you may present at the end of the decade. I thought Dacres was moved by a fine sense of compassion. I thought that with his admirable perception he had put a finger on the little comedy of fruitfulness in my life that laughed so bitterly at the tragedy of the barren woman, and was attempting, by delicate manipulation, to make it easier. I really thought so. Then I observed that myself had preposterously deceived me, that it wasn't like that at all. When Mr Tottenham joined us, Cecily and me, I saw that he had listened more than he talked, with an ear specially cocked to register any small irony which might appear in my remarks to my daughter. Naturally he registered more than there were, to make up perhaps for dear Cecily's obviously not registering any. I could see, too, that he was suspicious of any flavour of kindness; finally, to avoid the strictures of his upper lip, which really, dear fellow, began to bore me, I talked exclusively about the distant sails and the Red Sea littoral. When he no longer joined us as we sat or walked together, I perceived that his hostility was fixed and his *parti pris*. He was brimful of compassion, but it was all for Cecily, none for the situation or for me. (She would have marvelled, placidly, why he pitied her. I am glad I can say that.) The primitive man in him rose up as Pope of nature and excommunicated me as a creature recusant to her functions. Then deliberately Dacres undertook an office of consolation; and I fell to wondering, while Mrs Morgan spoke her convictions plainly out, how far an impulse of reparation for a misfortune with which he had nothing to do might carry a man.

I began to watch the affair with an interest which even to me seemed queer. It was not detached, but it was semi-detached, and, of course, on the side for which I seem, in this history, to be perpetually apologising. With certain limitations it didn't matter an atom whom Cecily married. So that he was sound and decent, with reasonable prospects, her simple requirements and ours for her would be quite met. There was the ghost of a consolation in that; one needn't be anxious or exacting.

I could predict with a certain amount of confidence that in her first season she would probably receive three or four proposals, any one of which she might accept with as much propriety and satisfaction as any other one. For Cecily it was so simple; prearranged by nature like her digestion, one could not see any logical basis for difficulties. A nice up-standing sapper, a dashing Bengal Lancer — oh, I could think of half a dozen types that would answer excellently. She was the kind of young person, and that was the summing up of it, to marry a type and be typically happy. I hoped and expected that she would. But Dacres!

Dacres should exercise the greatest possible discretion. He was not a person who could throw the dice indifferently with fate. He could respond to so much, and he would inevitably, sooner or later, demand so much response! He was governed by a preposterously exacting temperament, and he wore his nerves outside. And what vision he had! How he explored the world he lived in and drew out of it all there was, all there was! I could see him in the years to come ranging alone the fields that were sweet and the horizons that lifted for him, and ever returning to pace the common dusty mortal road by the side of a purblind wife. On general principles, as a case to point at, it would be a conspicuous pity. Nor would it lack the aspect of a particular, a personal misfortune. Dacres was occupied in quite the natural normal degree with his charming self; he would pass his misery on, and who would deserve to escape it less than his mother-in-law?

I listened to Emily Morgan, who gleaned in the ship more information about Dacres Tottenham's people, pay, and prospects than I had ever acquired, and I kept an eye upon the pair which was, I flattered myself, quite maternal. I watched them without acute anxiety, deploring the threatening destiny, but hardly nearer to it than one is in the stalls to the stage. My moments of real concern for Dacres were mingled more with anger than with sorrow — it seemed inexcusable that he, with his infallible divining-rod for temperament, should be on the point of making such an ass of himself. Though I talk of the stage there was nothing at all dramatic to reward my attention, mine and Emily Morgan's. To my imagination, excited by its idea of what Dacres Tottenham's courtship ought to be, the attentions he paid to Cecily were most humdrum. He threw rings into buckets with her — she was good at that — and quoits upon the 'bull' board; he found her chair after the decks were swabbed in the morning and established her in it; he paced the deck with her at convenient times and seasons. They were humdrum, but they were constant and cumulative. Cecily took them with an even breath that perfectly matched. There was hardly anything, on her part, to note — a little discreet observation of his comings and goings, eyes scarcely lifted from her book, and later just a hint of proprietorship, as on the evening she came up to me on deck, our first night in the Indian Ocean. I was lying on my long chair looking at the thick, low stars and thinking it was a long time since I had seen John.

'Dearest mamma, out here and nothing over your shoulders! You *are* imprudent. Where is your wrap? Mr Tottenham, will you please fetch mamma's wrap for her?'

'If mamma so instructs me,' he said audaciously.

'Do as Cecily tells you,' I laughed, and he went and did it, while I by the light of the quartermaster's lantern distinctly saw my daughter blush.

Another time, when Cecily came down to undress, she bent over me as I lay in the lower berth with unusual solicitude. I had been dozing, and I jumped.

'What is it, child?' I said. 'Is the ship on fire?'

'No, mamma, the ship is not on fire. There is nothing wrong. I'm so sorry I startled you. But Mr Tottenham has been telling me all about what you did for the soldiers the time plague broke out in the lines at Mian-Mir. I think it was splendid, mamma, and so does he.'

'Oh, *Lord!*' I groaned. 'Good night.'

IV

It remained in my mind, that little thing that Dacres had taken the trouble to tell my daughter; I thought about it a good deal. It seemed to me the most serious and convincing circumstance that had yet offered itself to my consideration. Dacres was no longer content to bring solace and support to the more appealing figure of the situation; he must set to work, bless him! to improve the situation itself. He must try to induce Miss Farnham, by telling her everything he could remember to my credit, to think as well of her mother as possible, in spite of the strange and secret blows which that mother might be supposed to sit up at night to deliver to her. Cecily thought very well of me already; indeed, with private reservations as to my manners and — no, *not* my morals, I believe I exceeded her expectations of what a perfectly new and untrained mother would be likely to prove. It was my theory that she found me all she could understand me to be. The maternal virtues of the outside were certainly mine; I put them on with care every morning and wore them with patience all day. Dacres, I assured myself, must have allowed his preconception to lead him absurdly by the nose not to see that the girl was satisfied, that my impatience, my impotence, did not at all make her miserable. Evidently, however, he had created our relations differently; evidently he had set himself to their amelioration. There was portent in it; things seemed to be closing in. I bit off a quarter of an inch of wooden pen-handle in considering whether or not I should mention it in my letter to John, and decided that it would be better just perhaps to drop a hint. Though I could not expect John to receive it with any sort of perturbation. Men are different; he would probably think Tottenham well enough able to look after himself.

I had embarked on my letter, there at the end of a corner-table of the saloon, when I saw Dacres saunter through. He wore a very conscious and elaborately purposeless air; and it jumped with my mood that he had nothing less than the crisis of his life in his pocket, and was looking for me. As he advanced towards me between the long tables doubt left me and alarm assailed me. 'I'm glad to find you in a quiet corner,' said he, seating himself, and confirmed my worst anticipations.

'I'm writing to John,' I said, and again applied myself to my pen-handle. It is a trick Cecily has since done her best in vain to cure me of.

'I am going to interrupt you,' he said. 'I have not had an opportunity of talking to you for some time.'

'I like that!' I exclaimed derisively.

'And I want to tell you that I am very much charmed with Cecily.'

'Well,' I said, 'I am not going to gratify you by saying anything against her.'

'You don't deserve her, you know.'

'I won't dispute that. But, if you don't mind — I'm not sure that I'll stand being abused, dear boy.'

'I quite see it isn't any use. Though one spoke with the tongues of men and of angels — '

'And had not charity,' I continued for him. 'Precisely. I won't go on, but your quotation is very apt.'

'I so bow down before her simplicity. It makes a wide and beautiful margin for the rest of her character. She is a girl Ruskin would have loved.'

'I wonder,' said I. 'He did seem fond of the simple type, didn't he?'

'Her mind is so clear, so transparent. The motive spring of everything she says and does is so direct. Don't you find you can most completely depend upon her?'

'Oh yes,' I said; 'certainly. I nearly always know what she is going to say before she says it, and under given circumstances I can tell precisely what she will do.'

'I fancy her sense of duty is very beautifully developed.'

'It is,' I said. 'There is hardly a day when I do not come in contact with it.'

'Well, that is surely a good thing. And I find that calm poise of hers very restful.'

'I would not have believed that so many virtues could reside in one young lady,' I said, taking refuge in flippancy, 'and to think that she should be my daughter!'

'As I believe you know, that seems to me rather a cruel stroke of destiny, Mrs Farnham.'

'Oh yes, I know! You have a constructive imagination, Dacres. You don't seem to see that the girl is protected by her limitations, like a tortoise. She lives within them quite secure and happy and content. How determined you are to be sorry for her!'

Mr Tottenham looked at the end of this lively exchange as though he sought for a polite way of conveying to me that I rather was the limited person. He looked as if he wished he could say things. The first of them would be, I saw, that he had quite a different conception of Cecily, that it was illuminated by many trifles, nuances of feeling and expression, which he had noticed in his talks with her whenever they had skirted the subject of her adoption by her mother. He knew her, he was longing to say, better than I did; when it would have been natural to reply that one could not hope to compete in such a direction with an intelligent young man, and we should at once have been upon delicate and difficult ground. So it was as well perhaps that he kept silence until he said, as he had come prepared to say, 'Well, I want to put that beyond a doubt — her happiness — if I'm good enough. I want her, please, and I only hope that she will be half as willing to come as you are likely to be to let her go.'

It was a shock when it came, plump, like that; and I was horrified to feel how completely every other consideration was lost for the instant in the immense relief that it prefigured. To be my whole complete self again, without the feeling that a fraction of me was masquerading about in Cecily! To be freed at once, or almost, from an exacting condition and an impossible ideal! 'Oh!' I exclaimed, and my eyes positively filled. 'You *are* good, Dacres, but I couldn't let you do that.'

His undisguised stare brought me back to a sense of the proportion of things. I saw that in the combination of influences that had brought Mr Tottenham to the point of proposing to marry my daughter consideration for me, if it had a place, would be fantastic. Inwardly I laughed at the egotism of raw nerves that had conjured it up, even for an instant, as a reason for gratitude. The situation was not so peculiar, not so interesting, as that. But I answered his stare with a smile; what I had said might very well stand.

'Do you imagine,' he said, seeing that I did not mean to amplify it, 'that I want to marry her out of any sort of *good*ness?'

'Benevolence is your weakness, Dacres.'

'I see. You think one's motive is to withdraw her from a relation which ought to be the most natural in the world, but which is, in her particular and painful case, the most equivocal.'

'Well, come,' I remonstrated. 'You have dropped one or two things, you know, in the heat of your indignation, not badly calculated to give one that idea. The eloquent statement you have just made, for instance — it carries all the patness of old conviction. How often have you rehearsed it?'

I am a fairly long-suffering person, but I began to feel a little annoyed with my would-be-son-in-law. If the relation were achieved it would give him no prescriptive right to bully me; and we were still in very early anticipation of that.

'Ah!' he said disarmingly. 'Don't let us quarrel. I'm sorry you think that; because it isn't likely to bring your favour to my project, and I want you friendly and helpful. Oh, confound it!' he exclaimed, with sudden temper. 'You ought to be. I don't understand this aloofness. I half suspect it's pose. You undervalue Cecily — well, you have no business to undervalue me. You know me better than anybody in the world. Now are you going to help me to marry your daughter?'

'I don't think so,' I said slowly, after a moment's silence, which he sat through like a mutinous schoolboy. 'I might tell you that I don't care a button whom you marry, but that would not be true. I do care more or less. As you say, I know you pretty well. I'd a little rather you didn't make a mess of it; and if you must I should distinctly prefer not to have the spectacle under my nose for the rest of my life. I can't hinder you, but I won't help you.'

'And what possesses you to imagine that in marrying Cecily I should make a mess of it? Shouldn't your first consideration be whether *she* would?'

'Perhaps it should, but, you see, it isn't. Cecily would be happy with anybody who made her comfortable. You would ask a good deal more than that, you know.'

Dacres, at this, took me up promptly. Life, he said, the heart of life, had particularly little to say to temperament. By the heart of life I suppose he meant married love. He explained that its roots asked other sustenance, and that it throve best of all on simple elemental goodness. So long as a man sought in women mere casual companionship, perhaps the most exquisite thing to be experienced was the stimulus of some spiritual feminine counterpart; but when he desired of one woman that she should be always and intimately with him, the background of his life, the mother of his children, he was better advised to avoid nerves and sensibilities, and try for the repose of the common – the uncommon – domestic virtues. Ah, he said, they were sweet, like lavender. (Already, I told him, he smelled the housekeeper's linen-chest.) But I did not interrupt him much; I couldn't, he was too absorbed. To temperamental pairing, he declared, the century owed its breed of decadents. I asked him if he had ever really recognised one; and he retorted that if he hadn't he didn't wish to make a beginning in his own family. In a quarter of an hour he repudiated the theories of a lifetime, a gratifying triumph for simple elemental goodness. Having denied the value of the subtler pretensions to charm in woman as you marry her, he went artlessly on to endow Cecily with as many of them as could possibly be desirable. He actually persuaded himself to say that it was lovely to see the reflections of life in her tranquil spirit; and when I looked at him incredulously he grew angry, and hinted that Cecily's sensitiveness to reflections and other things might be a trifle beyond her mother's ken. 'She responds instantly, intimately, to the beautiful everywhere,' he declared.

'Aren't the opportunities of life on board ship rather limited to demonstrate that?' I inquired. 'I know – you mean sunsets. Cecily is very fond of sunsets. She is always asking me to come and look at them.'

'I was thinking of last night's sunset,' he confessed. 'We looked at it together.'

'What did she say?' I asked idly.

'Nothing very much. That's just the point. Another girl would have raved and gushed.'

'Oh, well, Cecily never does that,' I responded. 'Nevertheless she is a very ordinary human instrument. I hope I shall have no temptation ten years hence to remind you that I warned you of her quality.'

'I wish, not in the least for my own profit, for I am well convinced already, but simply to win your cordiality and your approval — never did an unexceptional wooer receive such niggard encouragement! — I wish there were some sort of test for her quality. I would be proud to stand by it, and you would be convinced. I can't find words to describe my objection to your state of mind.'

The thing seemed to me to be a foregone conclusion. I saw it accomplished, with all its possibilities of disastrous commonplace. I saw all that I have here taken the trouble to foreshadow. So far as I was concerned, Dacres's burden would add itself to my philosophies, *voilà tout*. I should always be a little uncomfortable about it, because it had been taken from my back; but it would not be a matter for the wringing of hands. And yet — the hatefulness of the mistake! Dacres's bold talk of a test made no suggestion. Should my invention be more fertile? I thought of something.

'You have said nothing to her yet?' I asked.

'Nothing. I don't think she suspects for a moment. She treats me as if no such fell design were possible. I'm none too confident, you know,' he added, with a longer face.

'We go straight to Agra. Could you come to Agra?'

'Ideal!' he cried. 'The memory of Mumtaz! The garden of the Taj! I've always wanted to love under the same moon as Shah Jehan. How thoughtful of you!'

'You must spend a few days with us in Agra,' I continued. 'And as you say, it is the very place to shrine your happiness, if it comes to pass there.'

'Well, I am glad to have extracted a word of kindness from you at last,' said Dacres, as the stewards came to lay the table. 'But I wish,' he added regretfully, 'you could have thought of a test.'

V

Four days later we were in Agra. A time there was when the name would have been the key of dreams to me; now it stood for John's headquarters. I was rejoiced to think I would look again upon the Taj; and the prospect of living with it was a real enchantment; but I pondered most the kind of house that would be provided for the General Commanding the District, how many the dining-room would seat, and whether it would have a roof of thatch or of corrugated iron — I prayed against corrugated iron. I confess these my preoccupations. I was forty, and at forty the practical considerations of life hold their own even against domes of marble, world-renowned and set about with gardens where the bulbul sings to the rose. I smiled across the years at the raptures of my first vision of the place at twenty-one, just Cecily's age. Would I now sit under Arjamand's cypresses till two o'clock in the morning to see the wonder of her tomb at a particular angle of the moon? Would I climb one of her tall white ministering minarets to see anything whatever? I very greatly feared that I would not. Alas for the aging of sentiment, of interest! Keep your touch with life and your seat in the saddle as long as you will, the world is no new toy at forty. But Cecily was twenty-one, Cecily who sat stolidly finishing her lunch while Dacres Tottenham talked about Akbar and his philosophy. 'The sort of man,' he said, 'that Carlyle might have smoked a pipe with.'

'But surely,' said Cecily reflectively, 'tobacco was not

discovered in England then. Akbar came to the throne in 1526.'

'Nor Carlyle either for that matter,' I hastened to observe. 'Nevertheless, I think Mr Tottenham's proposition must stand.'

'Thanks, Mrs Farnham,' said Dacres. 'But imagine Miss Farnham's remembering Akbar's date! I'm sure you didn't!'

'Let us hope she doesn't know too much about him,' I cried gaily, 'or there will be nothing to tell!'

'Oh, really and truly very little!' said Cecily, 'but as soon as we heard papa would be stationed here Aunt Emma made me read up about those old Moguls and people. I think I remember the dynasty. Babur, wasn't he the first? and then Humayon, and after him Akbar, and then Jehangir, and then Shah Jehan. But I've forgotten every date but Akbar's.'

She smiled her smile of brilliant health and even spirits as she made the damaging admission, and she was so good to look at, sitting there simple and wholesome and fresh, peeling her banana with her well-shaped fingers, that we swallowed the dynasty as it were whole, and smiled back upon her. John, I may say, was extremely pleased with Cecily; he said she was a very satisfactory human accomplishment. One would have thought, positively, the way he plumed himself over his handsome daughter, that he alone was responsible for her. But John, having received his family, straightway set off with his staff on a tour of inspection, and thereby takes himself out of this history. I sometimes think that if he had stayed − but there has never been the lightest recrimination between us about it, and I am not going to hint one now.

'Did you read,' asked Dacres, 'what he and the Court poet wrote over the entrance gate to the big mosque at Fattehpur-Sikri? It's rather nice. "The world is a looking-glass, wherein the image has come and is gone − take as thine own nothing more than what thou lookest upon." '

'My daughter's thoughtful gaze was, of course, fixed upon the speaker, and in his own glance I saw a sudden ray of consciousness; but Cecily transferred her eyes to the opposite wall, deeply considering, and while Dacres and I smiled across the table, I saw that she had perceived no reason for blushing. It was a singularly narrow escape.

'No,' she said, 'I didn't; what a curious proverb for an emperor to make! He couldn't possibly have been able to see all his possessions at once.'

'If you have finished,' Dacres addressed her, 'do let me show you what your plain and immediate duty is to the garden. The garden waits for you − all the roses expectant −'

'Why, there isn't one!' cried Cecily, pinning on her hat. It was pleasing, and just a trifle pathetic, the way he hurried her out of the scope of any little dart; he would not have her even within range of amused observation. Would he continue, I wondered vaguely, as, with my elbows on the table, I tore into strips the lemon-leaf that floated in my finger-bowl − would he continue, through life, to shelter her from his other clever friends as now he attempted to shelter her from her mother? In that case he would have to domicile her, poor dear, behind the curtain, like the native ladies − a good price to pay for a protection of which, bless her heart! she would be all unaware. I had quite stopped bemoaning the affair; perhaps the comments of my husband, who treated it with broad approval and satisfaction, did something to soothe my sensibilities. At all events, I had gradually come to occupy a high fatalistic ground towards the pair. If it was written upon their foreheads that they should marry, the inscription was none of mine; and, of course, it was true, as John had indignantly stated, that Dacres might do very much worse. One's interest in Dacres Tottenham's problematical future had in no way diminished; but the young man was so positive, so full of intention, so disinclined to discussion — he had not reopened the subject since that morning in the saloon of the *Caledonia* — that one's feeling about it rather took the attenuated form of a shrug. I am afraid, too, that the pleasurable excitement of such an impending event had a little supervened; even at forty there is no disallowing the natural interests of one's sex. As I sat there pulling my lemon-leaf to pieces, I should not have been surprised or in the least put about if the two had returned radiant from the lawn to demand my blessing. As to the test of quality that I had obligingly invented for Dacres on the spur of the moment without his knowledge or con-nivance, it had some time ago faded into what he appre-hended it to be — a mere idyllic opportunity, a charming background, a frame for his project, of prettier sentiment than the funnels and the handrails of a ship.

Mr Tottenham had ten days to spend with us. He knew the place well; it belonged to the province to whose service he was dedicated, and he claimed with impressive authority the privilege of showing it to Cecily by degrees — the Hall of Audience to-day, the Jessamine Tower to-morrow, the tomb of Akbar another, and the Deserted City yet another day. We arranged the expeditions in conference, Dacres insisting only upon the order of them, which I saw was to be cumulative, with the Taj at the very end, on the night precisely of the full of the moon, with a better chance of roses. I had no special views, but Cecily contributed some; that we should do the Hall of Audience in the morning, so as not to interfere with the club tennis in the afternoon, that we should bicycle to Akbar's tomb and take a cold luncheon — if we were sure there would be no snakes — to the Deserted City, to all of which Dacres gave loyal assent. I endorsed everything; I was the encouraging chorus, only stipulating that my number should be swelled from day to day by the addition of such persons as I should approve. Cecily, for instance, wanted to invite the Bakewells because we had come out in the same ship with them; but I could not endure the Bakewells, and it seemed to me that our having made the voyage with them was the best possible reason for declining to lay eyes on them for the rest of our natural lives. 'Mamma has such strong prejudices,' Cecily remarked, as she reluctantly gave up the idea; and I waited to see whether the graceless Tottenham would unmurmuringly take down the Bakewells. How strong must be the sentiment that turns a man into a boa-constrictor without a pang of transmigration! But no, this time he was faithful to the principles of his pre-Cecilian existence. 'They are rather Boojums,' he declared. 'You would think so, too, if you knew them better. It is that kind of excellent person that makes the real burden of India.' I could have patted him on the back.

Thanks to the rest of the chorus, which proved abundantly available, I was no immediate witness to Cecily's introduction to the glorious fragments which sustain in Agra the memory of the Moguls. I may as well say that I arranged with care that if anybody must be standing by when Dacres disclosed them, it should not be I. If Cecily had squinted, I should have been sorry, but I would have found in it no personal humiliation. There were other imperfections of vision, however, for which I felt responsible and ashamed; and with Dacres, though the situation, Heaven knows, was none of my seeking, I had a little the feeling of a dealer who offers a defective *bibelot* to a connoisseur. My charming daughter – I was fifty times congratulated upon her appearance and her manners – had many excellent qualities and capacities which she never inherited from me; but she could see no more than the bulk, no further than the perspective; she could register exactly as much as a camera.

This was a curious thing, perhaps, to displease my maternal vanity, but it did; I had really rather she squinted; and when there was anything to look at I kept out of the way. I can not tell precisely, therefore, what the incidents were that contributed to make Mr Tottenham, on our return from these expeditions, so thoughtful, with a thoughtfulness which increased, towards the end of them, to a positive gravity. This would disappear during dinner under the influence of food and drink. He would talk nightly with new enthusiasm and fresh hope – or did I imagine it? – of the loveliness he had arranged to reveal on the following day. If again my imagination did not lead me astray, I fancied this occurred later and later in the course of the meal as the week went on; as if his state required more stimulus as time progressed. One evening, when I expected it to flag altogether, I had a whim to order champagne and observe the effect; but I am glad to say that I reproved myself, and refrained.

Cecily, meanwhile, was conducting herself in a manner which left nothing to be desired. If, as I sometimes thought, she took Dacres very much for granted, she took him calmly for granted; she seemed a prey to none of those fluttering uncertainties, those suspended judgements and elaborate indifferences which translate themselves so plainly in a young lady receiving addresses. She turned herself out very freshly and very well; she was always ready for everything, and I am sure that no glance of Dacres Tottenham's found aught but direct and decorous response. His society on these occasions gave her solid pleasure; so did the drive and the lunch; the satisfactions were apparently upon the same plane. She was aware of the plum, if I may be permitted a brusque but irresistible simile; and with her mouth open, her eyes modestly closed, and her head in a convenient position, she waited, placidly, until it should fall in. The Farnham ladies would have been delighted with the result of their labours in the sweet reason and eminent propriety of this attitude. Thinking of my idiotic sufferings when John began to fix himself upon my horizon, I pondered profoundly the power of nature in differentiation.

One evening, the last, I think, but one, I had occasion to go to my daughter's room, and found her writing in her commonplace-book. She had a commonplace-book, as well as a Where Is It?, an engagement-book, an account-book, a diary, a Daily Sunshine, and others with purposes too various to remember. 'Dearest mamma,' she said, as I was departing, 'there is only one "P" in "opulence," isn't there?'

'Yes,' I replied, with my hand on the door-handle, and added curiously, for it was an odd word in Cecily's mouth, 'Why?'

She hardly hesitated. 'Oh,' she said, 'I am just writing down one or two things Mr Tottenham said about Agra before I forget them. They seemed so true.'

'He has a descriptive touch,' I remarked.

'I think he describes beautifully. Would you like to hear what he said to-day?'

'I would,' I replied, sincerely.

' "Agra," ' read this astonishing young lady, ' "is India's one pure idyl. Elsewhere she offers other things, foolish opulence, tawdry pageant, treachery of eunuchs and jealousies of harems, thefts of kings' jewels and barbaric retributions; but they are actual, visualised, or part of a past that shows to the backward glance hardly more relief and vitality than a Persian painting' − I should like to see a Persian painting − 'but here the immortal tombs and pleasure-houses rise out of colour delicate and subtle; the vision holds across three hundred years; the print of the court is still in the dust of the city." '

'Did you really let him go on like that?' I exclaimed. 'It has the licence of lecture!'

'I encouraged him to. Of course he didn't say it straight off.

He said it naturally; he stopped now and then to cough. I didn't understand it all; but I think I have remembered every word.'

'You have a remarkable memory. I'm glad he stopped to cough. Is there any more?'

'One little bit. "Here the Moguls wrought their passions into marble, and held them up with great refrains from their religion, and set them about with gardens; and here they stand in the twilight of the glory of those kings and the noonday splendour of their own." '

'How clever of you!' I exclaimed. 'How wonderfully clever of you to remember!'

'I had to ask him to repeat one or two sentences. He didn't like that. But this is nothing. I used to learn pages letter-perfect for Aunt Emma. She was very particular. I think it is worth preserving, don't you?'

'Dear Cecily,' I responded, 'you have a frugal mind.'

There was nothing else to respond. I could not tell her just how practical I thought her, or how pathetic her little book.

VI

We drove together, after dinner, to the Taj. The moonlight lay in an empty splendour over the broad sandy road, with the acacias pricking up on each side of it and the gardens of the station bungalows stretching back into clusters of crisp shadows. It was an exquisite February night, very still. Nothing seemed abroad but two or three pariah dogs, upon vague and errant business, and the Executive Engineer going swiftly home from the club on his bicycle. Even the little shops of the bazaar were dark and empty; only here and there a light showed barred behind the carved balconies of the upper rooms, and there was hardly any tom-tomming. The last long slope of the road showed us the river curving to the

left, through a silent white waste that stretched indefinitely
into the moonlight on one side, and was crowned by Akbar's
fort on the other. His long high line of turrets and battle-
ments still guarded a hint of their evening rose, and dim and
exquisite above them hovered the three dome-bubbles of the
Pearl Mosque. It was a night of perfect illusion, and the
illusion was mysterious, delicate, and faint. I sat silent as we
rolled along, twenty years nearer to the original joy of things
when John and I drove through the same old dream.

Dacres, too, seemed preoccupied; only Cecily was, as they
say, herself. Cecily was really more than herself, she ex-
hibited an unusual flow of spirits. She talked continually, she
pointed out this and that, she asked who lived here and who
lived there. At regular intervals of about four minutes she
demanded if it wasn't simply too lovely. She sat straight up
with her vigorous profile and her smart hat; and the sil-
houette of her personality sharply refused to mingle with the
dust of any dynasty. She was a contrast, a protest; positively
she was an indignity. 'Do lean back, dear child,' I exclaimed
at last. 'You interfere with the landscape.'

She leaned back, but she went on interfering with it in
terms of sincerest enthusiasm.

When we stopped at the great archway of entrance I
begged to be left in the carriage. What else could one do,
when the golden moment had come, but sit in the carriage
and measure it? They climbed the broad stone steps together
and passed under the lofty gravures into the garden, and I
waited. I waited and remembered. I am not, as perhaps by
this time is evident, a person of overwhelming sentiment, but
I think the smile upon my lips was gentle. So plainly I could
see, beyond the massive archway and across a score of years,
all that they saw at that moment – Arjamand's garden, and
the long straight tank of marble cleaving it full of sleeping
water and the shadows of the marshalling cypresses; her wide

dark garden of roses and of pomegranates, and at the end the Vision, marvellous, aerial, the soul of something — is it beauty? is it sorrow? — that great white pride of love in mourning such as only here in all the round of our little world lifts itself to the stars, the unpaintable, indescribable Taj Mahal. A gentle breath stole out with a scent of jessamine and such a memory! I closed my eyes and felt the warm luxury of a tear.

Thinking of the two in the garden, my mood was very kind, very conniving. How foolish after all were my cherry-stone theories of taste and temperament before that uncal-culating thing which sways a world and builds a Taj Mahal! Was it probable that Arjamand and her Emperor had loved fastidiously, and yet how they had loved! I wandered away into consideration of the blind forces which move the world, in which comely young persons like my daughter Cecily had such a place; I speculated vaguely upon the value of the subtler gifts of sympathy and insight which seemed indeed, at that enveloping moment, to be mere flowers strewn upon the tide of deeper emotions. The garden sent me a fragrance of roses; the moon sailed higher and picked out the little kiosks set along the wall. It was a charming, charming thing to wait, there at the portal of a silvered, scented garden, for an idyl to come forth.

When they reappeared, Dacres and my daughter, they came with casual steps and cheerful voices. They might have been a couple of tourists. The moolight fell full upon them on the platform under the arch. It showed Dacres measuring with his stick the length of the Sanscrit letters which declared the stately texts, and Cecily's expression of polite, perfunc-tory interest. They looked up at the height above them; they looked back at the vision behind. Then they sauntered towards the carriage, he offering a formal hand to help her down the uncertain steps, she gracefully accepting it.

'You — you have not been long,' said I. 'I hope you didn't hurry on my account.'

'Miss Farnham found the marble a little cold under foot,' replied Dacres, putting Miss Farnham in.

'You see,' explained Cecily, 'I stupidly forgot to change into thicker soles. I have only my slippers. But, mamma, how lovely it is! Do let us come again in the daytime. I am dying to make a sketch of it.'

Mr Tottenham was to leave us on the following day. In the morning, after 'little breakfast', as we say in India, he sought me in the room I had set aside to be particularly my own.

Again I was writing to John, but this time I waited for precisely his interruption. I had got no further than 'My dearest husband,' and my pen handle was a fringe.

'Another fine day,' I said, as if the old, old Indian joke could give him ease, poor man!

'Yes,' said he, 'we are having lovely weather.'

He had forgotten that it was a joke. Then he lapsed into silence while I renewed my attentions to my pen.

'I say,' he said at last, with so strained a look about his mouth that it was almost a contortion, 'I haven't done it, you know.'

'No,' I responded, cheerfully, 'and you're not going to. Is that it? Well!'

'Frankly — ' said he.

'Dear me, yes! Anything else between you and me would be grotesque,' I interrupted, 'after all these years.'

'I don't think it would be a success,' he said, looking at me resolutely with his clear blue eyes, in which still lay, alas! the possibility of many delusions.

'No,' I said, 'I never did, you know. But the prospect had begun to impose upon me.'

'To say how right you were would seem, under the circumstances, the most hateful form of flattery.'

'Yes,' I said, 'I think I can dispense with your verbal endorsement.' I felt a little better. It was, of course, better that the connoisseur should have discovered the flaw before concluding the transaction; but although I had pointed it out myself I was not entirely pleased to have the article returned.

'I am infinitely ashamed that it should have taken me all these days — day after day and each contributory — to discover what you saw so easily and so completely.'

'You forget that I am her mother,' I could not resist the temptation of saying.

'Oh, for God's sake don't jeer! Please be absolutely direct, and tell me if you have reason to believe that to the extent of a thought, of a breath — to any extent at all — she cares.'

He was, I could see, very deeply moved; he had not arrived at this point without trouble and disorder not lightly to be put on or off. Yet I did not hurry to his relief, I was still possessed by a vague feeling of offence. I reflected that any mother would be, and I quite plumed myself upon my annoyance. It was so satisfactory, when one had a daughter, to know the sensations of even any mother. Nor was it soothing to remember that the young man's whole attitude towards Cecily had been based upon criticism of me, even though he sat before me whipped with his own lash. His temerity had been stupid and obstinate; I could not regret his punishment.

I kept him waiting long enough to think all this, and then I replied, 'I have not the least means of knowing.'

I can not say what he expected, but he squared his shoulders as if he had received a blow and might receive another. Then he looked at me with a flash of the old indignation. 'You are not near enough to her for that!' he exclaimed.

'I am not near enough to her for that.'

Silence fell between us. A crow perched upon an opened venetian and cawed lustily. For years afterwards I never heard a crow caw without a sense of vain, distressing experience. Dacres got up and began to walk about the room. I very soon put a stop to that. 'I can't talk to a pendulum,' I said, but I could not persuade him to sit down again.

'Candidly,' he said at length, 'do you think she would have me?'

'I regret to say that I think she would. But you would not dream of asking her.'

'Why not? She is a dear girl,' he responded, inconsequently.

'You could not possibly stand it.'

Then Mr Tottenham delivered himself of this remarkable phrase: 'I could stand it,' he said, 'as well as you can.'

There was far from being any joy in the irony with which I regarded him and under which I saw him gather up his resolution to go; nevertheless I did nothing to make it easy for him. I refrained from imparting my private conviction that Cecily would accept the first presentable substitute that appeared, although it was strong. I made no reference to my daughter's large fund of philosophy and small balance of sentiment. I did not even – though this was reprehensible – confess the test, the test of quality in these ten days with the marble archives of the Moguls, which I had almost wantonly suggested, which he had so unconsciously accepted, so disastrously applied. I gave him quite fifteen minutes of his bad quarter of an hour, and when it was over I wrote truthfully but furiously to John . . .

That was ten years ago. We have since attained the shades of retirement, and our daughter is still with us when she is not with Aunt Emma and Aunt Alice – grandmamma has passed away. Mr Tottenham's dumb departure that day in February – it was the year John got his C.B. – was followed, I am thankful to say, by none of the symptoms of unrequited affection on Cecily's part. Not for ten minutes, so far as I was aware, was she the maid forlorn. I think her self-respect was too robust a character, thanks to the Misses Farnham. Still less, of course, had she any reproaches to serve upon her mother, although for a long time I thought I detected — or was it my guilty conscience? — a spark of shrewdness in the glance she bent upon me when the talk was of Mr Tottenham and the probabilities of his return to Agra. So well did she sustain her experience, or so little did she feel it, that I believe the impression went abroad that Dacres had been sent disconsolate away. One astonishing conversation I had with her some six months later, which turned upon the point of a particularly desirable offer. She told me something then, without any sort of embarrassment, but quite lucidly and directly, that edified me much to hear. She said that while she was quite sure that Mr Tottenham thought of her only as a friend — she had never had the least reason for any other impression — he had done a service for which she could not thank him enough — in showing her what a husband might be. He had given her a standard; it might be high, but it was unalterable. She didn't know whether she could describe it, but Mr Tottenham was different from the kind of man you seemed to meet in India. He had his own ways of looking at things, and he talked so well. He had given her an ideal, and she intended to profit by it. To know that men like Mr Tottenham existed, and to marry any other kind would be an act of folly which she did not intend to commit. No, Major the Hon. Hugh Taverel did not come near it — very far short, indeed! He had talked to her during the whole of dinner the night before about jackal-hunting with a bobbery pack — not at all an elevated mind. Yes, he might be a very good fellow, but as a companion for life she was sure he would not be at all suitable. She would wait.

And she has waited. I never thought she would, but she has. From time to time men have wished to take her from us, but the standard has been inexorable, and none of them have reached it. When Dacres married the charming American whom he caught like a butterfly upon her Eastern tour, Cecily sent them as a wedding present an alabaster model of the Taj, and I let her do it − the gift was so exquisitely appropriate. I suppose he never looks at it without being reminded that he didn't marry Miss Farnham, and I hope that he remembers that he owes it to Miss Farnham's mother. So much I think I might claim; it is really very little considering what it stands for. Cecily is permanently with us − I believe she considers herself an intimate. I am very reasonable about lending her to her aunts, but she takes no sort of advantage of my liberality; she says she knows her duty is at home. She is growing into a firm and solid English maiden lady, with a good colour and great decision of character. That she always had.

I point out to John, when she takes our crumpets away from us, that she gets it from him. I could never take away anybody's crumpets, merely because they were indigestible, least of all my own parents'. She has acquired a distinct affection for us, by some means best known to herself; but I should have no objection to that if she would not rearrange my bonnet-strings. That is a fond liberty to which I take exception; but it is one thing to take exception and another to express it.

Our daughter is with us, permanently with us. She declares that she intends to be the prop of our declining years; she makes the statement often, and always as if it were humorous. Nevertheless I sometimes notice a spirit of inquiry, a note of investigation in her encounters with the opposite sex that suggests an expectation not yet extinct that another and perhaps a more appreciative Dacres Tottenham may flash across her field of vision − alas, how improbable! Myself I can not imagine why she should wish it; I have grown in my old age into a perfect horror of cultivated young men; but if such a person should by a miracle at any time appear, I think it is extremely improbable that I will interfere on his behalf. (1903)

ALICE PERRIN
The Centipede

The Indian winter was over, and it was just at the time when the hot winds are waiting to begin, and punkah-frills are being mended and renewed, and when the up-country trains are crowded with English women and children on their way to the hills. The large hotel, wherein for a few hours I was breaking a long journey, was a well-known resting-place at a busy junction, and the ugly white building resounded with the voices of *ayahs* and babies. In the verandas were piled boxes and packages of every size and appearance.

I was weak from the effects of recent malaria, the night travelling had tired me, and I was resting in a cool, lofty bedroom that smelled of whitewash and bats. As I lay on the narrow webbing bedstead, that dipped in the middle like a hammock, I listened drowsily to quick sounds in the corridors, the squabbling of servants in the compound, and the chirrup of a grey squirrel that whisked industriously up and down the transparent blind of split bamboo that hung before the open window.

Through the blind I could see into the veranda where a pile of luggage cast a patch of shadow, and presently two *ayahs*, shrouded in their white garments, came and seated themselves in this shelter from the roasting sun to gossip and chew betel-nut. They had evidently but just become acquainted, and I was amused to hear them exchanging polite remarks, in affected tones, concerning the market price of food – a topic that with natives holds much the same position as does the weather amongst people in England. While they talked, the fretful wail of an infant rose and fell from a room further down the veranda.

'Thy *mem-sahib* cannot quiet the babba?' said one of the women when preliminary civilities were over. She was very old and shrivelled, with pock-marked features, and sunken, anxious black eyes. She looked shabby and dirty — a complete contrast to her new friend, who was young and fat, with spotless clothing and tinkling silver ornaments.

'She cannot,' replied the other, and she spoke as one with a grievance, 'and the child cries, cries, and always cries. But that the *mem-sahib* has been long in Hindustan and knows too much, would I place a little, a very little, opium under my finger-nail and permit the babba to suck and bite at it. Then would there be peace for all and without harm. But it is forbidden, because these sons of owls, the English, prefer their children to wail and cry till everyone is dead with fatigue! It is a true saying that a demon took a monkey to wife, and the result by the grace of the gods was the English.'

'Doubtless,' said the old woman. 'But it were wiser to do naught, whether the *mem-sahib* knows much or nothing at all. I am old, and was in service with the sahib-people from my girlhood upwards, and some years back did I lose my place, and receive my dismissal without pay or testimonial, only because I endeavoured to save the life of the babba that was then in my charge. Undoubtedly should I have saved her but for the ignorance and stupidity of the *mem-sahib*. But it is ever the same. "Tell a lie and get sweets: tell the truth and lose your life." Now am I forced to take humble and uncertain employment in the compound of a hotel, receiving no regular wages but only the *backsheesh* from the travellers, which is not sufficient to fill my stomach or buy me clothing for the cold weather. My life departs from me, and often do I remember with sorrow the time when I had ten rupees a month, and a blue cloth coat with red braid, and was a power in the compound, till that evil day came when I tried to cure the babba of her sickness, and was falsely told that I had caused her death. I – *I* who had loved her as a mother, who had held her in mine arms and sung her to sleep since she was born. Ai! Ai! it was long ago, but even now, when I have, maybe, eaten curried meat with my rice, which is seldom enough, God knows, do I dream of it all and awake weeping.'

The younger *ayah* made a sound of interrogation, her mouth being too full of betel-nut to speak. I felt glad I understood the language so well, for I was curious to hear what was coming.

'The *mem-sahib* was young,' continued the old woman in a dreary, reminiscent voice, 'and the sahib but little older. They were married before they came across the black water to our country, and when the child was born they were as babes themselves, knowing nothing. The *mem-sahib* was very ill, and there was a nurse-mem present, and the doctor-sahib. But all of them were English, and none of them knew aught of the magic bread that brings delivery, and when I offered to fetch one costing two rupees from the bazaar, they were angered and bade me be silent or take my leave. The child proved a weakling, as I knew full well it would be, for had I not seen the evil night-bird fly over the *mem-sahib's* head the evening before the birth? – and also, after the little one was born, did they not permit the mother to sleep the night through, making no noise or talk to keep away bad spirits?

'But in spite of all this foolishness the child lived, though a weakling, and her eyes were blue as indigo and her hair the colour of a brass cooking vessel that has been newly rubbed. She was of a sweet and gentle disposition, and it was to me she said her first word, calling "*Ayah! ayah!*" It was I who held her when she made her first steps, and it was I who knew when her first tooth came through the gum. She grew stronger when she had turned the twelve months, and all went well. In the hot weather the *mem-sahib* did not go away to the hills, for she was well also, and the doctor-sahib said that the child would do better in the plains, while still so young, than in the hills where the climate will often cause belly trouble to the very little ones.

'The babba throve through the hot season, eating her food, and laughing and playing; but when the rains came, and the air was heavy with the wet heat, she grew listless and would not eat so much or play so often, and one night she awoke crying and pointing with her little hands to her ear. The *mem-sahib* sent with all haste for the doctor-sahib, who was but a youth himself and could know little of the ailments of children, and he said it was cold in the ear. Cold! – when day and night the punkahs were needed, and the ice ever ran short because of the quantity that was used, and the very rain that fell was as hot water to the touch!

'The days and nights went by, and still the babba cried and beat her head, and none of the doctor-sahib's remedies caused relief. Fever came upon her also, and the father and mother were distraught. They could not now take her to the hills because she had grown too weak for the long hot journey. By day and by night I would stay with the *mem-sahib* as she sat white and still beside the babba, who was *behosh* and we listened to her moanings and movements in her pain that could not be stilled. All the time I understood in my mind what it was that made the babba ill and caused the pain in her head, and the true remedy was known to me; but I feared to speak and tell the *mem-sahib*, remembering her anger about the delivery bead, and the evil spirits, and how she ever mocked at the customs of our folk during sickness. We, the people of Hindustan, know well that pain in the ear, such as the babba was suffering, is caused by a centipede that enters the head – though how, the gods alone can tell – and grows and grows till it brings death if it be not removed. There is one cure only, and that even is useless if applied too late.

'Then the hour came when the doctor-sahib told the *mem-*

sahib something that made her weep sorely, and she said to me in her tears, "Oh! *ayah*, the life is passing from my babba, and if sleep comes not to her she will die!"

'I told her, *"Mem-sahib*, weep not; the child shall live!" And, saying no word of my intention I went out, during my dinner hour, into the compound to a corner where an old brick wall was falling into ruin, and I searched amongst the stones, taking care that I touched not a scorpion, of which there were plenty, and once moving aside as a black snake came forth, hissing, and crawled away into the grass. I beheld many evil creatures, for in the rainy season do they increase and multiply, preying one upon the other, and it is the time when snakes, and scorpions, and such like, have come to their full size.

'I turned the bricks over with care till I found that which I sought − a large centipede, yellow, and a great length, with hundreds of feet spread out from its body like wires. I caught it in the duster I had brought with me, and then I searched for its mate, knowing that the centipede, like the cobra and karait, is seldom found alone. But I looked in vain, and my food-time was nearly over, therefore was I forced to be content with that which I had got.

'I went to my outhouse and prepared the remedy. The centipede that I had caught did I fry in clarified butter, and pounded it with certain herbs, and spells written on paper, making a poultice; and I rejoiced at what I had done, for I knew that when the mixture was laid on the child's head, the centipede that was already within her brain, causing the pain and sickness, would come forth out of her ear and she would live.

'With caution did I take the poultice into the bungalow hidden beneath my wrapper. The *mem-sahib* was sitting by the babba's cot, and as I entered she held up her finger and whispered to me that the little one seemed quieter and perhaps she would sleep. The tears were running down her white face, and my heart strained within me as I beheld her so weary with sorrow and watching. I desired greatly to tell her I had that beneath my wrapper which would give her back her child, but I withheld my words and urged her to lie down on her bed and rest, saying that I would watch faithfully by the babba and call her should there be need.

'But she would not move, and I sat on the floor and waited, for she had not slept for many nights, and now that the child was quieter, I thought, maybe, in the heat and silence of the afternoon she would doze. It was even as I hoped. The *mem-sahib*'s eyes closed and her head sank down on the little one's cot. I arose and looked at the child; her breathing was quick and faint, her little face was troubled, and oh! so thin and white — white as the folds of my wrapper. The centipede was there, killing her slowly, and it was I only who had the means of saving her life. I looked at the *mem-sahib*; she lay still. Then I put the poultice on the child's head just above the ear, leaving room for the insect to crawl out, and I held it there bending lower over the cot.

'My wrapper slipped from my head and fell on to the bed, touching the face of the *mem-sahib*, who moved, and I became frightened. I left the poultice on the little one's head, gathered up my wrapper, and went softly back to my corner. The room was very still, and the babba had ceased to stir and moan — already was the evil one loosing his hold and preparing to issue forth. The punkah waved to and fro, and mine eyes grew heavy. I know not how it came about but I must have slept. I was awakened by a loud cry, and when I raised my head the *mem-sahib* was holding the babba, and screaming, and plucking at something on the child's neck.

'I ran to the bed, and saw a long yellow centipede lying just below the poultice. It had come forth, the evil one, and I cried out for gladness. Then I saw that it had fastened its poison feet into the child's flesh, and in a moment all was bewilderment and disturbance, and I cannot rightly recall what happened. The sahib ran in, and the doctor-sahib came at once, and they asked me questions. When I answered, and spoke truth concerning what I had done, the doctor-sahib called me bad names, and said that the child had been on the point of sleep, and might have recovered but for my wickedness. That, unwittingly, I must have brought from the ruins, in the folds of my garments, another centipede that had crawled on the bed and clung to the child's flesh, and that now would she die, and all through my fault. I — that had held her in my arms since she was born, and had guided her first steps, and heard her first utterance; I — who loved her as mine own offspring!

'I wept, and explained, and told them that the centipede had been drawn by the poultice from the child's ear; but they paid no heed, and so was I cast forth as a leper and a murderess, without character or payment, reviled and accursed for what I had not done.

'The babba died? Yes. But had the *mem-sahib* not screamed and clutched her when she beheld the evil one, the child would have slept on and awakened cured. The centipede that had issued forth from her ear would have crawled away doing no harm. Whereas the *mem-sahib* endeavoured to pluck it away, and so, as is the custom of its kind, the creature clung with its poison feet, which are as red-hot wires. Thus it all happened through the foolishness and ignorance of the white people, who think they know all and that the dark people know nothing — '

The old *ayah* paused and looked away across the compound with troubled remembrance in her weary eyes.

'Wah! wah!' said the other, and spat red betel-nut juice on the stone floor.

A peevish cry of '*Ayah — ayah*,' came through the doorway

further down the veranda, and the younger woman rose with reluctance.

'Salaam, *ayah-ji*,' she said with condescending civility. 'It hath been pleasant talk and I would that I might remain longer, but my *mem-sahib* calls and her voice is impatient.'

She padded away on her bare feet, and after a few moments the old *ayah* got up with an effort and moved stiffly out of the veranda. I watched her go, and then lay thinking of the tragic little story. Could it be true, or had I fallen asleep and dreamed it all? I rose and looked into the veranda. There stood the boxes casting their patch of shadow, and on the stone floor were splashes of red betel-nut juice. Through the further door came the fretful wail of an infant, and an *ayah*'s voice crooning a native lullaby.

(1906)

ALICE PERRIN
The Rise of Ram Din

It was in the year of the famine when my father, Ram Bux of Kansrao in the Mathura district, bade me make ready to go with him to the City of Kings — which is two days' journey by road from the village — that I might there obtain employment as dish-washer in the service of a sahib; for there were many of us in my father's house, and his crops had failed for want of rain, so that there was not enough food to fill our stomachs.

In his youth my father, Ram Bux, had himself served the Feringhees, and having heard him speak much of those days I felt that I should learn my duties with the greater ease; and as we journeyed through the dry, empty fields in the early morning time, he also told me many more things concerning the ways of the sahibs, which are not the ways of the dark people. I was but a stripling, and knew little of what happened beyond the village of my birth where I worked in the fields and tended the cattle until the day came of which I now speak; and I learned from my father that it is well to obey the orders of the master without thought or question, even when it might be hard to understand the reason of his wishes.

'Thou art somewhat of an owl,' my father told me, 'and not so sharp or clever as was I, who rose to be head-servant in my master's house. But thou hast enough sense to understand an order, and maybe with diligence and obedience thou mayest rise from dish-washer to table-servant, and from table-servant to *khansamah*, and then will it be easy with the bazaar accounts in thy keeping, and power in the establishment, to gather rupees till thou canst return to thy home a person of wealth and importance, even as I did.'

'And what if the sahib beats me for no fault, as thou sayest will happen on occasions?'

'Take thy beating and say nothing. Above all things, do not run away. The Feringhees themselves are brave, though they are dogs and sons of dogs, and when they behold courage in others do they respect it. A beating does little harm. I lived once with a colonel-sahib who gave medicine as a punishment, and that was bad. There are certain sahibs who neither drink, nor beat, nor swear, but it is hard for a new-comer without recommendations or experience to obtain service with such, and the sahibs whom I served in the old days have now all died or gone back across the black water many years since. Thou must be content at first with what thou canst get; only remember this – obey orders without question, quarrel not with thy fellow-servants, and squander not thy wages in the bazaar.'

I pondered over the wise words of my father and laid them up in my heart, and I resolved that I would rise, even as he had done, to be the headservant of a sahib's household, that in time I might return to my village with riches and influence.

When we reached the city, we stayed for the night in the *serai*, and until dawn I could not sleep for the strange sights and sounds, and the crowd that came and went; never before had I seen so many men together. In the morning sunshine we went through the streets, and I stared at the glittering vessels in the brass-shops, at the display of sweetmeats, toys, and jewels, and the gay materials shown by the cloth-merchants. My father bought me a white muslin coat, a pair of calico trousers tight below the knee, and a new *puggaree*; and we took seats in the *ekka* and drove out to the part where the sahibs dwell beyond the city. Here it was all open space and broad roads, with trees of mango, teak, and tamarind, and the gardens were very beautiful. My father told me that, though the native city was wide and full of people, there were now but few sahibs, and no regiments at all; whereas he remembered that before the Mutiny there had been a large cantonment and many sepoys.

There was no service to be had at the house of the magistrate-sahib, or with the colonel-sahib of police, nor with the doctor-sahib, so we went to the bungalow of the engineer-sahib who looked after the roads and buildings of the district. There we heard that a dish-washer was needed, and the *khansamah-jee* said that if my father gave him a *backsheesh*, and I promised him a percentage of my pay, he could get me the place without any recommendation. He also said that the engineer-sahib was a good sahib, and the service to be desired, and that I should be well treated. So after some argument my father paid the *khansamah*, who was named Kullan, and I gave the promise. My father told me again to obey orders and answer not to abuse, and then he left me and went back to his village.

But after he had gone I learned from the bearer, who was also a follower of the Prophet, that no servant ever stayed long with the engineer-sahib. 'For,' he said, 'the sahib is truly a devil, and when I am near him my fear of him is such that my liver melts. Sometimes for weeks will he be quiet, and then he will drink too much whisky, and for days we go in fear of our lives.'

I felt angered that Kullan should have told my father naught of this, and though I said nothing I determined that, should the chance arise to do him an evil in return, I would remember how he had lied and taken my father's money, and bound me to give him percentage on my pay.

When I beheld my master I could well believe that what the bearer had told me was true, for the sahib had hair that was the colour of a polished copper cooking-vessel, and the flesh of his face was like unto raw meat; he ate his food with haste like a pariah dog, and looked about him as though he feared an enemy. Nevertheless, I stayed in his service, for was I not

more or less in bondage to the *khansamah-jee*? And also for
the first few weeks matters went well. The sahib sometimes
beat and abused the other servants, but not badly, and me he
never noticed. I took care to be diligent over my work, I
learned the ways of the compound, Kullan taught me how to
cook (for this spared him trouble when he wished to stay late
in the bazaar), and I helped the bearer to brush the sahib's
clothes and to keep the rooms tidy.

But the peace did not continue. The sahib began to drink
much whisky, and one evening, when some matter dis-
pleased him during dinner he sprang at the bearer, who was
also table-servant, and smote him heavily, using words that
burned mine ears as I sat in the pantry washing the dishes.
The bearer cried out that he was hurt unto death; his *puggaree*
came off, and the sahib kicked it through the open door and
across the veranda into the bushes; then he shook the man as
a dog will shake vermin, and all the time he smote and kicked
him, and roared abuse.

For some hours afterwards the bearer lay in his outhouse
groaning, and later in the night-time he rose and took his
belongings and ran away without his arrears of wages or a
written recommendation. Thus was the *khansamah* forced to
do the bearer's work as well as his own, whereat he grumbled
sorely; and my duties were doubled also, for I now helped to
wait at table; and all the time I watched for a chance of letting
the sahib see that I feared him not, for I remembered my
father's words.

Two days later, when the sahib was sitting at breakfast
eating but little and drinking whisky, the *khansamah* spilt
some sauce on the tablecloth, and my knees shook as the
sahib rose slowly from his seat, and, looking at Kullan with
eyes like those of a tiger, walked towards him just as the
striped-one approaches its victim. Kullan knelt and prayed
for mercy, but the sahib dragged him over the floor till his
coat came off in the sahib's hand, and he kicked the man

along the ground like a game ball, driving him into the veranda. Kullan rose quickly, looking like a beast that is hunted, but before he could flee the sahib caught him and pushed him into the lamp-closet that led from the veranda, and locked the door. He laughed as he put the padlock key in his pocket, and heard Kullan crying and smiting at the door from the darkness within the go-down. When he turned and saw me looking, he shook his fist at me, and told me to go to my work.

Then the sahib went to his room and lay on the bed and slept, and I cleared away the breakfast and washed up everything; afterwards I went to the kitchen and found it empty; the servants' houses were also empty, and none answered to my call. They had all fled in fear, having doubtless heard the noise of the sahib's rage, and there was no one left save I, Ram Din the dish-washer, and Kullan the *khansamah*, who was crying and calling in the lamp go-down.

Towards sundown a telegram came for the sahib, and not without misgiving in my heart I took it to his room. He awoke and read the telegram, and then arose in haste, speaking of trouble concerning a bridge in the district, and bidding me pack his bag with clothes sufficient for a day and night, and order his trap to be got ready, and bring him whisky.

I packed the bag and brought the whisky, and I said, 'Your highness, there is no syce in the stables, they have all run away. But thy slave can harness the horse.'

I went straightaway, and with trouble and patience I put the horse to the cart and brought it to the door. The sahib did not beat me, though from want of knowledge I had done it badly, and when I told him there were no servants left at all he cursed their souls to hell, and bade me stay and take care of everything till he should return.

I asked him, 'What are the orders concerning Kullan *Khansamah* who is imprisoned within the lamp go-down?'

He laughed, and the sound was like the cry of the hyena

round the walls of the village at dusk. 'The order is that he stay there till I return. Dost thou understand?'

I salaamed, and he drove away.

Then did my heart glow within me, for now had my time come, and the sahib should see that I was of use, and could obey. All that evening was I alone in the kitchen, and Kullan cried in the go-down. I fed the horses and the fowls, and after locking up the house at night I took my bed and placed it in the veranda that I might guard against thieves. But I could not sleep by reason of the noise made by the *khansamah*, and I answered him not, for I feared he might persuade me to disobey orders and break open the padlock, and I remembered my father's words. Also did I rejoice that Kullan was in trouble, for had he not deceived my father and taken money under false pretences, and did he not exact percentage from my miserable pay as dish-washer? So I smiled when I heard him beating on the door and calling, and I only feared that when the sahib returned and let him out Kullan might kill me for heeding not his entreaties.

But the sahib did not return the next evening nor the next, and I was forced to move my bed from the front veranda to the back of the house on account of the howling of Kullan in the go-down. I slept the other side of the house, and I kept away from the front veranda, but still could I hear him wailing and calling, and I refrained from bursting open the padlock on the door because of the orders of the sahib.

On the fourth day the sahib had not returned; and the voice of Kullan was hoarse and faint. By the sixth day it was altogether silent, and I thought, 'Now shall I rise to be chief servant, and I shall appoint and have dominion over the other servants; also now will the household accounts be in my hands, and I shall amass wealth.'

When the sahib came back on the morning of the seventh day he looked weary, and as though he had suffered much care and anxiety; he took no notice of me nor did he ask me any questions. I led his horse and trap to the stables, I got his bath and laid out his clean clothes, and brought his breakfast. All the time he was deep in thought and was making figures with a pencil on a piece of paper. I wished to speak, and remind him about Kullan, but it was hard to attract his attention. I coughed and walked about the room, and moved the plates on the breakfast-table, and I took a fly-trap and killed flies with some noise.

At last, when the sahib began to light a big cheroot, I craved permission to speak, and he told me to say what I had to say quickly and not to disturb him.

'Sahib,' I said, with humility, 'concerning the matter of Kullan *khansamah* who is in the go-down, it is necessary to get out the lamp oil.'

He stared at me maybe for one minute, and then he dropped his cheroot, and his red face became white as my clean muslin coat. He rose and pushed me aside, saying no word, and strode into the veranda, I following him. He searched for the key of the padlock in his pockets, but found it not: so he wrenched the chain from the woodwork of the door with great force, and the dead body of Kullan *khansamah* fell out of the go-down face downwards on the veranda floor.

Then the sahib caught me by the shoulder and shook me backwards and forwards, shouting in mine ear and calling me names, and his voice sounded as though his throat were filled with dust. He cried out that he had meant to return in a day and a night, but that the damage to the bridge had delayed him, and he had forgotten all about Kullan the *khansamah*. He cursed me for a fool because I had not broken open the padlock.

'Sahib,' I said, and bowed my head before him, 'the order was that Kullan should stay in the go-down until the day of thine honour's return. This slave did but obey thy commands.'

Then the face of the sahib grew purple, and he choked and gasped, and fell at my feet with foam on his lips; and with much effort I got him into the house, and laid him on his bed.

Afterwards he was ill for many days; but no one, not even the doctor-sahib, or the nurse-mem who came to take care of him, ever knew what had happened, for before I fetched the doctor-sahib I pushed the body of Kullan *khansamah* báck into the go-down and left it there till the night-time, when I buried it in a corner of the compound with all precaution.

There were none to witness the burial or to ask any question, for he was a down-country man, and I said in the bazaar that he had departed to his home.

While the sahib lay sick I made for him jelly, soup and custard, for I had learned from Kullan how to cook. I took my turn in watching by his bedside, and when his health returned I told him privately of what I had done.

For many years after this was I the sahib's head servant on thirty rupees a month, and he was as wax in the hands of his slave, Ram Din. I it was who had charge of the sahib's keys and kept his money. It was I appointed the other servants, and exacted percentage from their wages. It was I who made payments and gave the orders, and the sahib ever settled my accounts without argument. I had authority in the compound. I grew prosperous, and had a large stomach, and a watch and chain.

Now has the sahib retired from the service of the Government and has gone to England, and I, Ram Din, have bought land in mine own district and have married four wives and am a person of importance in the village.

So is it true what my father had told me: that by obeying orders and being fearless may a man rise in the service of the sahib people, and gain wealth and honour.

(1906)

OTTO ROTHFELD

The Crime of Narsingji

'I do hereby charge you, Narsingji Jevansingji, as follows: —
That you, on or about the 15th of March at the railway station
of Partabgadh, first, did strike with your sword Khanderao
Sakaram with intent to kill him and did thereby cause his
death; second, did strike with your sword Lakshmiram
Dhuleram with intent to kill him and did thereby cause his
death; third, did strike with your sword Ranchod Umed with
intent to kill him and did thereby cause his death; fourth, did
strike with your sword Bai Galal with intent to kill her and
did thereby cause her death; fifth, did strike with your sword
Bai Motibai with intent to kill her and thereby cause her
death; and that you are therefore guilty of offences of murder
under S. 302 of the Indian Penal Code, cognisable by the
Court of the Political Agent; and I therefore direct that you
be tried for the said offences by the Court of the Political
Agent.'

The words rang drowsily through the hot tent. The sun
hung straight above the world in the burning sky, and the
very birds were asleep. Two blue-coated and blue-turbaned
policemen leaned upon their Sniders, and between them
stood Narsingji Jevansingji, prisoner and Rajput, accused of
murder. On neck and ears and ankle was the gleam of gold,
and the jauntily twisted turban of yellow silk cocked gallantly
over the left ear. The carefully-curled beard curved from the
parting on the chin round the small ears. For Narsingji was a
Rajput of the blood, a 'son of the kingdom', the descendant
of princes.

The prisoner moved uneasily, looked at his seated judge,
was silent for a moment, and then burst into the story of his
crime.

'Am I guilty, Sahib? I must be, for you tell me I am. Yet I had no intention of killing. Am I not a Rajput, born of the sun? Why should I stain my sword with the blood of women? My father slew the proud Mussulman troopers with steel. Should the blade be dirtied with murder? If you will listen, Sahib, I shall tell you the truth. Why should I speak a lie? I am guilty in your English law, and you will hang me by the neck. Your honour is master. Who shall tell lies in the presence of the master?

'Yet you must know, O Sahib, I, Narsingji, son of Jevansingji, am a Rajput, and of noble house. The Rajah himself is no better, for it is but his destiny that he sits upon the lion-throne. But we are of one blood, he and I. So it was that I lived in his house. I, Narsingji, son of Jevansingji, lived as one of his officers, one of his cadets who shared in his bread and his drink. Since I was a child of twelve have I lived in his house, and been faithful to his salt. Much time has passed since then. But we are of one blood, he and I, O Sahib.

'Well, Sahib, the Rajah had a necklace of emeralds which he wished to have reset in Bombay. So the Rajah sent for me, Narsingji, son of Jevansingji, of the royal blood, to the ante-room on the upper storey, which looks over the river which flows from the hills in the pools among the rocks, and upon the temple of Mahadev where we sacrifice the buffaloes. The Rajah sent for me, and he put the necklace into my hands, the necklace of emeralds, and he ordered me to take it to Bombay and give it into the hands of Shivlal, goldsmith, in the Marwari Bazaar. And I laughed, for the task was light, and I had in me desire of seeing Bombay and the dancing girls of the Girgaum Road. Then a household page came to me out of the inner part of the house, and he handed me silks for matching in the Bhendi Bazaar. And I took the silks, for it was an order of the Lady, the Rani of my Rajah.

'Next morning I rose early, and I rolled up the necklace of emeralds and the silks and my own clothes in my carpet, and I rode forth to the station. And at the station all smiled upon me and wished me well, for all knew me, Narsingji, of the Rajah's household. And all through the day I travelled, in the fire-carriage which the Sahibs have brought into the land. And the seats were hard, and the flies buzzed in the carriage and the dust flew thick and the sun beat hotter and hotter. Many lay down and slept, for the noontide is hot and sleep is good. But I slept not; for, look you, I was alone amongst strangers, and with me were the silks and emeralds. And I have been ever faithful to my salt. So the day passed, O Sahib.

'It was night when the train reached Partabgadh, where it is established for us to change into another train which runs from the North to Bombay. The mail, they said, would arrive in the early morning, before the crowing of the cocks. I was hungry, see you, for I had not broken fast all the long day. So I took my carpet to the end of the platform and sat upon the pebbles and ate bread of wheat-flour and picklings of green-stuffs, which they had given me from my house. For such is our custom upon journeyings. And when I had eaten, I filled my brass cup with water and drank. Evil is the water of Partabgadh. Assuredly he who drinks of it is defiled. Then – why should I tell a lie? – I undid the twist of my turban, and opened the little silver box that nestles therein, and cut off for myself the evening opium dose. Ours is the rich black juice of the Malva poppy, sweet, the giver of strength. Of such did I taste as is ever my custom, neither more nor less. Perhaps – who knows? – it may have been a little more, for I was tired and the day had been long. Then, being at ease, I leant back upon my bundle and looked up to the skies of the night. Stately and fair hung the splendour of the moon, white as of living silver, and the dark green of the shadows stood forth upon the earth, mystic and wonderful. Beautiful shone the moon amongst the sparkling stars, like the face of the loved one by twilight, when she waits decked in her sixteen jewels and the curtains are brilliant with gems. I looked; and the wing-feathers of slumber brushed upon my eyelids. For I was at peace and had been tired.

'Then a fear took me by the heart for that I was in a strange place, and with me the silks and the trinkets. Say they not, "In a strange place all men are thy enemies"? Verily such was my fate at Partabgadh. So, rousing myself, I lifted my carpet and went to the passage where they take the tickets, beside the office of the Master. And there stood a policeman, he whose name you have written first, O Sahib. One of the low-born was he, a rude Mahratta from the plundering Deccan, one of these petty lordlings whom ye have put to be a burden upon us, even unto our Rajput lands, ye rulers from the West. Seeing him, in spite of his surly brow and his dark skin, dark as a baseborn robber's should be, I went to him and said, "Brother" — a curse on my tongue that it ever called such as he Brother — 'I am tired and I have with me a bundle. Watch you it while I sleep, and it will be a kindness." He scowled — the low-born — and said, 'Who are you that I should be your servant? Call me Sahib, brother-in-law.' I was angry, see you, but thinking that the emeralds were of my Rajah and that I must keep them safe, be-thinking me also that I was in a strange land and the Government, I humbled myself and entreated him, even of the Mahratta. Then said he, 'What things of value have you, man from the hills, that you are afraid? Give me twenty rupees and I will watch them. Else shall I surely charge you with a theft.'

'Then I was more angry, for I was no thief, I, Narsingji, son of Jevansingji. But even in my wrath I kept hand on the rein of forbearance and said, "Know thou, son of all the world, that I am a Rajput of the prince's household and no thief.

Twenty rupees I cannot give thee, for so much have I not. But I will give you two rupees to let me sleep here and to look upon my bundle and see that it is safe." Then he laughed aloud — a curse upon his master! — and his dark skin grew yet darker. He mocked me, taunting, and said, 'Sleep here thou shalt not, but under guard.' And then he miscalled my wife and my mother, and my heart grew even fuller. So, speaking ill of my honour, he came to lay hand on my bundle, saying he would see what it held and take his twenty rupees without gift. Then, in my anger, I told him that to put finger on the property of my king was as death. But he laughed and called me base-born.

'There was blood in my eyes and the station was deep coloured with red of blood, blood of the slaying of men. The dress of the man had turned crimson, and the smell of blood took me sharp and bitter in the nostrils. The breath of the Mother, the Mother of Death, lay upon me. In my arms lay my sword and the hilt fitted itself with a caress to the palm of my right hand. I drew it out with a scream and the edge already seemed red ere the killing. He cried and turned to flee, but the sword was already leaping in my hand, and it caught him on the skull with the crash of steel on the victim. I laughed, but I knew not why. I shouted, and knew not wherefore. But all around was the red of battle, and the smell of slaughter. '*Jai Kali!*' — the drumming was in my ear! I turned round to see some form of man come and again bend to go. And he too was garbed in red; and he fell also. So I ran forth upon the platform, shouting and slashing. This alone I know and no more. Only I felt the blade whistle and heard the crash of blow upon flesh, and I longed to kill and kill. And so — so I dropped and was bound, and they told me I had slain five. It may be so, and I know I have killed, though I know not how many. Therefore give the order to hang, for such is your law. There shall be weeping in my house.

'But it is my prayer, O Sahib, that first you give an order to send the emeralds to Shivlal, goldsmith, of the Marwari Bazaar. For never have I or my house, my lord, been faithless to our trust.'

(1909)

LIONEL JAMES
The Honour of Daud Khan

The last of the laggard camels from the *kafila* were out of the
Khyber and crawling over the plain towards Jumrud; the
great shadows from the Bagiari Dhara were creeping across
the white dust-driven *tonga* road; the pickets of Khyber
Rifles from the southern end of the Pass, their day's vigil
done, were climbing down from the heights to concentrate at
Fort Maude, thanking God for a respite from the fierce
refraction of the sun's rays which, on the summits of the
Khyber's iron-stone bastions, at this season of the year, is
almost unbearable.

Turning his back upon the awe-inspiring panorama of
barren rock which the gut of the Pass presents, the officiating
Commandant of the Khyber Rifles pressed leg to his pony's
flanks and cantered along the dusty mile to Jumrud, avoiding
the spirals of pungent dust hovering wearily above the trail of
the belated *kafila*. He had had a long and tedious day; he was
sick of the dust-laden air, and the ride down from Ali Musjid,
through the sweltering heat of a breathless June afternoon,
had wearied him of everything except the thought of his
cooler quarters in Jumrud. Yet he had reason to congratulate
himself. Since he had taken over the officiating reins in the
Khyber nothing untoward had happened, which in this section of the Borderland was almost a record. The fair young
Englishman prided himself that his own handling of these
wild frontiersmen was responsible for the present calm. But
perhaps Jemadar Ali, the grim red-bearded Soubadar-Major
waiting in Jumrud for his commanding officer's return,
could have told a different story — a story of inter-tribal feuds
which at the moment were more engrossing than mere raids

across the frontier and sniping off trading *kafilas* in the Pass. But the Soubadar-Major was not ruminating on these matters, he was waiting for the captain sahib, to whom he had to impart information of another nature.

Presently the sahib arrived at the sloping causeway which leads up to the great brown pile of Jumrud Fort. Dismounting, he tossed his reins to the orderly who had ridden close at his heels, and turned to greet the Soubadar. The latter saluted with the dignified decorum of a well-bred native officer, and made some simple remark concerning the state of the Pass.

'Yes, Soubadar, it has been a very hot day!' and as the sun was down the youthful Commandant pushed back his brown *lungi* and mopped his brow. Dressed in *chupkan* and *lungi*, and with his fair moustache powdered with the fine Khyber dust, he might almost have been taken for a native albino. He watched, with the keen eye of a cavalryman, the gait of his pony as the orderly led her away. The day had been long in the Khyber and the way hard; he looked for the signs of wear and tear in her tread. The Soubadar stood passively by, waiting such time as his superior officer should see fit to re-open the conversation. He had important information to impart, but with the true oriental restraint he showed in face or attitude no trace of mental agitation.

The young Commandant turned from the scrutiny of his mare.

'A good piece of stuff that, Jemadar Ali; we'll make a fine little animal of her yet!'

'She is a good mare, Sahib: may she serve as well as you wish. I myself never have favoured that colour in horse-flesh when of that sex.'

The boy looked up keenly. 'Jemadar Ali, I believe you are right. See how she picks her way as if she were shod with satin. Chestnuts outrage convention in more walks in life than one. But to business, Soubadar — is there any news to-day?'

The two men were now strolling up the zigzag which leads to the keep of the Fort.

'Sahib, Sharif Khan was in Peshawar Bazaar yesterday; to-day he is in Jum!'

The Commandant stopped dead in his tracks and turned to his Soubadar. The latter imparted this information, which so interested his senior, as phlegmatically as if he were repeating a roll-call.

'Sharif Khan has had the audacity to make his way into Peshawar — are you sure of this, Jemadar Ali? Why, it is only three days since we had news of him in the Rajgul Valley, and our informant said that he was then aware that the Government had placed 500 Rupees upon his head. Are you sure that you are not mistaken? Who brings the news of his return? It is incredible that even such a desperate scallywag as Sharif should have the effrontery to reappear in Peshawar within ten days of the price being fixed for his head.'

'The Sahib must remember that there are two sides to this dog's character. While of rifle-thieves the most expert, yet he is a very *cicisbeo*, and though his nostrils are full of the smell of blood, yet they ever pine for the jasmine scent of a woman's hair! Is he not a Pathan?'

'But who gives this information?' persisted the Commandant, as he continued the ascent to the main terrace of the Fort.

'Duffadar Mirza Khan. He is a Kuki Khel, and comes from Sharif Khan's own village. He would not be mistaken in the matter of a man's identity at a thousand yards, and he claims to have had speech with the outlaw!'

'Is the Duffadar to be trusted?' queried the Commandant.

'In so far as all matters that concern Sharif Khan. They are men of the same kidney, and I would be surprised if

yesterday's meeting between the two did not take place over
the lap of some woman!'·

'And where does he say that Sharif is now?'

'Over there,' and the Soubadar-Major waved his hand
across the parapet to the north. He indicated the village of
Jum, which lies at the foot of Jumrud Fort. The young
Englishman glanced down at the brown medley of flat-
topped houses. Even though it was evening, the village of
Jum conveyed to the mind that impression of baked brick
which is inseparable from every Punjab village. A burnt bush
here and there, an occasional splash of whitewash, a few thin
spirals of smoke, and the everlasting tawny brown of roof,
wall, and outhouse.

But from this same terrace of the Jumrud pile a magnificent view presents itself. Behind you lies the Peshawar
Vale, with all its memories and bloodstained history. In
front, from between the black sentinel crags of the Bagiari
defile, the Khyber winds its tortuous way amid a labyrinth of
iron-stone hills. Although Jumrud Fort is an edifice built
upon the plain, yet as you stand upon its keep you find a
marvellous landscape. Far away to either hand stretch the
low hills of Yagistan — scenes of blood and fighting for three
thousand years or more. To the left lies the Kohat Pass and
Jowaki country, and the entrance to the awful Bara Valley.
To the right lie the foothills of the Mohmund country, the
historic Shab-kadr plateau, where within the last sixty years
the British have five times crossed weapons with the tribesmen. Still farther to the right rises the black peak of
Malakand, a modern landmark in Indian Frontier history.

And now, as the Commandant turns southwards, away
over the green irrigated pastures of the fertile Peshawar *tehsil*,
he can see the pillar of dust which marks the trail of the
snake-like line of burdened animals which, clear of the Pass,
are now toiling foot-wearily past Hari Singh Ke Burj, until lost

in the shadow of the plantations which coop in Peshawar city. At the foot of Jumrud itself a portion of the most belated caravan, more leg-weary than the rest, is camping in the open. The evening stillness is broken by the gurgling complaint of the shaggy camels, as, obedient to their drivers' will, they kneel in rows, the better to surrender the heavy packs which throughout the day have galled them unmercifully.

In some measure it is a view of pathetic interest, for of a truth from the days of Alexander to the present moment may the mouth of the Khyber be called the Gate of Blood.

'And so he has sought a haven in the village of Jum?' The Commandant of the Khyber Rifles turned from the parapet. 'What makes you think he is there?'

'He told Duffadar Mirza Khan he would spend three days in Jum. Also he sent a message to your Excellency which it is not necessary to repeat.'

The Commandant leaned back against the mud-plastered parapet and drummed thoughtfully with his toe to the time of the trumpet sounding 'Hay up' in his lines. As the last note petered out amid the whinnying of the expectant troop horses, the Commandant braced himself against the wall and delivered himself of this prophetic judgement:

'Jemadar Ali, if Mirza Khan's story be true, then it is obvious that Sharif Khan only proposed his visit to Jum as a blind. If, however, with 500 rupees on his head and a new Lee-Enfield in his hand he will trust to the salt of his relatives in Jum, why, he will be a dead man before we start a new week.'

The Soubadar-Major was dismissed. He saluted and made his way down to the lines. The Commandant went straight to his bath. As he looked out of the loophole in his dressing-room he could see the twinkling lights breaking out in the village of Jum.

It all looked so quiet and peaceful in the rapidly dying

twilight, yet the Wild West of America in its worst day was never half so dangerous as that apparently peaceful hamlet of baked brick and plaster, situated within a pistol-shot of the British Border-line.

Well might the Commandant of the Khyber 'Catch-'em-alive-ohs' think that the village of Jum looked peaceful. It was only just this hour after sundown that the shooting eased off for a time. There was not a greybeard in the village, nor on that particular Border for that matter, who remembered a blood feud that had been maintained with such acrimony and pursued with such persistence as the present. It had a more definite origin than the majority of Pathan blood feuds. Each family has several feuds that have been intermittent in the sept for generations. But this one had come to a fresh head in a matter of filial affection between the two *maliks* of the village. It does not matter whether the lady was beautiful or otherwise. She was the girl-wife of Roshan Khan, *malik* of Jum, and she was living in Peshawar in security and sin with Ramzan Khan, son of the junior *malik* of Jum and son-in-law to Roshan Khan the aforesaid aggrieved one. As a consequence, in daylight the male adherents of the Roshan Khan faction shot the male *clientèle* of the junior Malik on sight if the latter stirred from the security of their baked mud walls; and the partisans of the nefarious Ramzan, having suffered rather heavily in the early reprisals which followed hot upon the elopement, lay in wait from dawn to sundown for anything male that claimed the hospitality of the house of Roshan. Never could the greybeards recall a feud so bitter: men, boys, bullocks, dogs, even fowls went down under the frenzy of this lust for vengeance engendered by the vagaries of a worthless baggage still in her teens.

Daud Khan, being just beyond the prime of life, took less interest in the working out of feuds than he had done ten years previously, when single-handed he lay up for and exterminated the house of Ahmed Ali, the Malikdin Khel, killing in four hours Ahmed Ali, his four sons, and one grandson. With increasing years the blood had commenced to course more thinly through his veins; his mind turned rather to agriculture than to love and war. His interest in the present feud was rather defensive. His eye was as quick as ever it had been, and the two new notches on the stock of his trusted Martini told that his hand was still as quick as his eye. But his heart was not in the feud business as it had been; besides, he was more intimately mixed up with the origin of the present trouble than he cared to think about, as a man who had reached that stage in life when peace is more attractive than war. Daud Khan was the nephew of the *malik*, Roshan Khan; also he had married the sister of the malik's erring wife.

It was the latter fact that chiefly troubled Daud Khan, since his wife was adjudged a great beauty and prize on the Borderland. She had been the wife of another, had been discovered in an illicit embrace, and through her wit and beauty had survived to be the second wife of Daud Khan's choice. Such success on the Border is consistent with virtue. But the elopement of the *malik*'s wife, his own wife's sister, had induced the Daud Khan, of middle age, to doubt the wisdom of having allied himself to such a 'virtuous' family. It irked him thus always to be on the defensive-offensive. But Daud Khan had visions of a worse state of affairs. What if his wife's 'virtue' should develop still further and make the offensive imperative? In that case who would look after his twenty *bigahs* of arable land?

As night fell Daud Khan busied himself with his yoke of draught oxen. It was only possible nowadays to tend the soil by night. Even this was becoming dangerous, as, about midnight, a young moon climbed over the hill-tops. With the stealth of an officer's patrol in touch with the enemy, Daud

Khan sent his yoke of two oxen down into the *nullah,* while he covered its advance from the lip of the ravine. A couple of shots on the far side of the village told him that other nocturnal agriculturists like unto himself were in trouble. Not that this was unusual. When eventually Daud Khan arrived at his fields he sullenly congratulated himself that he had made half his journey without wasting a cartridge. Daud Khan, with his rifle across his kneee, settled down on the particular point of vantage which best permitted him to supervise the ploughmen as well as to scrutinise the approaches.

It wanted perhaps half an hour of midnight, when almost simultaneously the two wooden ploughs broke. Daud Khan looked at the damage and, considering that the sky had suddenly clouded, determined to dart home and find duplicates for the broken pieces, intending, in view of the approaching rain, to risk a late ploughing. Nothing human can approximate the invisibility and stealth of movement of a lithe Pathan when, wrapped in his slate-coloured cloth, he perambulates at night. Daud Khan, almost invisible, was back in his house without even disturbing the dogs. One whimpered, and then, nosing its master, curled down to sleep again. The spare parts of agricultural instruments were in a go-down, which was locked. The keys were in the inner chamber.

Like a shadow Daud Khan passed from the courtyard to the inner chamber. The *chirag* flickered fitfully in its niche, its oil guttering in warning of exhaustion. Daud Khan felt for the clumsy keys of the Cashmere locks and, missing them from their accustomed place, turned to his wife's *charpoy* to enlist her assistance. The five-year-old boy, son of his former wife, with his skull-cap down well over his eyes, was lying with outstretched arms on the string-woven bed. He was almost naked, and the dingy light just reflected the shine of moisture on his brown body. Daud Khan wondered why he was sleeping in the chamber and not on the house-top or in the verandah, when suddenly he realised that his wife's *charpoy* was vacant. Nor did it appear that she had used the bed that night. Thinking that, finding the inner chamber too hot, she had crept to some secluded verandah, Daud Khan returned to the courtyard and raising his voice called to his wife. There was no answer. This seemed to Daud Khan to be strange. He had called loud enough to have waked her. He shouted out again with sufficient voice to carry to the sentries and Fort Jumrud. This time there was an answering call – a muffled, hesitating cry. It came from above, from certain caves in the sandstone heap against which Daud Khan's home was built.

The Pathan is a creature of impulse, but impulse qualified by a certain instinct; that peculiar sense which is only found in races who carry their lives in their hands. The moment Daud Khan heard his wife's voice he flung his rifle loose and, slipping out of the courtyard, glided up to the mouth of the nearest cave. He had heard something in that quavering response that had sent the blood coursing through his veins with all the fire and imagination of youth. Instinct taught him how to act.

He was within fifteen paces of the cave, on the edge of a *nullah*, when a figure flitted past him. It was his wife. He let her pass. A second later another figure, a foot or more taller than the first, appeared. Just as it definitely separated from the gloom, the slip of the moon pushed out clear of the clouds. Daud Khan was in shadow. He dropped on to one knee. A moment's pause – and then the dull bark of his Martini roused a host of sleeping dogs, and quickened the vigilance of the Jumrud sentries. Daud Khan rarely missed at a thousand yards; at fifteen, in a gleam of moonlight, he was certain of his quarry. In this case, under the paralysing impact of the lead, his wife's luckless lover just reeled, swung round and dropped.

Daud Khan, with his lips twitching in his ferocity, made two steps forward to deliver, if necessary, the *coup de grâce*. To act first and think afterwards is typical of the Pathan; but in this instance a desire, not altogether unintelligible, to have last speech with the unknown spoiler of his home seized Daud Khan. The lover lay motionless. Daud Khan crouched by his side.

'Art dead, pariah?'

For answer the wounded man suddenly sat up, threw his arms round the man he had wronged, and, with a strength that seemed to the astonished Daud Khan superhuman, pressed him back to the brink of the *nullah* and forced him over its edge. The descent was not great, but by the time that Daud Khan had collected his senses and recovered his rifle, the lover had disappeared. By the pale light of the moon Daud Khan discovered his tracks.

He must have been grievously wounded, for the soil where he had lain was soft with blood, and Daud Khan's *chupkan* was drenched with the same thick fluid. But it was impossible for Daud Khan to follow up the trail. Already the village was alarmed. When feud-tension is at its height agitation is infectious, and already spasmodic shooting had broken out.

Daud Khan returned to his homestead. He found his wife sitting on the verandah, rocking her body to and fro and beating her breast in the throes of her lamentations. He asked no questions of her; taking her roughly by the shoulder he cast her into an inner go-down, slammed the door, and shot the bolt. The 'virtues' of his wife were in the ascendant.

Shortly after daybreak on the following morning it was known through the length and breadth of the village of Jum that Sharif Khan, the outlaw, upon whose head, alive or dead, the White Sirkar had placed the price of 500 rupees, had, shortly after midnight, crawled to the courtyard of one Jan Dad Khan. Grievously wounded in the body, he had claimed, and had been accorded, the asylum which no Pathan will refuse the bleeding supplicant. How and why he was wounded no man knew. For the sake of the honour of the woman he had wronged Sharif Khan's lips were sealed, and Daud Khan had not the mien of a man who would blab of his home's disgrace until a full measure of vengeance had satisfied the code of morality which rules such matters on the Border. Men spoke of the grievous nature of the outlaw's wound and, seeing there was a price upon his head, queried whether it was the act of some too zealous sentry in the Khyber Rifles. For the most part this was the accepted theory, since none connected the grim Daud Khan with the outlaw's agony. For three days and nights Sharif Khan tossed upon the *charpoy* in Jan Dad Khan's courtyard, his cries by day and his groans by night testifying to the desperate character of his hurts.

By the end of the third day the customary period of mutual respite from the *malik*'s feud had arrived. Men mingled freely in the village, and for the first time for weeks the rifle was carried slung by the principals in the feud. Men spoke of Sharif Khan's case and shook their heads. It was evident that the skill of the local leeches could not save him. From the first Jan Dad Khan and his sons had counselled the wounded man to allow them to carry him to the English doctor at Jumrud Fort. But the outlaw thought of his liberty and the price upon his head. Between his clenched teeth he reviled his benefactors for their humane suggestions, and accused them of cupidity of the reward. But after the third night the agony conquered the spirit and iron frame of the proud Pathan. His lip was bitten through, and his pores streamed with the sweat of his torment. He besought them to take him to Jumrud. In the cool of the evening Jan Dad and his sons acquiesced. They placed him on a lighter *charpoy*, and bore him away towards the British frontier.

Another hundred yards and he would have been across, when a tall Pathan stopped the little procession. It was Daud Khan. The bearers put the *charboy* down. Daud Khan did not wait even to look into the wounded man's eyes, he just blew out his brains as he lay. Turning to Jan Dad he explained —

'There is a lady in my house who preferred this carrion to me!'

There was a knock at the door of the Commandant's room.

'What is it, Soubadar?' queried the Commandant of the Khyber Rifles, as the native officer pushed the purdah aside and saluted.

'There is a wonderful gathering on the plain in front of the village of Jum; your Excellency should come and see it!'

'What is it about?'

'Your Excellency knows all about the affair of the popinjay Sharif Khan and Daud Khan?'

The Commandant nodded.

'Good; in five minutes Daud Khan turns loose his faithless wife!'

'Turns her loose? What do you mean by that, Soubadar?'

'Will not your Excellency come and see?'

The commandant accompanied the native officer to the main terrace of the Fort. Beneath them lay the open *maidan* which separates the curtain of the Fort from the village of Jum. The *maidan* was packed with villagers: they sat in a vast semicircle. Not only was there a huge concourse on the *maidan*, but all the women of the settlement seemed to be gathered upon the house-tops. It was evident that some affair of unusual interest was about to take place.

It was all so close that the Commandant did not require his glasses. Presently there was a movement in the crowd. Two men were conducting a third person to the *maidan*. The Commandant rubbed his eyes, and then involuntarily unfastened his glasses. He had not been mistaken. A naked woman was being conducted to the arena. The progress was slow, as the poor creature, half demented at the indignity thus placed upon her, tried to hide her overwhelming shame by sinking to the ground and crouching at her tormentors' feet. At last they brought her to the fringe of the *maidan*. With a wail she sank to the ground. A man leaned over her and appeared to remonstrate with her. She grovelled at his feet, and tried to hide her nakedness and her shame in the long loose folds of his nether garments.

'Her husband is telling her that she has only to run to the Border to be free,' said the Soubadar grimly. And then he added in the same monotone, 'See, she believes him, the fool!'

The Soubadar had divined the truth. The forlorn creature, dazed beyond reason, believed her husband's words: that there was a haven for her if she faced the few yards to the British Border. She came to this conclusion just at the moment that the Commandant dropped his glasses, and excitedly cried out in Pushtu:

'Great God, what brutes! We must stop this!'

But the understanding had come too late. The girl – for she was barely more – gave one shudder, jumped nimbly to her feet, and darted into the open space with the swiftness and frenzied grace of a startled hare. In a moment Daud Khan's Martini spoke. The little figure gave one bound in the air and fell nerveless on the dusty plain. Instantly the crowd fell upon the lifeless body and beat it out of recognition. Daud Khan stood on the fringe of the pack of village pariahs, running a pull-through down the barrel of his rifle. The

Commandant of the Khyber Rifles, blanched in face and trembling like an aspen, could even hear his callous laugh as he jested with his neighbours.

Thus were two more notches added to the stock of Daud Khan's rifle; and thus was the honour of his house satisfied.

The blood-money still remains unclaimed.

-(1909)

EDMUND CANDLER
Mecca

The great commotion of oars and the chant of rowers became
an actual menace. Half-an-hour before, the rhythmic
murmur of it had agitated a herd of cheetal on the mud flat.
Now, air and water vibrated with the disturbance. The
muggers in the creek slipped off their beds of slime into the
water; the kingfisher left his perch, and the deer standing by
the edge of the *khal* glided farther into the forest. Only an
impassive heron remained to see the black ark of a vessel
swing noisily into the channel.

The boat was high out of the water, with a bamboo-and-
wattle shanty perched on it from stern to amidships, leaving
the fore-part open for the six rowers. Four of them sat on the
thwarts, and two squatted on the beak and pulled like slaves
with their long twelve-foot oars, which were lashed to the
side with rope and struck the water almost perpendicularly.

As the vessel swung into the channel, oars and chant
slackened simultaneously. The anchor was let down to a
quicker tune, and the bamboos were taken from the eaves of
the thatch and driven into the mud to guard the boat from
swinging round with the tide.

Old Abdul Munim sat on the poop watching the débris of
fallen twigs, the burnished *hental* fronds, and the golden
clubs of the *gol-patta*, as one by one they yielded to the slowly
rising tide, lifting themselves imperceptibly to its caress with
a demure and hesitating reluctance. Wrapped in pious
thought and parable he followed each frond with his eyes as it
was carried away from the mud-bank by the same mysterious
agency that had disposed it there for a term, maybe to shelter
the loves of thin grey crabs, whose ends are as essential to the

general scheme — though the old man knew it not — as the activities of *pirs* and *hajis*. One by one they were borne out to the stream, nosing their way through the tangled mangrove roots until they were sucked into the tide that was setting one way, even as he, yielding to an instinct that had long been planted in him by the inscrutable Director of all energies, was being sucked into the human tide that was setting all ways to Mecca.

He might have read a parable in the submission of the palm fronds which were borne out through many tangled obstructions, and with such slow persistence, to the sea. But he was impatient. Looking up from his abstraction, he saw the *manjhi* gazing at him.

'Why have you stopped?' he said. 'You have a strong current.'

'The boat needs bailing; the men are tired; it is time for a meal.'

'Always baling; always many delays. The moon is in the second quarter, and in a few days the pilgrim ship leaves Chittagong.'

'There is no safety for the passenger but in the experience of the navigator. By bailing the boat is saved and the cargo is kept dry.'

'How many days is it to Chittagong?'

'We will certainly reach there the day after to-morrow,' said Gopi Manjhi for the tenth time in as many days, and fell again into moody abstraction.

Old Abdul Munim watched the *mallahs* at their work until his eyes were drawn again into the vortex of dancing palm fronds that circled solemnly in an eddy under the bank, moving to some subtle harmony of the waters, a rhythm modulated by the moon, until one by one the clubs and leaves obeyed the call, detached themselves from the maze, and floated away on their obscure errand. He had not the moralising bent, or the deliberateness of it all might have increased his dejection, seeing that material things are marshalled and directed smoothly to their ends, while things of the spirit are clogged and obstructed by appetite and will. No, that was a text for *pandits* and *ganis*. What philosophy had his seventy years taught him? They had given him a calm brow, patient eyes, and the grey beard of eld; but one thought made his heart sob like a child's. It burned through all his meditations. And now it filled him with a great fear.

The old man sat on the poop, a knife-like face and spirit, but a knife sheathed. He wore the dignity of arms in peace. In his mouth the words of the Prophet rang like a battle-cry. When he called the *Azan* from the deck, as he had done for thirty years from his mosque in Mirzapur, old Gopi Manjhi blinked sulkily, and his infidel crew, Sital, and Kallu, and Bodhi, and Thamman, and the two Pasis, Mussai and Jaga-bandham, bent more intently over their oars, or looked into the bilge-water, or affected sleep. He dreaded lest the journey he was making to glorify God, and vindicate his being, should be interrupted by Allah's inscrutable will. Had not seventy years been directed to this end?

Abdul Munim was known to some fifty souls in Mirzapur as the mullah of an obscure mosque on the Arrah road. His congregation were poor, small shopkeepers and servants, whose humble marriages and funerals afforded him a scanty income in fees, which with the contribution of grain, some thirty maunds in the year, sufficed his needs, but left little margin for the *haj* fund, towards which he put by a few rupees a-year, devoting his life's savings to the pilgrimage as men of lesser faith do to investments, purchases, and an-nuities. Sometimes in a lean year the hoard diminished and Mecca receded. These were days of small hope, when he even grudged the *zakat*, the religious tax of a fortieth part of his income to feed the poor. He gave unstintingly and withheld nothing; but he never forgot that in forty years these contributions delayed him one. Then he had uneasy scruples about his father. At one time he had saved for the pilgrimage of both, but the old man had become feeble in mind. He lived in a dark room crooning the *Wazifa*, the ninety names of God, and only went out to disgrace Abdul Munim by gathering sticks, over which he bent feebly like a hireling. When the old father died Abdul Munim was in his sixty-sixth year, and he had saved nearly three hundred rupees. The goal was in sight. It was but a matter of five years.

Then came the *Shab-i-barat*, on which the Mullah said, 'One year to-day I start to the Holy City.' On that very night Abdul Munim met Gopi Manjhi searching for a few passengers to take with him by river to Chittagong. The boatman visited all the mullahs of the city, and hung about the mosques talking of the new pilgrim ship that was to leave Chittagong for Mecca on the first of Baisakh. The journey that way, he said, was fifteen rupees cheaper than by Bombay. A *haji* hung on the skirts of the crowd that had collected round him, crying out in a loud voice to all:

'Go at once. Go to-day. Next year ye may be gathered in the dust. Thousands leave the world every day and none return. What remedy for death did the Physician Bu Ali find? He came in to the world and is gone. When the hour comes there is not granted a moment's delay. When ye depart the desires and aspirations of the heart are locked, every one, up within the bosom.'

'Fifteen rupees cheaper,' Abdul Munim murmured. 'This is a miracle; with me a year has passed in a day.'

Gopi Manjhi and his hammer-tongued *haji* led the way to the riverside, where a group of the curious had already collected. A rustic was asking one of the sailors when the boat would reach Mecca.

'This boat doesn't go,' he said.

'Not go?'

'No. At Chittagong the pilgrims will change into another one, as big as a city.'

'Ah! a fine story. Bigger than that!' the old man said with a smile, and began to gaze at the vessel with the half-pitying amusement that such toys provoke in the self-contained and sufficiently-rounded villager.

Meanwhile the coolies were unloading a train of bullock-carts, and carrying sacks of mustard and poppy-seed along the swaying planks to the boat. A consequential-looking man, who had arrived in a palanquin, watched the work with the air of a proprietor. He beckoned Gopi Manjhi to him.

'How many have you?' he asked in a low voice.

'Three have paid, and I think the lean mullah over there is coming.' He nodded at Abdul Munim.

'That is right. More would be dangerous. Besides, it will be enough. You will pay off the interest on this voyage.' Then as he waddled towards the boat he turned back and added grimly, 'Take half now and half in Chittagong.'

A lane opened for the *zemindar*, for it was none other than Baldeo Rai of Dhantsuli – a usurer of great wealth. Half the *manjhis* on the river borrowed money of him and paid ex-orbitant rates. Gopi Manjhi owed his very boat to him, and had paid more in interest on it than its original cost. So he watched without anxiety the narrow planks swaying beneath the fat man's presence, and half hoped they would subside with him into the stream. It was not likely that any ob-sequious bystander would be concerned enough to pull him out.

A few days later the boat left her moorings with a cargo of oil- and poppy- and mustard-seeds, potatoes and curry stones, and four pilgrims, bound for Chittagong. Nearly three weeks had passed, and Gopi Manjhi was loitering somewhere in the tidal creeks of the Sundarbans. The pilgrims were ill at ease.

Muhammad Salih joined Abdul Munim on the deck.

'We have seen no craft coming or going,' he said. 'Is it not possible that the *manjhi* has lost his way?'

'There are a thousand channels here and a great deal of mud, and it appears that there is no purpose in going one way more than another.'

'Why are we stopping?'

'Baling, always baling.'

'Why can't they bale while they are moving? They have the tide. It is a vessel of indolence. Call Fazl Karim and Mirza Yahya. Have they forgotten it is Friday and on the stroke of noon?'

On the other side of the awning Fazl Karim was airing Titar, the partridge, and pensioned fighter, whom he paraded morning and evening on the deck and fed when no one was looking with grain that he bored out of the sacks with an awl.

On that boat, where no one kept a timepiece and the hours passed unheeded, the bird's familiar cry at sunrise, and the *Azan* of the Mullah were the morning and the evening gun. Fazl Karim watched the bird contentedly. He did not fret at halts. A month or two before, the old man had been pensioned from the treasury of a native state, where he had sat over a metal chest all his days, counting money until he began to believe it was his own. His broad face had come to wear a benign look, which his gold-rimmed spectacles and square beard dyed with the red of new bricks enhanced. The young man Mirza Yahya sat beside him regarding the parade of Titar vacantly, as he listened to the tale of his past victories. This *Kaboota-baz*, trifler, pigeon-flier, ne'er-do-well — had been sent on the pilgrimage by his uncle, Muhammad Nazim, the wealthy Kazi of Sultanpur, who had entrusted the boy to the care of Fazl Karim with some small hope of reform. To these the gaunt goat-like head of Muhammad

Salih appeared beyond the awning.

'It is noon,' he said. 'The Moulvie Sahib calls you to prayer.' Titar was put back in the cage and the two solemnly obeyed the call.

On the foredeck Abdul Munim stood facing his congregation. For the thousandth time Muhammad Salih, Fazl Karim, and Mirza Yahya quailed before the awful words of the *Khutbah*:

'Sons of Adam, arise and remember! Think of your forefathers who are no more. Remember death and its condition! Remember also the two angels Munkir and Nakir, who visit the dead in their tombs. Think of what befalls in the deep grave and forget not that you yourself will be flung into it. Verily this will be a great change. Where are your brothers? Where your race? Where your forefathers? Where your friends and associates who used to sit beside you in assemblies? Death has put an end to them all. They have become mould in their graves. Their beauty is gone. Their eyes are lustreless. They have become heaps without form. Their limbs have fallen apart. Their skins are broken. Their bones are fine dust. They are the food of worms. Take thought and consider that ye ere long will taste death and be laid under the earth. Then shall ye be enmeshed in the net of your misdeeds, and no compunction, no penitence, no regret will avail.'

When the Arabic portion had been read, Abdul Munim repeated the names of prophets, saints, kings, soldiers, poets, philosophers, and their illustrious companions, who stayed on the earth a brief space and are gone — Adam, and Noah of the Ark, Joseph and Jacob, Ishmael, Isaac, and Abraham the judge of the universe, Solomon of the Seal; the Prophets — Hud, Idris, Johan, Shish, Job, and Shuaib, who turned the people to Islam; Jesus and David and Moses, who received from the Lord each his own book; and Muhammad, the darling of the Most High, for whom the earth and universe were made. 'They and all the progenitors of man have gone. We will leave the world even as they. Our friends will speak of our death, even as we speak of theirs.' He urged his companions to repent, to prepare.

Then he stood, head erect, arms folded on the breast, his gaze fixed raptly on the West, penetrating mountains, deserts, cities, forest trees, the curvature of the ocean, through which devout eyes cleave a vista of faith, where at the end gleams the purple pall of the Kaabah calling them to the *durbar* of God. Arms dropped to the knee, eyes fixed on the earth, back inclined fervently, still as a chrysalis, and as informed with the winged spirit, confined, encompassed, and aspiring. Up again, head erect, arms folded on the breast, eyes fixed raptly on the West, and as he, the Imam, led the prayer and bent and swayed and knelt and stood, erect and awed in the presence of God, the others bent and swayed with him, moved with one rhythmic impulse, perfectly attuned, body and soul, in the Prophet's inspired discipline of supplication.

The prayer ended, there was silence awhile. Then Abdul Munim exhorted his companions, dwelling on the glory of the pilgrimage. He told them how one day they would see from a high hill the trees of the city of Medina; how their eyes would rest on the four glittering towers and the green dome of Muhammad's tomb; how they would enter and pray even where the Prophet himself had stood and prayed, saying, 'One prayer in this my mosque is more helpful than a thousand elsewhere.'

Then the old man spoke of Mecca. The day would come when they would behold with their own eyes the city walls. For years he had listened to the rhapsodies of *hajis*. In spirit he had walked round the House of Allah, touched the hem of the *Kiswah*, the gloomy golden-banded pall, and heard above him the rustling of angels' wings. Often had he pressed his cheeks on the smooth walls of the sanctuary, and his lips on the black stone. Often in his dreams he had run swiftly between Safa and Marwah to the two green pillars, crying the *Takbir* and imploring pardon for his sins. Often had he listened to the Friday sermon, and stoned the devil at Arafat, drunk the water of Zemzem and fed the pigeons of Allah's mosque.

In burning words he celebrated the glory of the quest, the felicity of victory or death in the accomplishment.

'Allah will shadow thee in that day when there is no shade but His shadow, and cause thee to drink from the cup of His Prophet Muhammad, after which is no thirst to all eternity.'

As he spoke the devoted Muhammad Salih bowed his head as if in the presence of the Lord. The beard of Fazl Karim shone like a brand lit by the fire of his eyes; and a spark from the fire of this consecration fell on the dull spirit of Mirza Yahya, and quickened him till he too glowed in response.

II

Old Munim was celebrating his sacred theme when Kallu and Sital lowered the *dongi* into the stream. A breeze had sprung up, and the skiff, which was decked and carried a double sail, glided smoothly over the water, Kallu steering it with his sal-wood paddle. 'The first creek round the corner,' he said. The sails dropped and the nose of the boat was driven into the ooze of a shoal. The two unwound their lines.

'What is Gopi Manjhi waiting for?' Sital said. 'He will settle the business of the *baipari* first; you will see that will be to-night, with good luck. Thamman says the jute boat is anchored in the Khulna channel four miles to the west. It will be the turn of these sons of pigs to-morrow.'

'Gopi is slow. It should have been on Monday in the Bogee

Khal. The woodcutters have not been there for five years.'

'Or who would have looked for them at Kenjotolla, where they left the cutting on account of the man-eater?'

'It is five days since Monday, and much rice has been wasted. To each two seers a day. That is forty seers.'

'True, though it was not our expense.'

'The rice should have been ours. Four mouths have been busy too long.'

'Why did he not take in the stones at Rampal?'

'Indolence! What need to sink them?' he said. 'Are there not muggers enough? And what business should take men up these *khals*?'

'Gopi is slow. Jaswant was a sharp blade in these things, quick to strike. He sent his men to the bottom the first night he was in the jungle, and no man has seen them since. He employed stones.'

'Stones are better.'

Sital drew in his line and rebaited. The becktie were not feeding.

'How much do you think Abdul Munim has?' he asked.

'Gopi says he must have three hundred and fifty rupees, perhaps four hundred. Reckon it thus: There is the price of the journey to Mecca and back from Chittagong. That will be a hundred and fifty rupees. Then there is food on the way, and the cost of living at Mecca and the journey to Medina and to and from the coast. Without alms that will be thirty rupees a month; with charity more, and the Mullah is a pious man. Also, there is the second half of the fare. That we have earned. Gopi gave the first half to Baldeo Rai, the great devil! Altogether, perhaps three hundred and fifty rupees.'

'And the others?'

'Fazl Karim and Mirza Yahya should have more, but I doubt Muhammad Salih. He may have three hundred. It would be very improvident to undertake the journey with less.'

'I have my fears about him. He is a lean dog.'

'Still, it will be a good voyage.'

'Not bad for these hard times,' Kallu said. 'Old Jaswant and his crew would have reckoned it a poor business. Five times the profit in one voyage, from Goalpara to Barisal, and the next month up at Khana in the log trade, or in the raft traffic on the Ganges above Hardwar. Then an opium cargo from Nepal to Chittagong with nine thousand rupees in the chest for the month's journey. Those were good days; better still when he was a young man. No police on the river from Khulna to Goalundo, no questions asked, no registration, no patrol, no gazette, and for every mullah who swung on the bloody banyan tree twenty were rich men, owned their own boats, and lived on their own land. They were proud days too, and every gang sailed under their own bunting.'

'It would not be a bad trade now, if it were not for the *mahajan*.'

'The *mahajan*! Curse him!' Kallu said. 'But he was no match for Jaswant.' Then he told the story once more of how Jaswant Manjhi had overreached Jitoo Rai, *zemindar* of Kankinara. The *zemindar* lent him money for his boat, employed him with his own cargo, sent an agent with him down the river – a man who would not overlook a pin-prick in a sack – and Jaswant put the fellow quietly overboard with a stone round his neck. Then he sold the boat and cargo at Goalundo – it was an *ulank* of 1200 maunds – and appeared openly at Kankinara with a story that it had capsized in a bore with all hands save himself and two of the crew, who had beached the *dongi* at Jagira Char and were repairing a leak when their comrades went under in mid-stream. Jaswant returned the *dongi* to the *zemindar* like an honest man. It was a real bore in the morning that gave him the idea. It did a great deal of damage and was much talked about, which came in well in the evidence. Two policemen saw the *ulank* go down, and that only cost four rupees.

'Luck of the stars!' Sital said enviously.

'There was luck, no doubt. But it is not every *manjhi* who can make thousands of rupees out of a bore. It had not passed five minutes when he throttled the agent and sank him, and tore off the brass plate from the bows. In the evening he bought the witnesses and arranged the sale. I and the others went north to the Brahmaputra by the waterway between Godaveri and Mathura Bazaar. We met at the Baruna Mela at Munshiganj, and Jaswant gave me a hundred and fifty rupees. It was just such a place as this we sent the agent to the bottom.'

Sital looked out to the main channel as if he expected to see the man's ghost. The neighbourhood was a perfect paradise for the fresh-water pirate. There were deep *khals* full of fish, beautiful *churs* where they might bask in the sun, an intricate network of channels known only to themselves and the woodcutters, and within a few miles a channel where richly-laden boats passed daily to and from Khulna and Barisal, inviting plunder, and there was only one patrol boat within a hundred miles.

'Jaswant was a quick blade,' repeated Kallu. 'He never paid for his jute. Gopi Manjhi is slow.'

'But how safe!' said Sital. 'Where has he not his agent? Every channel pilot from the Meghna to Manhari Ghat belongs to his people, and from Dhubri to Chittagong. He knows all the receivers from Khulna to Mirzapur. He has men in the yards of the steam companies; no boat-owner or villager dare give evidence against him, and he has more folk among the police than any Mullah on the river.'

'Gopi is safer, but Jaswant would turn over a *lakh* of rupees in half the time it takes Gopi to make a thousand.'

'Jaswant had three sentences, and in the end he was hung. Gopi has never been inside a *thana*. He is careful. He has not been seen for weeks. See how he got news of to-night's business. He did not even land at Khulna: Thamman went ashore and met the priest, Durga Saran Pande, in an out-house of the *hauli* drinking shop.'

Again they fell to talking of profits. It seemed that the *baipari* of the jute boat they were waiting for had half finished his rounds. He must have paid out hundreds of rupees to *ryots* in advance for the crop, all of which was money lost.

'Curse it!' Sita said. 'If Gopi had not been so slow we might have met the man farther up the river.'

'We might never have crossed his tracks,' said Kallu. 'But wait until we see what is in the chest.'

When they reached the boat Gopi was squatting on the deck where they had left him, unperturbed, like a gross god. He looked the kind of man for whom jails yawn instinctively. A sallow, wheat-coloured complexion, hard, set eyes, round face, boil marks on each calf, both ears bored with straws let in, a mole on the left side of his noise, and a lump on his forehead. The man was so marked you would think that, if he were wise, crime must have come to him as an afterthought. He could not pass in the street unnoticed. Yet it was true that he had never received a sentence. Every member of the crew had left his thumb-mark somewhere in Bengal or the United Provinces, or seen the inside of a jail except Gopi Manjhi, and he belonged to a proclaimed clan.

Gopi was still sitting on the deck ruminating crime, with the moon shining on his placid, malign face, when the *dongi* was lowered again, and Thamman and Sital and Kallu and the two Pasis rowed swiftly into the night. As they went off Mirza Yahya woke from an uneasy sleep.

'What is amiss?' he cried. 'Where are they going?'

'Be at peace,' Gopi Manjhi said, 'they have gone fishing.'

'Fishing! Five of them?'

'Even so. In the moonlight the becktie feed well.'

Mirza Yahya sank back on the deck, and covered his face in a blanket. His sleep was troubled.

Mirza Yahya was awake when the *dongi* came back. The breeze had dropped and he heard the swish-swish of the paddles a long way off. He lay still as a stone, feigning sleep, and breathed through his nose. As the boat came alongside he heard Bodhi whisper:

'What have you got?'

Thamman answered, 'We have got the chest.'

'Have you opened it?'

'Not yet. Get the double file. We will break it open round the bend lest we disturb the pilgrims. By the weight of it there should be over a thousand rupees.'

Then, while Bodhi was ransacking a locker astern, Mirza gathered the whole story through the answers to Beni's impatient questions. The *dongi* had approached the jute boat unperceived, and the two Pasis had boarded her. The *baipari* and the crew were sleeping on the deck, and they found the chest where they expected it, lashed to the mast under one of the thwarts. They were lowering it into the *dongi* when Mussai slipped and the box struck the edge of the boat. Somebody shouted, '*Dohai Sahheb-ka!*' A dozen figures rose up and there was a great commotion on board.

'Were there any blows?' Beni asked.

'I struck one of them who stood on the edge, and he fell in the water,' Thamman answered. 'I did not mean to kill him; but he was fated to die. We got away in the darkness. The moon had set when we entered the channel.'

'They might hunt a hundred years,' said Beni, 'and not find us here; and if they did find us, what then?'

'What then?' Thamman repeated; and the words struck a chill into Mirza's heart.

At that moment Bodhi appeared with the file. He slipped into the *dongi*, and they rowed away. Mirza lay still, paralysed with fear, while the sound of the oars receded. Soon he heard across the river the faint tap-tap- of beaten metal and the rasping of a file, a hard merciless message – the echo of Thamman's 'What then?' Mirza felt the despair of the trapped beast, listening for the steps of the hunter in the morning after a night of pain. He looked all round him, but there was no refuge, no sail, no traffic, nor had there been for the last forty-eight hours. They were isolated – a flock driven into the shambles, each one waiting the assassin's caprice. There was the bank hard by, and the jungle projecting over it, inviting shelter; but what help was there in that – a sunless maze choked with thorn and tangled creepers, intersected everywhere by waterways, frequented by the obscene mugger, miles from the haunt of man, with deep squelching mud underfoot, in which every step would shriek treacherously to pursuers? 'Here I am,' Fear whispered, 'fly!' And again Fear whispered, 'Stay! Turn not the back. The nape of the neck is the enemy's desired mark. It precipitates the stroke. The blow falls there unseen.'

Mirza opened his eyes and looked across the deck to where Fazl Karim lay, shrouded in his homely red shawl. He longed to approach and wake him, but he heard the oars again, and hid his face in his blanket, until he felt the sun's rays creep on to it and saw the light steal through.

Long before this the vessel was astir. Every movement on the deck appalled him; but as the footsteps came near and passed by he made an effort to construe each sound into the normal routine of the day. He lifted his head and found it was so. The *mallahs* were going about their business as usual. Fazl Karim had lit his hookah. Then Titar called imperiously. It was the hour of the first parade and grain-pecking. The cry warmed Mirza's heart.

When he joined Fazl Karim he was saying to himself, 'It is light and warm now, and we are all alive just as yesterday, and the *mallahs* are laughing and cooking their food, and the old Gopi Manjhi is playing chess. It must have been a bad dream.' On the poop Abdul Munim was already at prayer. His high brow pressed the deck. As he lifted it the slanting sun shone upon it, and the *dejecta* of Titar became glorified there. Mirza gathered hope. Muhammad Salih crossed the deck like a dignified old goat and placed his mat beside the *mallahs*. The old man's familiar gait reassured him. Here was a touch of home. How often had he seen him enter the Mullah's mosque on the trunk road! How familiar was that ragged beard and the face beneath the high turban, lean and shrunken save for a puffy inch on each side of the nose, where no hair grew. His shop in the Sudder bazaar was not half the size of the bamboo shanty in which Gopi Manjhi sat, and no one ever seemed to halt by it. Mirza wondered how he had collected money enough for the pilgrimage. Then he remembered his surprise one day when he had seen the old man on the Id-ul-Bakra, wearing a green velvet *jubba* braided with gold. He wore it a day or two after the festival, and not entirely to glorify Allah. All these memories soothed him. They were remote from tragedy. He was calmer when he unburdened himself to Fazl Karim.

'We have fallen amongst thieves and assassins,' he said, and he told his tale.

Fazl Karim was greatly agitated, but he argued against their peril.

'They are bad men,' he said, 'but they would not dare.'

'Then why have they brought us here? Why don't they go on? They murdered one man for the chest, and they would have murdered more had there been need. We are only four. If they rob us they will not leave us to escape.'

'They would not dare,' Fazl Karim repeated. 'They may rob and kill strangers in the night and hear nothing of it. But we entered their boat at Mirzapur in the light of day. If we are killed every man will hang.'

'But what are they doing here? We shall lose the pilgrim ship. Why do they not go on? Certainly they intend some evil.'

'Perhaps they heard of the jute boat, and left the course for it.' Mirza was reassured. But Fazl Karim's ray of comfort was short-lived. As he sat brooding over the business he remembered hearing of a boatful that had been lost on the river some years back. The captain and three of the crew had gone off in the *dongi*, and they had brought home a tale that the vessel had capsized in a storm and sunk with all on board. He had not thought of the matter from that day to this.

The story increased Mirza's fears. Many of the *manjhi's* doings had appeared strange. It was easy now to apply sinister motives to them. For a week or more he had avoided all villages. He had passed through Khulna in the night, and only anchored for an hour in mid-stream, sending the *dongi* ashore with Thamman and Bodhi. In these forsaken creeks time seemed of no value to him, but he had never loitered in populous districts. Why should he loiter at all? He had all Baldeo Rai's cargo on board. When did he expect to land it at Chittagong?

The question was answered for him oracularly. Muhammad Salih had crossed the deck, and was standing with his head thrust into the cabin.

'When do we reach Chittagong?' he asked sourly.

Gopi Manjhi looked up from his chess. 'Perhaps to-morrow,' he said. 'Perhaps next week.' He seemed to speak with studied indifference. There was no attempt to explain matters, or even to appear plausible.

Muhammad Salih answered angrily, 'You will miss the ship, and you have taken half our passage-money; may you suffer here and hereafter.'

Gopi Manjhi seized an oar as if to strike the old man; but he put it down, and muttered something about being aground and waiting for the tide, and all men being the servants of Fate; and Kallu laughed.

'This is how men talk to captives,' Fazl Karim said. 'Let us acquaint Abdul Munim with what has passed.'

The old man's suspicions had long been awake, but he had no wordly comfort for them. Rather he spoke of Paradise.

'Do not fear,' he said. 'He created man of crackling clay like the potter's, and He created the firmament from the smokeless fire.

'There is no God but He, the Creator of everything; then worship Him, for He over everything keeps guard.

'And do not say of those that are slain in the way of God that they are dead, yea, they are living. But ye do not understand.

'They shall be in gardens 'neath which streams flow, in the midst of outspread shades and abundant fruits neither failing nor forbidden.'

The morning wore on, and the lazy noon crept by, and the crew slept, or conferred together in the wattle shanty. Not a word had been spoken since Muhammad Salih's outbreak, but an impalpable barrier had risen up between the *mallahs* and the pilgrims. The hours were burdened with an apathy intense and foreboding; but underneath it something active was stirring, something sinister was afoot. A hand had been raised somewhere in menace. The stroke was imminent, yet it was mysteriously delayed. The net was closing in on the pilgrims; in everything they read the hand of Fate: in their isolation, in the great silence, in the enfolding forest, in the awful inertness of man, the intentness of Nature, in the lisp of the water against the bows and the busy indifference of the grey crabs on the shoal. Kallu and Sital and Bodhi and the two Pasis appeared to them mysteriously commissioned, aware of their errand and obedient without malice, conscious of being the tools of an imminent will. Fear and guilt tainted the air. The Moslems sat huddled together, now whispering, now brooding in silence; and when Mirza Yahya looked up he saw the hard cold eye of Thamman fixed upon him, and he said in his heart, 'Thus the butcher regards the doomed sheep.'

All hope died within him; he lay in a very ague of fear. His lips and throat were dry. His ears tingled to the sound of beaten metal and the rasping of a file. They were haunted with Thamman's inexorable 'What then?'

In the long silence Titar called, and Abdul Munim cried out in response:

'Dost thou not perceive that all creatures in heaven and earth praise God, and the birds also?'

He was overbold. At the words, so sudden and unexpected, the sweat broke out on Mirza Yahya's brow. The *mallahs* stirred uneasily, and the silence closed in on them again, like rings on the surface of a forest pool disturbed by a falling bough.

After a silence Fazl Karim whispered, 'What shall we do if they attack us to-night?'

They conferred, but were incapable of a strategical plan.

The evening wore away, and the pilgrims prostrated themselves in prayer. The sun set, the last rays of light were dispersed, the last defence of the innocent. The night fell, grim and terrible, shield of the assassins, the shadows their scouts and picquets, the stillness and the faint night voices their gathered strength and secret malign allies.

The four pilgrims lay across the empty shanty, but in the stillness of the night Mirza Yahya crept inside. 'When they strike,' he thought, 'these three will lie between me and them,' and he passed his hand nervously over the wattle, seeking to loosen the woof of dried palm fronds and bamboos. But the crackling woke echoes that frightened him more. He sat up rigidly against the wall, one hand clutching the aperture he had made, ready to spring — where he knew not.

Hour after hour passed, and Mirza heard nothing save his own straining breath and the beating of his heart. His grip on the wattle had slackened through sheer exhaustion, and he was falling asleep, when he became alert somehow and aware of a presence outside. He heard whisperings and uneasy stirrings at the threshold of the cabin; then — after a pregnant silence — a tremendous blow and the crushing and splintering of bone against the deck. It was the head of Fazl Karim. The noise awoke Abdul Munim by his side, and he had a moment to lift his head and cry:

'Here I am at Thy call O Allah! Here I am at Thy call!' when the blow crashed on his skull, and he fell beside his companion. Someone leapt into the water, and Thamman called:

'Muhammad Salih has gone overboard, curse him! The other is inside!'

Mirza tore desperately at the wattle. The gap rent and opened for him, and he plunged through into the stream as the assassins entered.

III

Mirza plunged ankle-deep in mud, breasting the tangled undergrowth till dawn. The brittle *shulas* crackled under his feet and conspired to betray him. He fancied he heard in the commotion the footsteps of his pursuers. Even if he outdistanced them escape was hopeless, for nothing but a cyclone, or a flood, could wash out his tracks. He stopped and listened; the forest was still! An early jungle-cock crowed familiarly and called up a blurred vision of home — his father's shop, the *zilla* school, and the courtyard where he

used to build mud mosques with his sister and plant mari-
golds in the four corners of minarets. The crowing filled him
with illogical hope, and made the strange net of horror that
had been cast round him in his vigil unreal, the illusion of a
sick mind. The sound recalled caresses, familiar household
things, and the sheltered life into which the thought of a
bloody and cruel death had not entered. But the horror grew
again with the stillness that followed the call. The jungle was
savage and unresponsive. For a moment he leant against a
tree, struggling for breath, while the grey light began to
penetrate the forest. Then the thought that he could be seen
goaded him on. He reached a creek, and swam along it until
he found a branch of a tree overhanging the water; he caught
at it, and lifted himself up and crept along the branch to the
trunk, and dropped far from the bank, so that his tracks
might be hidden from the other side. A faint hope that
Thamman would lose the track fluttered weakly beside the
certainty that he would follow. Still, it was a check. He
struggled on through the jungle, which no eye could penetrate. But he could not hide. The mud weighed him down,
and every time he dragged a foot forward gave a churlish
menace of betrayal, which echoed alternately with the crackling of the brittle *shulas*. The water oozing into his deep
footprints made treacherous puddles. It was a malevolent
place for a fugitive.

Just before dawn he heard the breakers. He did not know
the meaning of the sound, but instinct led him to the sea. As
the sun rose he broke pantingly through the mangrove roots
into the surf, and ran along the beach where the waves
washed out his footprints. It was a salvation he had not
dreamed of, and he knew that if he could turn a spit of land
before his pursuers reached the edge of the jungle he might
be safe. Every now and then he came on the outlet of a creek
and swam it; but he was brought up by one of the main

channels and driven inland again. 'Allah hates me!' he cried. But he would not surrender himself to the mud. He struggled against the stream, until it became too deep and strong. Then he climbed a *keora* tree that grew out of the water, and hid in its branches that he might live another day.

Here he was safe awhile in the deep shade with no betraying footsteps, and he thought of the others for the first time. Poor old Fazl Karim! His head was splintered on the deck, and his bright beard would be seen no more in the streets of Mirzapur. And Abdul Munim, where was he? He had delivered his message and performed his trust. How readily had he answered the summons with his: 'Here I am at Thy call, O Allah! Here I am at Thy call!' But the pilgrimage of which he spoke always, what of that? Would he never see the *Bayt Allah* after all? He was dead, so surely it was impossible. Yet how sad it was — never to look on the House of the Prophet, or touch the golden-banded gloomy pall, the *Kiswah*, veil of the *Kaabah;* never to stone the devil at Arafat, or listen to the Friday sermon, or run between Safa and Marwah, or perform the *Tawaf*, the circumambulation; never to press his cheeks to the walls of the sanctuary, or his lips to the black stone; never to drink of the water of Zemzem, or to feed the pigeons of Allah's mosque! There was old Muhammad Salih also! He had jumped overboard and he could not swim. They were all dead. What then? He, too, would die; but he did not care. He was surprised that he did not care, that he was no longer afraid. He only feared Thamman's eyes. Now he was very tired. When he was more tired he would drop into the water from the tree, and the stream would lull him to sleep. He only prayed that he might never see the *mallahs* again. Then he thought of home. As he became drowsy, his ears were filled with sound; he thought he heard the rattle of his mother's loom. But the noise came nearer; it was regular, mechanical. Mirza became aware that it was a boat. Had the fiends discovered him? He crept along the branch into the thickest shade.

The boat moored on the opposite bank. Had they seen him? He peered through the leafy screen, and saw a strange craft — broad and squat in the prow as a barge — loaded with stacks of grey muddy shells and huge earthenware *chattis* of fresh water. He was dumb for a moment. The sense of life's renewal came on him like a flood; the horror was dissipated and became a malignant dream.

He hailed the boat with a loud, 'Ah ho! Ah ha! Ah yee! *Manjhi!*' and two dark-skinned, shockheaded men rose from behind the *chattis*, spoke a few words, and put to shore in a canoe. They were shell-gatherers from Barisal. He told them that he had been shipwrecked, thinking that they would be afraid to harbour him if they suspected the truth. They were of the faith — Muhammadans of Barisal — and Allah had sent them him in his need. No boat but theirs ever disturbed the solitude of the creek; but for them he might have wandered in the mud until he became food for the muggers and the crabs. Allah had ordained the hour, and led him to the place. After the day's gathering the cargo would be full; the shell-gatherers were returning with the flood tide. For him, the least worthy, Allah had stretched out his arm. He knelt in prayer a moment, then he lay at the bottom of the boat and slept.

IV

Dawn broke on a bloody ship. Someone had thrown a sheet over the Mullah and Fazl Karim, but when the sun rose it lit up congealed streams of blood that had crossed and re-crossed, flowing from two fountains where the sheet had been sucked down from its spontaneous grey folds and undulations by something that attracted it underneath, publishing the nature of its scarlet pulp to the authors who would hide it.

Thamman and Sital and Bodhi had put ashore in the *dongi* when Mirza Yahya went overboard. They pursued him through the darkness, which was so dense that they never caught sight of him, though they heard him crashing through the brushwood ahead. The noise grew fainter, for the pursuers had to stop every few minutes to make sure of the direction Mirza was taking. At last, when the sounds were so faint that they could scarcely be distinguished from the cheep-cheep of the water oozing into their own footprints, Thamman called a halt.

'Let him go!' he said. 'What can save him?'

It was evident that Mirza was lost. Great rivers lay between him and the dwellings of man. No human being ever visited the jungle except the woodcutters, who were at work far away on the Khulna side. He was isolated in an inaccessible block of the forest. If the tigers and muggers spared him he would die of hunger, or of thirst, for everywhere the water was salt.

'Come, let us go back,' Thamman said. 'He will certainly die, and we will tell old Gopi that we have done for him.'

So they returned on their tracks to the boat. When they reached the boat Kallu and Beni were hauling something out of the water on to the deck. It was Muhammad Salih. In his tin trunk they had found only a hundred and sixty rupees, so they concluded the rest must be in his belt. They had been searching the river since the first ray of light. At last they had found him. As Kallu lifted the distended corpse on to the boat Thamman said:

'See, the old starveling has become fat. His belly was never so full.'

But the jest was soon turned against himself. When they stripped the old man and tore off his belt they found a paltry twenty rupees.

'What cursed improvidence!' Thamman said. 'He could

not have paid his way back.'

Eight voices were raised in disgust, and for a while the peace of the creek was disturbed with angry chatter.

Then Gopi lifted a corner of the sheet. 'We must clear up,' he said.

The Moulvie Sahib and Fazl Karim were stripped, and their stained clothes laid in a bundle on one side. The treasurer's gold-rimmed spectacles were broken beyond repair.

'A pity you spoilt them,' Thamman said, as he detached them from the clotted beard and hair. 'They would have fetched three rupees, eight annas in the bazaar.'

For the burial there was no need of stones. Bodhi had found a water-sodden branch of a *keora* tree, heavy as lead. They sawed it into three pieces and tied its burden to each with fibres of jute. One by one they were dropped into the *khal*. As the Moulvie Sahib was lowered into the water, Gopi Manjhi said good-humouredly:

'Ah, *Haji*, sleep in Paradise!'

There was no malice in the obsequies. If Muhammad Salih had deceived them, they found enough in the chests of Mirza and the treasurer to make amends.

When the funeral was over they fell to cleaning the deck, while Thamman prepared the morning meal, grumbling all the while that the rice of the deceased was such poor stuff. At eight o'clock Titar, the partridge, became uneasy. The hour was long past when Fazl Karim should release him for his morning parade and grain-peckings. He called three times to wake his master, but drew on himself instead the hard eye of Thamman.

Thamman stretched a hand into the cage and wrung the bird's neck. Sital put him into the pilau.

'That is four of them,' he whispered to Thamman, with a smile. 'I wish we had the other.'

'He will surely die,' Thamman answered.

But he was wrong. Mirza lives to-day, and for those four lives four pirates hung.

When Mirza Yahya, a chastened and God-fearing young man, heir to the Kazi of Sultanpur, tells the story of the trial, it pleases him to say:

'So four of these assassins were destroyed in Khulna jail. That is law — a life for a life. For Abdul Munim, Gopi Manjhi swung; for Fazl Karim, Sital; for Muhammad Salih, Kallu; and for Titar, Thamman.'

(1911)

LEONARD WOOLF
Pearls and Swine

I had finished my hundred up — or rather he had — with the Colonel and we strolled into the smoking-room for a smoke and a drink round the fire before turning in. There were three other men already round the fire and they widened their circle to take us in. I didn't know them, hadn't spoken to them or indeed to anyone except the Colonel in the large gaudy uncomfortably comfortable hotel. I was run down, out of sorts generally, and — like a fool, I thought now — had taken a week off to eat, or rather to read the menus of interminable table d'hôte dinners, to play golf and to walk on the 'front' at Torquay.

I had only arrived the day before, but the Colonel (retired), a jolly tubby little man — with white moustaches like two S's lying side by side on the top of his stupid red lips and his kind choleric eyes bulging out on a life which he was quite content never for a moment to understand — made it a point, my dear Sir, to know every new arrival within one hour after he arrived.

We got our drinks and as, rather forgetting that I was in England, I murmured the Eastern formula, I noticed vaguely one of the other three glance at me over his shoulder for a moment. The Colonel stuck out his fat little legs in front of him, turning up his neatly shoed toes before the blaze. Two of the others were talking, talking as men so often do in the comfortable chairs of smoking rooms between ten and eleven at night, earnestly, seriously, of what they call affairs, or politics or questions. I listened to their fat, full-fed assured voices in that heavy room which smelt of solidity, safety, horsehair furniture, tobacco smoke, and the faint civilised aroma of whisky and soda. It came as a shock to me in that atmosphere that they were discussing India and the East: it does, you know, every now and again. Sentimental? Well, I expect one is sentimental about it, having lived there. It doesn't seem to go with solidity and horsehair furniture: the fifteen years come back to one in one moment, all in a heap. How one hated it and how one loved it!

I suppose they had started on the Durbar and the King's visit. They had got on to Indian unrest, to our position in India, its duties, responsibilities, to the problem of East and West. They hadn't been there of course, they hadn't even seen the brothel and *café chantant* at Port Said suddenly open out into that pink and blue desert that leads you through Africa and Asia into the heart of the East. But they knew all about it, they had solved, with their fat voices and in their fat heads, riddles, older than the Sphinx, of peoples remote and ancient and mysterious whom they had never seen and could never understand. One was, I imagine, a stock jobber, plump and comfortable with a greasy forehead and a high colour in his cheeks, smooth shiny brown hair and a carefully grown small moustache: a good dealer in the market: sharp and confident, with a loud voice and shifty eyes. The other was a clergyman: need I say more? Except that he was more of a clergyman even than most clergymen. I mean that he wore tight things — leggings don't they call them? or breeches? — round his calves. I never know what it means: whether they are bishops or rural deans or archdeacons or archimandrites. In any case I mistrust them even more than the black trousers: they seem to close the last door for anything human to get in through the black clothes. The dog collar closes up the armour above, and below, as long as they *were* trousers, at any rate some whiff of humanity might have eddied up the legs of them and touched bare flesh. But the gaiters button them up finally, irremediably, for ever.

I expect he was an archdeacon; he was saying: 'You can't impose Western civilisation upon an Eastern people — I believe I'm right in saying that there are over two hundred millions in our Indian Empire — without a little disturbance. I'm a liberal, you know. I've been a Liberal my whole life — family tradition — though I grieve to say I could not follow Mr Gladstone on the Home Rule question. It seems to me a good sign, this movement, an awakening among the people. But don't misunderstand me, my dear Sir, I am not making any excuses for the methods of the extremists. Apart from my calling — I have a natural horror of violence. Nothing can condone violence, the taking of human life, it's savagery, terrible, terrible.'

'They don't put it down with a strong enough hand,' the stock-jobber was saying almost fiercely. 'There's too much Liberalism in the East, too much namby-pambyism. It is all right here, of course, but it's not suited to the East. They want a strong hand. After all they owe us something: we aren't going to take all the kicks and leave them all the halfpence. Rule 'em, I say, rule 'em, if you're going to rule 'em. Look after 'em, of course: give 'em schools, if they want education — schools, hospitals, roads, and railways. Stamp out the plague, fever, famine. But let 'em know you are top dog. That's the way to run an eastern country. I am a white man, you're black; I'll treat you well, give you courts and justice; but I'm the superior race, I'm master here.'

The man who had looked round at me when I said 'Here's luck!' was fidgeting about in his chair uneasily. I examined him more carefully. There was no mistaking the cause of his irritation. It was written on his face, the small close-cut white moustache, the smooth firm cheeks with the red-and-brown glow on them, the innumerable wrinkles round the eyes, and above all the eyes themselves, that had grown slow and steady and unastonished, watching that inexplicable, meaningless march of life under blazing suns. He had seen it, he knew. 'Ah,' I thought, 'he is beginning to feel his liver. If he would only begin to speak, we might have some fun.'

'H'm, h'm,' said the Archdeacon. 'Of course there's something in what you say. Slow and sure. Things may be going too fast, and, as I say, I'm entirely for putting down violence and illegality with a strong hand. And after all, my dear Sir, when you say we're the superior race you imply a duty. Even in secular matters we must spread the light. I believe – devoutly – I am not ashamed to say so – that we are. We're reaching the people there, it's the cause of the unrest, we set them an example. They desire to follow. Surely, surely we should help to guide their feet. I don't speak without a certain knowledge. I take a great interest, I may even say that I play my small part, in the work of one of our great missionary societies. I see our young men, many of them risen from the people, educated often, and highly educated (I venture to think), in Board Schools. I see them go out full of high ideals to live among those poor people. And I see them when they come back and tell me their tales honestly, unostentatiously. It is always the same, a message of hope and comfort. We are getting at the people, by example, by our lives, by our conduct. They respect us.'

I heard a sort of groan, and then, quite loud, these strange words:

'*Kasimutal Rameswaramvaraiyil terintavan*'.

'I beg your pardon,' said the Archdeacon, turning to the interrupter.

'I beg yours. Tamil, Tamil proverb. Came into my mind. Spoke without thinking. Beg yours.'

'Not at all. Very interesting. You've lived in India? Would you mind my asking you for a translation?'

'It means "he knows everything between Benares and Rameswaram". Last time I heard it, an old Tamil, seventy or eighty years old, perhaps – he looked a hundred – used it of one of your young men. The young man, by the bye, had been a year and a half in India. D'you understand?'

'Well, I'm not sure I do: I've heard, of course, of Benares, but Rameswaram, I don't seem to remember the name.'

I laughed; I could not help it; the little Anglo-Indian looked so fierce. 'Ah!' he said, 'you don't recollect the name. Well, it's pretty famous out there. Great temple – Hindu – right at the southern tip of India. Benares, you know, is up north. The old Tamil meant that your friend knew everything in India after a year and a half: *he* didn't, you know, after seventy, after seven thousand years. Perhaps you also don't recollect that the Tamils are Dravidians? They've been there since the beginning of time, before we came, or the Dutch or Portuguese or the Muhammadans, or our cousins, the other Aryans. Uncivilised, black? Perhaps, but, if they're black, after all it's *their* suns, through thousands of years, that have blackened them. They ought to know, if anyone does: but they don't, they don't pretend to. But you two gentlemen, you seem to know everything between Kasimutal – that's Benares – and Rameswaram, without having seen the sun at all.'

'My dear sir,' began the Archdeacon pompously, but the jobber interrupted him. He had had a number of whiskies and sodas, and was quite heated. 'It's very easy to sneer: it doesn't mean because you've lived a few years in a place . . . '

'I? Thirty. But they – seven thousand at least.'

'I say, it doesn't mean because you've lived thirty years in a place that you know all about it. Ramisram, or whatever the damned place is called, I've never heard of it and don't want to. You do, that's part of your job, I expect. But I read the papers, I've read books too, mind you, about India. I know what's going on. One knows enough – enough – data: East and West and the difference: I can form an opinion − I've a right to it even if I've never heard of Ramis what d'you call it. You've lived there and you can't see the wood for the trees. We see it because we're out of it − see it at a distance.'

'Perhaps,' said the Archdeacon, 'there's a little misunderstanding. The discussion − if I may say so − is getting a little heated − unnecessarily, I think. We hold our views. This gentleman has lived in the country. He holds others. I'm sure it would be most interesting to hear them. But I confess I didn't quite gather them from what he said.'

The little man was silent: he sat back, his eyes fixed on the ceiling. Then he smiled.

'I won't give you views,' he said. 'But if you like I'll give you what you call details, things seen, facts. Then you can give me *your* views on 'em.'

They murmured approval.

'Let's see, it's fifteen, seventeen years ago. I had a district then about as big as England. There may have been twenty Europeans in it, counting the missionaries, and twenty million Tamils and Telegus. I expect nineteen million of the Tamils and Telegus never saw a white man from one year's end to the other, or if they did, they caught a glimpse of me under a sun helmet riding through their village on a flea-bitten grey Indian mare. Well, Providence had so designed it that there was a stretch of coast in that district which was a barren wilderness of sand and scrubby thorn jungle − and nothing else − for three hundred miles; no towns, no villages, no water, just sand and trees for three hundred miles. Oh, and sun, I forget that, blazing sun. And in the water off the shore at one place there were oysters, millions of them lying and breeding at the bottom, four or five fathoms down. And in the oysters, or some of them, were pearls.

'Well, we rule India and the sea, so the sea belongs to us, and the oysters are in the sea and the pearls are in the oysters.

Therefore of course the pearls belong to us. But they lie in five fathoms. How to get 'em up, that's the question. You'd think being progressive we'd dredge for them or send down divers in diving dresses. But we don't , not in India. They've been fishing up the oysters and the pearls there ever since the beginning of time, naked brown men diving feet first out of long wooden boats into the blue sea sweeping the oysters off the bottom of the sea into baskets slung to their sides. They were doing it centuries and centuries before we came, when − as someone said − our ancestors were herding swine on the plains of Norway. The Arabs of the Persian Gulf came down in dhows and fished up pearls which found their way to Solomon and the Queen of Sheba. They still come, and the Tamils and Moormen of the district come, and they fish 'em up in the same way, diving out of long wooden boats shaped and rigged as in Solomon's time, as they were centuries before him and the Queen of Sheba. No difference, you see, except that we − Government I mean − take two-thirds of all the oysters fished up: the other third we give to the diver, Arab or Tamil or Moorman, for his trouble in fishing 'em up.

'We used to have a Pearl Fishery about once in three years, it lasted six weeks or two months just between the two monsoons, the only time the sea is calm there. And I had, of course, to go and superintend it, to take Government's share of oysters, to sell them, to keep order, to keep out K.D.'s − that means Known Depredators − and smallpox and cholera. We had what we called a camp, in the wilderness remember, on the hot sand down there by the sea: it sprang up in a night, a town, a big town of thirty or forty thousand people, a little India, Asia almost, even a bit of Africa. They came from all districts: Tamils, Telegus, fat Chetties, Parsees, Bombay merchants, Sinhalese from Ceylon, the Arabs and the Negroes, Somalis probably, who used to be their slaves. It was an immense gamble; everyone bought oysters for the chance of the prizes in them: it would have taken fifty white men to superintend that camp properly: they gave me one, a little boy of twenty-four fresh-cheeked from England, just joined the service. He had views, he had been educated in a Board School, won prizes, scholarships, passed the Civil Service Exam. Yes, he had views; he used to explain them to me when he first arrived. He got some new ones, I think, before he got out of that camp. You'd say he only saw details, things happen, facts, data. Well, he did that too. He saw men die – he hadn't seen that in his Board School – die of plague or cholera, like flies, all over the place, under the trees, in the boats, outside the little door of his own little hut. And he saw flies, too, millions, billions of them all day long buzzing, crawling over everything, his hands, his little fresh face, his food. And he smelt the smell of millions of decaying oysters all day long and all night long for six weeks. He was sick four or five times a day for six weeks; the smell did that. Insanitary? Yes, very. Why is it allowed? The pearls, you see, the pearls: you must get them out of the oysters as you must get the oysters out of the sea. And the pearls are very often small and embedded in the oyster's body. So you put all the oysters, millions of them, in dug-out canoes in the sun to rot. They rot very well in that sun, and the flies come and lay eggs in them, and maggots come out of the eggs and more flies come out of the maggots; and between them all, the maggots and the sun, the oysters' bodies disappear, leaving the pearls and a little sand at the bottom of the canoe. Unscientific? Yes, perhaps; but after all it's our camp, our fishery – just as it was in Solomon's time. At any rate, you see, it's the East. But whatever it is, and whatever the reason, the result involves flies, millions of them and a smell, a stench – Lord! I can smell it now.

'There was one other white man there. He was a planter, so he said, and he had come to 'deal' in pearls. He dropped in on

us out of a native boat at sunset on the second day. He had a
red face and red nose, he was unhealthily fat for the East: the
whites of his eyes were rather blue and rather red: they were
also watery. I noticed that his hand shook, and that he first
refused and then took a whisky and soda – a bad sign in the
East. He wore very dirty white clothes and a vest instead of a
shirt: he apparently had no baggage of any sort. But he was a
white man, and so he ate with us that night and a good many
nights afterwards.

'In the second week he had his first attack of D.T. We
pulled him through, Robson and I, in the intervals of watching over the oysters. When he hadn't got D.T., he talked: he
was a great talker, he also had views. I used to sit in the
evenings – they were rare – when the fleet of boats had got
in early and the oysters had been divided, in front of my hut
and listen to him and Robson settling India and Asia, Africa
too probably. We sat there in our long chairs on the sand
looking out over the purple sea, towards a sunset like blood
shot with gold. Nothing moved or stirred except the flies
which were going to sleep in a mustard tree close by; they
hung in buzzing clusters, billions of them on the smooth
leaves and little twigs: literally it was black with them. It
looked as if the whole tree had suddenly broken out all over
into some disease of living black currants. Even the sea
seemed to move with an effort in the hot, still air; only now
and again a little wave would lift itself up very slowly, very
wearily, poise itself for a moment, and then fall with a weary
little thud on the sand.

'I used to watch them, I say, in the hot still air and the smell
of dead oysters – it pushed up against your face like something solid – talking, talking in their long chairs, while the
sweat stood out in little drops on their foreheads and trickled
from time to time down their noses. There wasn't, I suppose,
anything wrong with Robson, he was all right at bottom, but

he annoyed me, irritated me in that smell. He was too cock-sure altogether, of himself, of his Board School education, of life, of his "views". He was going to run India on new lines, laid down in some damned Manual of Political Science out of which they learn life in Board Schools and extension lectures. He would run his own life, I dare say, on the same lines, laid down in some other text book or primer. He hadn't seen anything, but he knew exactly what it was all like. There was nothing curious, astonishing, unexpected, in life, he was ready for any emergency. And we were all wrong, all on the wrong tack in dealing with natives! He annoyed me a little, you know, when the thermometer stood at 99, at six p.m., but what annoyed me still more was that they – the natives! – were all wrong too. They too had to be taught how to live and die, too, I gathered.

'But his views were interesting, very interesting – espec-ially in the long chairs there under the immense Indian sky, with the camp at our hands – just as it had been in the time of Moses and Abraham – and behind us the jungle for miles, and behind that India, three hundred millions of them listen-ing to the piping voice of a Board School boy, are the inferior race, these three hundred millions – mark race, though there are more races in India than people in Peckham – and we, of course, are superior. They've stopped somehow on the bot-tom rung of the ladder of which we've very nearly, if not quite, reached the top. They've stopped there hundreds, thousands of years: but it won't take any time to lead 'em up by the hand to our rung. It's to be done like this: by showing them that they're our brothers, inferior brothers; by reason, arguing them out of their superstitions, false beliefs; by education, by science, by example, yes, even he did not forget example, and White, sitting by his side with his red nose and watery eyes, nodded approval. And all this must be done scientifically, logically, systematically: if it were, a

Commissioner could revolutionise a province in five years, turn it into a Japanese India, with all the *ryots* as well as all the *vakils* and students running up the ladder of European civilisation to become, I suppose, glorified Board School angels at the top. "But you've none of you got clear plans out here," he piped, "you never work on any system: you've got no point of view. The result is" — here, I think, he was inspired, by the dead oysters, perhaps — "instead of getting hold of the East, it's the East which gets hold of you."

'And White agreed with him, solemnly, at any rate when he was sane and sober. And I couldn't complain of his inexperience. He was rather reticent at first, but afterwards we heard much — too much — of his experiences — one does, when a man gets D.T. He said he was a gentleman, and I believe it was true; he had been to a public school; Cheltenham or Repton. He hadn't, I gathered, succeeded as a gentleman at home, so they sent him to travel in the East. He liked it, it suited him. So he became a planter in Assam. That was fifteen years ago, but he didn't like Assam: the luck was against him — it always was — and he began to roll; and when a man starts rolling in India, well — He had been a clerk in merchants' offices; he had served in a draper's shop in Calcutta; but the luck was always against him. Then he tramped up and down India, through Ceylon, Burma; he had got at one time or another to the Malay States, and when he was very bad one day, he talked of cultivating camphor in Java. He had been a sailor on a coasting tramp; he had sold horses (which didn't belong to him) in the Deccan somewhere; he had tramped day after day begging his way for months in native bazaars; he had lived for six months with, and on, a Tamil woman in some little village down in the south. Now he was "dealing in" pearls. "India's got hold of me," he'd say, "India's got hold of me, and the East."

'He had views too, very much like Robson's, with additions. "The strong hand" came in, and "rule". We ought to govern India more; we didn't now. Why, he had been in hundreds of places where he was the first Englishman that the people had ever seen. (Lord! think of that!). He talked a great deal about the hidden wealth of India and exploitation. He knew places where there was gold — workable too — only one wanted a little capital — coal probably and iron — and then there was this new stuff, radium. But we weren't go-ahead, progressive, the Government always put difficulties in his way. They made "the native" their stalking-horse against European enterprise. He would work for the good of the native, he'd treat him firmly but kindly — especially, I thought, the native women, for his teeth were sharp and pointed and there were spaces between each, and there was something about his chin and jaw — *you* know the type, I expect.

'As the fishing went on we had less time to talk. We had to work. The divers go out in the fleet of three hundred or four hundred boats every night and dive until midday. Then they sail back from the pearl banks and bring all their oysters into an immense Government enclosure where the Government share is taken. If the wind is favourable all the boats go back by six p.m. and the work is over at seven. But if the wind starts blowing off shore, the fleet gets scattered and boats drop in one by one all night long. Robson and I had to be in the enclosures as long as there was a boat out, ready to see that, as soon as it did get in, the oysters were brought to the enclosure and Government got its share.

'Well, the wind never did blow favourably that year. I sat in that enclosure sometimes for forty-eight hours on end. Robson found managing it rather difficult, so he didn't like to be left there alone. If you get two thousand Arabs, Tamils, Negroes, the Moormen, each with a bag or two of oysters, into an enclosure a hundred and fifty yards by a hundred and fifty yards, and you only have thirty timid native 'subordinates' and twelve native policemen to control them — well, somehow or other he found a difficulty in applying his system of reasoning to them. The first time he tried it, we very nearly had a riot; it arose from a dispute between some Arabs and Tamils over the ownership of three oysters which fell out of a bag. The Arabs didn't understand Tamil and the Tamils didn't understand Arabic, and, when I got down there, fetched by a frightened constable, there were sixty or seventy men fighting with great poles — they had pulled up the fence of the enclosure for weapons — and on the outskirts was Robson running round like a distracted hen with a white face and tears in his blue eyes. When we got the combatants separated, they had only killed one Tamil and broken nine or ten heads. Robson was very upset by that dead Tamil, he broke down utterly for a minute or two, I'm afraid.

'Then White got his second attack. He was very bad: he wanted to kill himself, but what was worse than that, before killing himself, he wanted to kill other people. I hadn't been to bed for two nights and I knew I should have to sit up another night in that enclosure as the wind was all wrong again. I had given White a bed in my hut: it wasn't good to let him wander in the bazaar. Robson came down with a white face to tell me he had "gone mad up there again". I had to knock him down with the butt end of a rifle; he was a big man and I hadn't slept for forty-eight hours, and then there were the flies and the smell of those dead oysters.

'It sounds unreal, perhaps a nightmare, all this told here to you behind blinds and windows in this — ' he sniffed — 'in this smell of — of — horsehair furniture and paint and varnish. The curious thing is it didn't seem a nightmare out there. It was too real. Things happened, anything might happen, without shocking or astonishing. One just did one's work, hour after hour, keeping things going in that sun which stung one's bare hands, took the skin off even my face, among the flies and the smell. It wasn't a nightmare, it was just a few thousand Arabs and Indians fishing up oysters from the bottom of the sea. It wasn't even new, one felt; it was old, old as the Bible, old as Adam, so the Arabs said. One hadn't much time to think, but one felt it and watched it, watched the things happen quietly, unastonished, as men do in the East. One does one's work — forty-eight hours at a stretch doesn't leave one much time or inclination for thinking — waiting for things to happen. If you can prevent people from killing one another or robbing one another, or burning down the camp, or getting cholera or plague or smallpox, and if one can manage to get one night's sleep in three, one is fairly satisfied; one doesn't much worry about having to knock a mad gentleman from Repton on the head with the butt end of a rifle between-whiles.

'I expect that's just what Robson would call not getting hold of India but letting India get hold of you. Well, I said I wouldn't give you views and I won't: I'm giving you facts: what I want, you know, too is to give you the feeling of facts out there. After all that is data for your views, isn't it? Things here feel so different; you seem so far from life, with windows and blinds and curtains always in between, and then nothing ever happens, you never wait for things to happen, never watch things happening here. You are always doing things somehow — Lord knows what they are — according, I suppose, to systems, views, opinions. But out there you live so near to life, every morning you smell damp earth if you splash too much in your tin bath. And things happen slowly, inexorably by fate, and you — you don't do things, you watch with the three hundred millions. You feel it there in everything, even in the sunrise and sunset, every day, the immensity, inexorableness, mystery of things happening. You feel the whole earth waking up or going to sleep in a great arch of sky; you feel small, not very powerful. But who ever felt the sun set or rise in London or Torquay either? It doesn't: you just turn on or turn off the electric light.

'White was very bad that night. When he recovered from being knocked down by the rifle, I had to tie him down to the bed. And then Robson broke down — nerves, you know. I had to go back to the enclosure and I wanted him to stay and look after White in the hut — it wasn't safe to leave him alone even tied down with cord to the camp bed. But this was apparently another emergency to which the manual system did not apply. He couldn't face it alone in the hut with that man tied to the bed. White was certainly not a pretty sight writhing about there, and his face — have you ever seen a man in the last stages of D.T.? I beg your pardon. I suppose you haven't. It isn't nice, and White was also seeing things, not nice either: not snakes, you know, as people do in novels when they get D.T., but things which had happened to him, and things which he had done — they weren't nice either — and curious ordinary things distorted in a most unpleasant way. He was very much troubled by snipe: hundreds of them kept on rising out of the bed from beside him with that shrill cheep! cheep! of theirs: he felt their soft little feathered bodies against his bare skin as they fluttered up from under him somewhere and flew out of the window. It threw him into paroxysms of fear, agonies. It made one, I admit, feel chilly round the heart to hear him pray one to stop it.

'And Robson was also not a nice sight. I hate seeing a sane man break down with fear, mere abject fear. He just sat down at last on a cane-bottomed chair and cried like a baby. Well, that did him some good, but he wasn't fit to be left alone with White. I had to take White down to the enclosure, and I tied him to a post with coir rope near the table at which I sat there. There was nothing else to do. And Robson came too and sat there at my side through the night watching White, terrified but fascinated.

'Can you picture that enclosure to yourself down on the sandy shore with its great fence of rough poles cut in the jungle, lighted by a few flares, torches dipped in coconut oil: and the white man tied to a pole raving, writhing in the flickering light which just showed too Robson's white scared little face? And in the intervals of taking over oysters and settling disputes between Arabs and Somalis and Tamils and Moormen, I sat at the table writing a report (which had to go by runner next morning) on a proposal to introduce the teaching of French in 'English schools' in towns. That wasn't a very good report. White gave us the whole history of his life between ten p.m. and four a.m. in the morning. He didn't leave much to the imagination; a parson would have said that in that hour the memory of his sins came upon him – Oh, I beg your pardon. But really I think they did. I thought I had lived long enough out there to have heard without a shock anything that men can do and do – especially white men who have 'gone under'. But I hadn't : I couldn't stomach the story of White's life told by himself. It wasn't only that he had robbed and swindled himself through India up and down for fifteen years. That was bad enough for there wasn't a station where he hadn't swindled and bamboozled his fellow white men. But it was what he had done when he got away "among the natives" – to men, and women too, away from "civilisation", in the jungle villages and high up in the mountains. God! the cold, civilised, corrupted cruelty of it. I told you, I think, that his teeth were pointed and spaced out in his mouth.

'And his remorse was the most horrible thing, tied to that post there, writhing under the flickering light of the flare: the remorse of fear – fear of punishment, of what was coming, of death, of the horrors, real horrors and the phantom horrors of madness.

'Often during the night there was nothing to be heard in the enclosure but his screams, curses, hoarse whispers of fear. We seemed alone there in the vast stillness of the sky: only now and then a little splash from the sea down on the shore. And then would come a confused murmur from the sea and a little later perhaps the wailing voice of one man calling to another from boat to boat across the water: "Abdulla! Abdulla!" And I would go out on to the shore. There were boats, ten, fifteen, twenty, perhaps, coming in from the banks, sad, mysterious, in the moonlight, gliding in with the little splashings of the great round oars. Except for the slow moving of the oars one would have thought they were full of the dead, there was not a movement on board, until the boats touched the sand. Then the dark shadows, which lay like dead men about the boats, would leap into life — there would rise a sudden din of hoarse voices, shouting, calling, quarrelling. The boats swarmed with shadows running about, gesticulating, staggering under sacks of oysters, dropping one after the other over the boats' sides into the sea. The sea was full of them and soon the shore too, Arabs, Negroes, Tamils, bowed under the weight of the sacks. They came up dripping from the sea. They burst with a roar into the enclosure: they flung down their sacks of oysters with a crash. The place was full of swaying, struggling forms: of men calling to one another in their different tongues: of the smell of the sea.

'And above everything one could hear the screams and prayers of the madman writhing at the post. They gathered about him, stared at him. The light of the flares fell on their dark faces, shining and dripping from the sea. They looked calm, impassive, stern. It shone too on the circle of eyes: one saw the whites of them all round him: they seemed to be judging him, weighing him: calm patient eyes of men who watched unastonished the procession of things. The Tamils' squat black figures, nearly naked, watched him silently, almost carelessly. The Arabs in their long dirty night-shirts, black-bearded, discussed him earnestly together with their guttural voices. Only an enormous Negro, towering up to six feet six at least above the crowd, dressed in sacks and an enormous ulster, with ten copper coffee pots slung over his back and a pipe made of a whole coconut with an iron tube stuck in it in his hand, stood smiling mysteriously.

'And White thought they weren't real, that they were devils of Hell sent to plague and torture him. He cursed them, whispered at them, howled with fear. I had to explain to them that the Sahib was not well, that the sun had touched him, that they must move away. They understood. They salaamed quietly, and moved away slowly, dignified.

'I don't know how many times this didn't happen during the night. But towards morning White began to grow very weak. He moaned perpetually. Then he began to be troubled by the flesh. As dawn showed grey in the east, he was suddenly shaken by convulsions horrible to see. He screamed for someone to bring him a woman, and, as he screamed, his head fell back: he was dead. I cut the cords quickly in a terror of haste, and covered the horror of the face. Robson was sitting in a heap in his chair. He was sobbing, his face in his hands.

'At that moment I was told I was wanted on the shore. I went quickly. The sea looked cold and grey under the faint light from the east. A cold little wind just ruffled the surface of the water. A solitary boat stood out black against the sky, just throbbing slowly up and down on the water close in shore. They had a dead Arab on board, he had died suddenly while diving, they wanted my permission to bring the body ashore. Four men waded out to the boat: the corpse was lifted out and placed upon their shoulders. They waded back slowly: the feet of the dead man stuck out, toes pointing up, very stark over the shoulders of the men in front. The body was laid on the sand. The bearded face of the dead man looked very calm, very dignified in the faint light. An Arab, his brother, sat down upon the sand near his head. He covered himself with sackcloth. I heard him weeping. It was very silent, very cold and still on the shore in the early dawn.

'A tall figure stepped forward, it was the Arab sheik, the leader of the boat. He laid his hand on the head of the weeping man and spoke to him calmly, eloquently, compassionately. I didn't understand Arabic, but I could understand what he was saying. The dead man had lived, had worked, had died. He had died working, without suffering, as men should desire to die. He had left a son behind him. The speech went on calmly, eloquently, I heard continually the word *khallas* — all is over, finished. I watched the figures outlined against the grey sky — the long lean outline of the corpse with the toes sticking up so straight and stark, the crouching huddled figure of the weeping man and the tall upright sheik standing by his side. They were motionless, sombre, mysterious, part of the grey sea, of the grey sky.

'Suddenly the dawn broke red in the sky. The sheik stopped, motioned silently to the four men. They lifted the dead man on to their shoulders. They moved away down the shore by the side of the sea which began to stir under the cold wind. By their side walked the sheik, his hand laid gently on the brother's arm. I watched them move away, silent, dignified. And over the shoulders of the men I saw the feet of the dead man with the toes sticking up straight and stark.

'Then I moved away too, to make arrangements for White's burial: it had to be done at once.'

There was silence in the smoking-room. I looked round. The Colonel had fallen asleep with his mouth open. The jobber tried to look bored. The Archdeacon was, apparently, rather put out.

'It's too late, I think,' said the Archdeacon, 'to — Dear me, dear me, past one o'clock.' He got up. 'Don't you think you've chosen rather exceptional circumstances, out of the ordinary case?'

The Commissioner was looking into the few red coals that were all that was left of the fire.

'There's another Tamil proverb,' he said. 'When the cat puts his head into a pot, he thinks all is darkness.'

(1915)

JOHN EYTON
The Dancing Fakir

Jackson was an incorrigible drifter. He was generally referred to as 'that Jackson', having no known first name, Christian or otherwise. In the bazaar also he was 'that Jackson', without the appendage of Sahib. The bazaar knew his kind too well. Yet he was an Englishman of a sort — the sort that drifts.

Once, in better days, he had spent two seasons with a third-rate variety company in one of the Calcutta music-halls. He had shown really marked ability as a mimic, and could take off a native to the life; his patter songs were popular; even when drunk, as was frequent, he could keep a wonderfully serious face. But one night he returned from a strange revel in the Chinese quarter, and proceeded to divest himself of his clothing on the stage — slowly and impassively. It took six men a considerable time to remove him. He had a rooted idea that he was a Dancing Fakir, and with a dead-white face he made rings round the manager and his minions, until he fell insensible among the footlights. His theatrical career ended in that faint.

Jackson drifted on. The Calcutta race-course knew him for a time in various capacities — none of them above suspicion. At one time he was concerned with bicycles, which he stole for another to hire out. This led to three months in jail. After his release he drifted from Calcutta to Bangalore, and thence to Bombay, where he helped in a motor garage, having a smattering of mechanics and a turn for touting. From Bombay too he passed. There was a story of a drunken assault on a Parsee by a pale, pock-marked Angrez dressed in a dirty white cotton suit, an old Khaki topi, and canvas shoes, who passed by a selection of names — Williams, Duveen, Riley, Smithers, and Jackson. The police got track of him in the bazaar, in a street where his predilection for the rawest arrack made his capture seem a certainty; but he escaped. It was thought that he had disguised himself as a native. The reward for the tall, stooping man with the pale, clean-shaven face and the pock-marks was never claimed. Jackson had passed on. He was never heard of again.

II

The apotheosis of Jackson was in this wise.

He became a Fakir. Perhaps his success at the Calcutta music-hall suggested this unusual course. His remarkable knowledge of native idiom stood him in good stead, and he found the part easier to play than he would have supposed. His patter, with the impassive face, procured him free meals — even free drinks on the wooden platforms of country liquor shops. He never gave himself away, however drunk; for the more drunk he was the more he believed himself a Fakir. In a Fakir a certain wildness is expected; his dancing was looked upon as an idiosyncrasy, and gained him a reputation. He cultivated long hair, which he made tawny with henna; he wore nothing but a yellow cloth round his middle, and brown beads round his neck; a wild, wispy beard was also grown gradually, and dyed red; and white dust on his brown, naked body, and red caste-marks barring his forehead were easy. No one ever recognised Jackson. He had no name now. His wanderings are unknown; he must have seen much — enough, at least, to make him forget that he had ever been Jackson.

Little wayside shrines knew him; he could puff out vile smoke from the earthenware pipe, and spit, and make strange guttural noises with any beggar priest in India. He ate no meat, but he throve on grain and milk, gifts of villagers; the Dancing Fakir became a finer figure on this fare than ever was Jackson. There is reason to believe that he drank less and less spirit. His diet must have stayed the craving. At any rate his physique improved vastly; he was really tall now, without the stoop; there was scarcely a taller Fakir in all the thousand villages he visited.

Though his wanderings have not been chronicled, it is certain that he was at Bijapur at the time of the riot. It was Ramlila time – a season of religious festival and plays and fairs. Bijapur was gay with people in their brightest clothes. The steps of the temple above the river were thronged. There were bathers in scarlet and in yellow; women in blue and in red; coloured strips of flags; and, beyond, the houses of the bazaar were bright in the sun – light blue and yellow and white. In the narrow streets the crowds were promenading, chaffering, and admiring all day. In the cloth shops country folk were buying finery for Ramlila time – bright cottons, and tinsel for the children. All the booths were full of merchandise placed on little wooden platforms just raised above the ground, and the sellers squatted by their goods. Red, golden, and white grain was piled in heaps before the shops of the grain merchants; farther on, a pyramid of oranges; and beyond – in the street of the workers in brass – a great pile of brazen vessels flaunted the sun. The Dancing Fakir doubtless saw all these things, as he sat at the street corner listening to the talk of two *Sadhus* with shaven heads and orange-coloured garb. He gathered that there was a good deal of ill-feeling under all the bustle and chatter. The Deputy Commissioner had forbidden the procession to pass down the Bara Bazaar on account of Mohammedan scruples about their mosque in that street. The procession was immemorial: curse that mosque; curse the Sircar, who ordered these things! There were extra police about too, who had arrived by rail — an officer and thirty men. There were to be speeches at the *mela* that afternoon; Babu Gopi Nath, the great speaker, was himself coming. He was the friend of Mahatma Gandhi Ji. The Sircar was afraid of Gopi Nath. He was no mere windbag either, for he had led the riot at Khaspur, when many men had been killed. So ran the talk; the Dancing Fakir was well used to it. Hatred of the English and their ways had become a common enough theme in the bazaar, and he generally disregarded it. This time he heard more than usual. There was a whisper about looting the liquor shops, and the arrival of two hundred wild men from Khaspur. The Dancing Fakir wandered on. He did not care.

That year the crowd at the *mela* beat all records, and the Bijapur *maidan* was filled to overflowing. On the outskirts, children rode on rough merry-go-rounds at two *pies* a time. There were conjurers who spent most of their time drum-beating to an audience always on the move. There were snake-charmers from Khaspur; a man who had crawled on all fours from Hyderabad, and who now lay on the ground yelling strangely; a travelling show from Benares, the actors wearing red masks; three bands of one sort and another; and a Dancing Fakir who never changed his face. But the main attraction was a rough platform in the centre of the open meadow, where Gopi Nath was speaking. He was not much to look at — a little dark man with a moustache, glasses, and a small round black cap on his head. But when he held up his hand and began to speak of wrongs, there was a subtle change in the crowd. Hitherto there had been idle bustle. Now there was a silence — then a restlessness; an atmosphere of expectation; something vaguely menacing. Gopi Nath did not rant; at first he spoke slowly then took advantage of the lull to grip his hearers, following with an appeal of swift eloquence. He had caught that crowd: eyes stared; breathing quickened;

men pressed forward without knowing it. One by one the side-shows ceased. The Dancing Fakir was still, listening on the outskirts. No one moved, except the police in their khaki coats and red turbans quietly patrolling the crowd. Then there was a rustle – a murmur, like the sea. Gopi Nath was urging the crowd to loot the liquor shops, sources of the Sircar's wealth. Then later – one could not miss the words; they were like a clarion call – 'Hotel' – 'Club' – 'Blood of the English dog!' There came that unmistakable low growl of an angry mob, for one moment before the rush – then pandemonium.

Babu Gopi Nath had won them. The mob was beyond control; respectable people were fleeing from the ground to lock themselves in their houses. The rest were as one man – and that man was mad and would soon be drunk as well. Bijapur was only a Civil Station; it had no garrison beyond fifty police; Government was credited with trusting to luck in these matters; the English ladies were at the Club, playing tennis.

Babu Gopi Nath slipped off quietly to the car placed at his disposal by the All-India Non-cooperation Society, and was soon far away. After all, he was not a man of action.

IV

Then came the awakening of the Dancing Fakir. He did not consider explanations; he had never cared an anna for the Government, and had been long estranged from his own kind. But he thought of the Club – half a mile away, at the bottom of the straight, broad road from the *maidan*. He had passed it the day before. It lay straight ahead, beyond the cross-roads, where you turned to the right for the Collector's Court and the Treasury, and to the left for the bazaar and the river. The crowd would keep straight on; it had one idea only: the Club was the goal suggested. At this thought, a little spark which had almost died in the Dancing Fakir glowed up and fired him. He became not Jackson, but Alfred Henry Jackson. He saw only the tennis players.

He would have to act very quickly; the police had been overpowered; the crowd were beating their dead bodies with *lathis*. Just as well — they would hardly move seriously for a few minutes. There was a struggling mass of humanity outside the liquor shop in the little street abutting on the *maidan*. The Dancing Fakir suddenly grew active. He ran, leaping and shouting, to the liquor shop, passing a group of men who were beating two *bunnias*. The shop was already alight; bottles and *pipas* were broken, and the contents were streaming into the road. The Dancing Fakir knelt down, with others, in the dust, and lapped and lapped at the liquor. The spirit, to which he had lately been a stranger, fired his brain and gave him great strength. He could lead now — lead ten thousand men. He must lead them to the right at those cross-roads, towards the Treasury. He had seen a strong armed guard on the Treasury. But there was no time to lose: the crowd had begun to move; they were leaving the bodies.

Suddenly the Dancing Fakir leapt to his feet, caught a sword from a man near him, and danced madly through the crowd, yelling. He danced up to the nearest dead policeman, with leaps like those of a charging animal, and wildly hacked off his head; he snatched a long *lathi*, and impaled the head, tying it firm with the red turban. Then he raised it on high. People noticed the wild Fakir dancing through the crowd; two or three followed him; then more and more. Faster he went, and faster — the head aloft — waving his wild hair, singing. And the crowd followed him with an ugly sound, filling the wide road with a mass of running, pushing figures. The Dancing Fakir had only one thought — Would they turn to the right? Now they were at the cross-roads; he brandished the head and danced facing them, adjuring them, screaming at them. And they followed him. For a crowd is one man, and the Dancing Fakir had hit upon an old secret of leading rabbles. They will follow something on high – and a head on a pole is the best leader of all. He was covered by dust; blood was on his face and body – and something unearthly in his eyes; but in his heart he triumphed as he had never triumphed before. He led them right down the road to the Treasury; the police reinforcements cut off their rear and barricaded the cross-roads behind them. The police guard on the Treasury held their fire till the crowd came very near, and then fired volley after volley.

The Dancing Fakir sprang high in the air at the first volley, and fell – quite dead.

(1922)

MAUD DIVER
The Gods of The East

We be the Gods of the East,
  Older than all:
Masters of Mourning and Feast—
  How shall we fall?

KIPLING

A breathless, shadeless day, a day of monotonous brilliance, was slowly nearing its close. The sun hung rayless, a disc of flame over a rock-studded horizon, whose uncompromising outline — broken at intervals by ragged clumps of date-palms — was carven, crisp and clear, along the lower edges of a turquoise sky.

Neither shredded cloudlet nor haze of evening lent a softening influence to the stretches of yellow-grey sand, the jagged volcanic rocks, and dusty scrub of Western Rajputana. North and south, east and west, the gaunt profitless desert rose and fell, in billowing waves, and the level light streamed unhindered over its tawny surface.

A few moments more, and the sun was gone, leaving a crimson-purple stain upon the blue. Again a few moments, and, in that same blue, quivered the first palpitating stars.

With a soft strong rush of wings, the grey crane and the wild duck flew to their reedy resting places. The night-jar and fox-headed bat flitted ghost-like through the twilight in search of food. Here and there a trailing cloud of dust marked the track of some local herdsman driving his cattle byre-ward for the night.

One after one, like dropped stars, a group of home-lights revealed a village, hitherto almost indistinguishable from its surroundings: a mere cluster of mud-walled, sun-baked huts, huddled together on a bare billow of sand, as if from an actual sense of the vast loneliness around; and towards it trailing clouds converged from every point of the compass — for herdsmen of the desert roam far afield in search of green food.

At the billow's base, seven bedraggled date-palms clustered about a well; and beside the well a diminutive Hindu shrine was hewn from a boulder of red laterite.

Here, under drooping palm fronds in the glimmer of starlight, could be dimly discerned the figure of a man — tall, spare, muscular, and still as the slumbering earth.

For two hours he had sat thus, wrapt in the profound meditation of a mind and soul unharassed by the restless energy of modern civilisation. Desert-born and desert-bred, the silence and lifelessness of his surroundings oppressed him not at all; so absorbed was he in the secret communing of his own soul with the great unknown Soul of Things, to one of whose countless manifestations the grotesque red shrine by the well was dedicated. For Ram Singh was a Brahman and Rajput of caste and lineage unimpeachable; and — his evening service ended — it was his habit to devote the first hours of darkness to meditation and prayer.

The stern modelling of his features suggested fighting blood in his veins; but the face, as a whole, was that of a thinker rather than a warrior — a thinker who still retained unshaken faith in the gods of his forefathers, in traditions and customs handed down, through countless generations, even to his own.

A loud and cheerful voice from the heart of an approaching dust-cloud recalled him to earth and the affairs of earth.

'Oh-oh, Rama-ji, thou abidest late by the holy well. Hast some special favour to ask of Mai Lakshmi that thou flatterest her with such long devotions?'

'Not so, Durga Das,' replied the Brahman, gravely. 'I am beset by many thoughts. Surely thou hast heard that Munda Ram, banker, having failed to procure his moneys from Narain Das, thy kinsman, hath sworn to obtain them by *dharna?* And I – I am the herald who set my dagger to his bond.'

The wreathed smiles vanished from the listener's face, and he pursed his thick lips with an air of tragic solemnity that sat strangely on his comedy countenance.

'*Hai* – *hai!* Thou hast need, then, brother, for thought and prayer. Who knows but thy life may be the payment? Then will there be much trouble with the police-*log*, whose eyes search out every hole and corner. For myself, I hold by the laws of the British Raj; and, if I mistake not, Narain Das is of the same opinion.'

'Ay, that he is – cowardly son of a jackal!' spoke the Brahman, a flicker of mirth in his deep eyes. 'But it will soon be seen whether his faith in their power will be of any avail in his dealings with me and mine. If the money be not paid, and that instantly, my death will be upon his head. There are but these two ways: and he will be loath to choose the last, chicken-hearted as he is.'

Durga Das turned the palms of his hands outward in expressive native fashion.

'Who knows? His cowries are dear to him as his own heart's blood; but yet – a Brahman's death' – he wagged his bullet head slowly – 'I would not be in *his dhoti* this day for all his hoarded treasure. Of a truth, thine house will grieve to hear thy things. Wilt along?'

'Nay, friend, not yet. Why should my feet make haste to bear ill news?'

The question needed no answer; and, with a sympathetic grunt, Durga Das went on his way, attended by trailing clouds of dust.

Ram Singh, left alone again with the darkening desert and the silence and the stars, faced unflinchingly the situation forced upon him by caste, custom, tradition — the all-powerful trinity of the East. This *dharna* he had spoken of was an ancient Hindu practice — the most singular and extravagant ever conceived by man — for enforcing the payment of a debt: a practice long since made punishable under the British penal code. But it takes time and harsh experience to convince the desert-bred Hindu that the penal code is a living power that snaps irreverent fingers at customs and traditions other than its own: so, in certain regions, *dharna* survived long after it had nominally been suppressed.

By its iron decree, if any injured suitor vainly demanded payment, he installed himself upon his neighbour's doorstep. There he squatted day and night — patient and inexorable as the grim gods he served — abstaining from all food and religious ordinances. His victim, if still obdurate, was compelled to follow his example; and, should the mutual fast be prolonged till the suitor died of starvation, the debtor was held responsible for his death. It need hardly be said that these strange proceedings were apt to prove more effectual if the applicant were a Brahman of birth and blood: so there had grown up a peculiar caste of heralds — known as *charan* — who made themselves responsible for the fulfilment of public engagements, bonds, or family contracts. The sign manual of their office was a dagger, which, in event of failure, they were bound to plunge into their own hearts. Nor was even this enough to satisfy the Hindu's innate love of the horrible and the grim. Should a herald have reason to fear

that the indelible disgrace of causing a Brahman's death
might fail to overawe the defaulter, he was constrained to
take, instead, a life more sacred than his own – to kill, in
open daylight, on the offender's doorsill, either his wife or his
mother.

To be a herald, then, was to live in close fellowship with
the idea of a sudden and violent end; and thus had Ram
Singh, and a long line of ancestors before him, lived from
their youth up. Yet, when the critical moment came, it found
him very humanly dismayed. A vision of his young wife, and
of two lusty men-children, made his strong heart contract
with fear of that which might shortly be in store for him and
them.

And while he sat thus, his mind divided between prayer
and foreboding, the moonless night fell round him like a
curtain hiding all things from view.

II

*What have women to do with thinking? They love and they
suffer.*   Kipling.

'*Hai, hai!* My lord tarrieth late. These goodly *chapattis* will
be quite unfit for his eating.'

The young Brahman's wife crouched low before a brick
oven, lamenting her husband's unpunctuality. A slim
creature, in pale-coloured draperies, she looked scarcely
capable of mothering the two plump babes who fought and
scrambled gleefully a few paces from her side.

'And if he tarry, he hath some good reason,' spoke a voice
from a corner of the dimly lighted room. 'Of what use are the
hands of a wife if they cannot achieve the making of a new
meal for a husband?'

It was the voice of Mai Chandebi, mother of the absentee.
Full and strong, it sorted well with the tall, deep-chested

figure that rose and moved into the area of flickering light
given out by three cotton wicks laid in earthenware saucers
filled with oil.

'Lo, even now, he cometh. Make ready with haste,
Golabi.'

And Golabi obeyed. Obedience was the first and last law of
her young life; and she fulfilled it with a glad heart.

On the entrance of her lord, all was in order; and the
women, as was meet, withdrew while he broke his fast.
Golabi, a bare brown son on either hip, ventured an upward
glance at him as she went; but his eyes were on his mother;
and it was to her he spoke in carefully lowered tones.

'I would have speech with thee, mother, afterwards —
alone.'

Golabi's quick ears caught the words; and her arms tightened round her men-children. In them, she well knew, lay all
her power.

Whilst the mother and wife sat together in an inner room,
Ram Singh ate his meal alone and in silence, according to
custom, squatting on the bare, baked earth, clad only in his
loin-cloth and mystic Brahminical cord. And even as he
blessed his wife's domestic skill, the touch of steel was sharp
against his heart.

When the meal was ended, and his mother rejoined him,
he arose, and the two faced one another — erect and silent.
Their eyes met on one plane — steady and searching, and
alight with a great love.

The woman spoke first.

'Hath it come so soon, my son? I might have known. Never
falls the sword upon the neck of the willing victim.'

'Thou knowest, then?'

'How should I *not* know? I have seen the sword's shadow in
other eyes than thine, Rama-ji. To whom goest thou for the
money?'

'To Narain Das, landholder.'

'It will go hard with thee, son of my heart,' she said, with a swift tightening of her finely carved lips.

'Ay; but it shall go hard with him also. I hate him and all of his mongrel breed. We shall see now whether his faith in the white man's law shall avail him against the decree of the gods.'

'Thou hast not yet seen him?'

'I come from his very door.'

'And of what like seemed his countenance?'

Her tone was steady, but the life had gone out of it.

'Even as I had foreseen. He laughed me to scorn, and bade me carry word to Munda Ram that he had best make application for his dues through the law courts of the English.'

'And thou?'

The words were a mere whisper.

'I answered him, that the white man's law was naught to me, but the honour of my caste was all; that on the morrow, soon after dawn, I should return and take up my post at his door. I said, moreover, that if my blood upon his head did not avail to shake his scorn, I would anoint his threshold with the blood of her − mother of my sons.'

A twitch of pain crossed the stern face, and he turned it from the scrutiny of his mother's eyes. It was not an easy thing the gods demanded of him; but the Great Ones take no count of such passing illusions, in a world of illusions, as the love of a man for his wife.

For a long moment neither was capable of speech. The inevitable lay like a stone upon their hearts.

At length, with purpose in every line of her powerful face, the old woman laid her hand on the man's arm.

'My son, thinkest thou that this thing shall be permitted while breath is in my body and blood in my veins? Is it for naught that I am thy mother, and the widow of thy father? . . . If there be any talk of death in this matter, it shall be *mine only*, . . . hearest thou, my son?'

The fire of youth, dominant and masterful, flashed from her eyes: for in Rajputana even the women are soldiers at heart. But the man's strength of purpose matched hers. Was it not of her own bestowing?

'Nay, mother,' he answered sternly. 'That is shameful talk. Thy life – '

'Is it more to thee than *hers*, Rama-ji?'

The agonised man caught her wrinkled hands in both his own.

'Mother, I entreat thee, speak not of this thing. Is not thy life sacred above all others? It cannot – it *shall* not be!'

Her excitement had subsided. She was erect again; eyes and mouth unflinching.

'And I say that it shall be, my son. Since when hast thou learnt to set thy will against mine? Let there be no more speech on the matter. To-morrow I go with thee to the house of this man. She is young, Rama-ji. She hath borne thee men-children and shall bear thee yet more. But I – I am old, and a widow, and my life is a very little thing to give for thine honour, son of my heart.'

Ram Singh could only clench his hands and groan, while she comforted him, tenderly, as though he had been a suffering child; but no further mention of the morrow's hideous necessity passed between them.

That night, lying beside his young wife, he felt her slender body shaken with stifled weeping. Very gently, he inquired the cause: and she answered him, brokenly, with another question:

'Hast naught to tell me also, O my husband? I am no weakling . . . I that bare thee two sons in one day. Wherefore hast thou locked thine heart against me?'

The man laid a hand upon her head, stilling its restless motion.

'Hush thee, light of my life. To-morrow thou shalt know all. The night is for rest; and I would have thee sleep, my pearl – sleep.'

III

Still Brahm dreams . . . and till he wakes the gods die not. Kipling.

The first flush of dawn found the doomed household astir and going about their customary duties, which must be carried out whether hearts were at breaking point or no.

Mother and wife worked in silence, each at her appointed task – Golabi with moist lashes, for all her heroic maternal achievement; Chandebi with stern lips and dry, bright eyes.

The two plump babes fought and rollicked as usual, laughing up into the faces of the silent women, whose fingers were mechanically manipulating rice-balls, flower-balls, and sweetmeats, to be offered during the *sraddha* ceremonies, for the nourishment of Chandebi's ghost, when it should have discarded its mortal body, and for the formation of a new body in the regions of the blest. A grim occupation; but to your orthodox Hindu, custom renders all things possible and most things endurable.

The ceremony was long and dreary and solemn to the verge of stupefaction, involving much sprinkling of water, droning of prayers, and propitiating of priests. Ram Singh himself performed the principal rites, clad in spotless loincloth and white Brahminical thread; while his younger brothers were privileged to sprinkle flower-balls with water, and offer sweetmeats to insatiable priests. Custom decreed, moreover, that the interminable affair should be carried through fasting, to the mournful accompaniment of wailing chants. And it was so; while the ghost-to-be awaited its close with stoicism born of lifelong submission to the decrees of caste and the gods.

The sun rose high in the blinding blue, when three tall, white-clad figures drew up before the threshold of Narain Das, defaulter.

The worthy landholder was a man of full habit, and of a cheerful, time-serving humour, inexorable only where his cherished hoard of silver was concerned.

In answer to the formal summons, he came forth, beaming a benevolent welcome, clad in the short jacket and *dhoti* of his class. In a gap between the two garments a roll of brown flesh showed like a girdle round his ample form.

'Ohé, Rama-ji, thou art ever welcome,' he began, in accents a shade too suave for sincerity: but at sight of Chandebi's draped figure and the bared blade in her son's hand, his flow of words forsook him, and uneasiness crept into his furtive eyes.

Not all his cringing reverence for the Sahib, or his dread of breaking the Great Queen's laws, could make him other than a Hindu of caste, which is to say that, in his eyes, the Great Queen herself was an inconsiderable personage compared with the man who stood before him, unflinching purpose in every line of his stern, spare face.

The landholder's small stock of valour was not proof against the flash of a naked sword in the sunlight. The prospect of seeing an old and reverend woman struck down in cold blood might well have shaken a braver man than he: and behind the horror of the whole thing lurked the hair-raising conviction that her blood, so spilt, would be upon his own head till the day of his death — and through untold lives beyond. A clammy dew broke out upon his forehead. The suavity of his smiles increased tenfold.

'Verily, I had forgot; 'tis to settle that little matter of the loan that thou art come – and in a fortunate hour, my friend. I was about to send word that at the month's end I may at length be able to pay my honoured creditor, Munda Ram. Then will all be well between us; as between brother and brother.'

His fat brown hands moved nervously one over the other, as he lifted cunning, conciliatory eyes to the Rajput's face.

Ram Singh merely turned to his mother; and she, without quiver of hand or lip, kneeled down before him, her grey head bared in the sunlight.

'Thine honoured creditor asks a plain answer to a plain question. Wilt thou make payment at once – or no?'

The Rajput's tone was business-like and decisive; but the movement of his right arm sent a snake-like shiver down the defaulter's sleek back.

'Yea, I will make payment – by all means,' he cried with a quavering assumption of cheerfulness; and the kneeling woman lifted her head. 'But to procure so many rupees at one moment's notice is not within the power of this slave.'

Chandebi bowed her head as before.

'At the in-gathering of harvest much money will accrue to me. Then, by the gods of my fathers, I will repay every cowrie I have borrowed from the great and worthy Munda Ram. He knows I am a poor man . . . a very poor man . . . '

His restless hands were clenched to hide the tremor that shook them. He dared not look again into the Brahman's face; but a blinding flash told him the sword had been swung high above the motionless grey head.

'Have done with thy goat's bleating, son of a jackal. Keep that for the law-courts Make answer . . . yea, or nay.'

Ram Singh's voice rang out like a trumpet; and the gaping crowd, that had gathered to look on at this unwonted *tamasha*, held its breath – knowing the end was near.

With lips visibly trembling, Narain Das spoke: 'Stay thine hand, O Rama-ji: and by all that is holy I will pay a portion at least before the crops are in – a month . . . a little month . . . ' His quavering assurances were unceremoniously cut short by a cry of horror that rang shudderingly upon the still air.

The curved sword had swept down with mighty force; and Chandebi's grey head lay in a pool of blood at the landholder's feet, to the lasting damage of his patent-leather shoes.

With a howl of terror he turned and fled into the house, closely followed by the Brahman's two brothers, who had still to enforce the customary mingling of his blood with that of the victim.

The awe-stricken crowd broke up into groups – and gradually drifted away. When the first gasp of horror had spent itself, the sleepy village buzzed with talk of the morning's tragedy; and within a very few hours a second deputation was drawn up before the house front of Narain Das.

It consisted of a company of yellow-turbaned native police, backed by an English civilian, pale and perspiring, demanding, in terms more peremptory than polite, the person of Ram Singh, Brahman and Rajput.

The man gave himself up with his habitual air of dignity. He acknowledged his act without a word of explanation or defence – and Golabi and her two lusty sons saw his face no more.

The law, being lamentably without sense upon so nice a point of family honour, and being concerned only for protection of life and limb, condemned Chandebi's high-minded son to transportation for life. He accepted its decree, as he had accepted most of life's ugly inevitables, stoically and in silence.

Not so Narain Das. His wailing was loud and long, and sleep forsook his eyes. A vision of that grey head, steeped in its own blood, was with him night and day; till this spurner of Brahm's decrees, in an agony of terror and remorse, voluntarily starved himself until he died.

(1924)

KATHERINE MAYO
The Widow

Countless is the number of unhappy women condemned
to widowhood even before they have ceased to be children.
The sin and misery of it all indescribable. And is it to be
said that there is to be no alleviation, no remedy, no end to
all this wretchedness and iniquity? Can such things which
are a disgrace to the sacred land of India be tolerated by
her sons any longer? Social reform, it is true, is difficult
work, and the populace will inevitably discredit and
malign the pioneers in this field. (Mrs Parvati Chan-
drasekhara Aiyar. Stri-Dharma, August 1927, p.149.)

A sun-cracked Bengali plain, streaked with the long bright
shadows of early morning. A solitary thatched-roofed hut of
smooth grey clay. In its doorway, squatting, a woman swathed
in white. Over beyond, half-veiled in floating dust, the grey
clay village that makes her world.

Sita, the woman, by count of the calendar, has lived
through twenty-nine years. By count of the Brahmanic code,
she is the ancient survival of an ancient sin. By count of her
mind, she is a child.

Her fleshless cheeks, drawn like a mummy's, expose the
contour of her teeth. Her short cropped hair that should be
black is coarse and grizzled grey. Each tendon of her little
hands stands out alone. Her great dark eyes stare void — eyes
of a doomed animal that, having exhausted both pain and
fear, knows there is no hope.

As for this hut, her home: One room. Clay floor and walls,
cow-dung-smeared. No window. A bare corded cot. A water-
jar. A food-pot suspended from a peg beside the door. A

grinding-stone. And that is all.

Her life belongs to the past. For hours each day through long drab years she has stared back into the past, seeing pictures without purpose. To-day, having risen with the dawn, having done her ceremonial bathing, having offered to the gods her ceremonial prayer, she sits in the doorway idle. What more is there to do? And, as ever, the pictures begin to come.

She sees herself a little child, happy in an affluent home, her mother's pet till a baby brother comes to fill all eyes. Then the women of the household take her in hand, teaching her all that a Hindu girl-child needs to know — the iron-bound rules of her caste that control each act of life, to break which is damnation; the prayers and propitiations of the gods lest they, who lie always in wait, find excuse to do one a harm; the duties of the wife to the husband, her personal god; the supplications that that husband be provided duly.

For the rest, to fill her days, just small games — and the talk of the women endlessly revolving all that they knew of life. They spoke of child-bearing, much of pain, and sometimes of disease that could eat their bodies with sores.

Somehow, the horror of flesh so defaced laid hold on the thought of the listening child — became in time the demon that haunted her sleep and awoke her nightly, sick and shivering. Secretly she dwelt on it, till, terror-driven, she framed a prayer all her own, adding to the ritual.

'Great Ones,' day by day she repeated, under her breath, 'givers of sons and gold and houses and cattle and all good gifts, to me you have given but one thing — this small body, in which I serve. Of your mercy, then, I beseech you, keep this my body clean, uncankered, undefiled.'

Also, of course, she prayed for a husband, laying her little offering of toys or fruits or flowers before the shrine. And in due season the husband had been procured, from the proper caste circle, not without payment of much money in dowry. In haste, they sent her home to him just before her twelfth birthday, the signs of womanhood having come upon her.

Well she recalled that 'home-going'. Her little mother and the women of the household had often told her all that it meant, yet somehow her child mind, for all the familiarity of the words, had escaped realisation. Such a big man, such an old, fat man, was Bimal her husband! Much bigger, much older than her father; and she at twelve was such a tiny thing!

Four wives had come before her, this new household said. But all had died barren. Now she, Sita, must surely give the master a son.

'I will pray the gods without ceasing,' said little Sita, obedient, trembling. And so she prayed, yet always added her secret prayer: 'Uncankered, Great Ones! Undefiled!'

A year passed. Childhood had vanished. Her frame had scarcely increased, all her vitality being daily sapped away.

'You grow thin and ugly and dull,' the women mocked her, 'and you bear no fruit. Our master will soon discard such a tree and set another in its place.'

Yet Fate worked otherwise in the mind of Bimal her husband, who one day said:

'To-morrow I send you to the temple of Kali, to pray that you give me a son. All day shall you pray, where the priests assign you. At night, you shall sleep where the priests assign you. After that you shall return to me, and in due season bring to birth him, the long-awaited, that shall save my soul from hell.'

So the serving folk had taken her to Kali's temple, cooped in the curtained bullock-cart, as became the station of rich man's wife, that none might see her face. All day in the temple she besought the goddess. And at night, filled with fear, she lay where the priests bade her, in a dark place apart.

'Had you a dream in the night season?' that priest inquired when morning came.

'Not a dream, but a strong Presence that visited me,' she had answered. 'And the voice of the Presence was like the voice of my lord priest.'

'Give thanks to Kali. It was a god,' quoth the other. 'Return to your husband and bid him send me much money at the birth of the child.'

But alas, the child when it came was a girl!

Years passed. Despite a second visit to the temple no other child was vouchsafed. And life became one long dull pain — to be borne with meekness, the will of the blessed gods.

'Yet, for all the pain, have they heard my own prayer!' she would whisper. 'Yet have they ever protected me from the Horror that Eateth the Flesh. They have kept my body clean!' And the thought stayed her secret soul to patience and peace.

Bimal, meantime, despairing, had adopted a son, that his skull might be cracked on the funeral pyre by a hand within the circle of the law.

As for the little daughter that Kali sent, she had been duly trained, duly married like her mother before her, and duly sent home in her eleventh year to her husband's house.

Then Bimal died, because of the sins of Sita his wife. What sins? In vain through succeeding years she had sought to discover them. They belonged to some former incarnation, of which the gods had wiped her memory clean.

But if a man dies, is it not always because of the sins of the wife who survives him? Wherefore she walks justly accursed of all orthodox Hindudom, a slave, a rightless thing of evil omen, till death releases the earth of her weight.

Obeying the explicit Hindu code, they had taken away her marriage token, had cut off her long black hair and shaved her head, had stripped her of all her jewels and her clothing.

Then clad in a single mantle — a *sari* of white cotton cloth —
widows' wear — they had turned her into the street to beg. In
which they, the rightful heirs, while saving to themselves all
Bimal's hoard, did but emphasise the verdict of high
Destiny.

But the gods had relented. Sarat, her daughter's husband,
a generous man, had lent her this clay hut, apart from the
village, to shelter her head. More still, Sarat gave her cop-
pers, now and again, enough to buy her the one scant meal a
day that is widows' fare. And, on the days when she walked to
the village market to find her food, Sarat even consented that
she creep into her daughter's presence, no festival being on
foot to be marred by her evil eye, that she might assure
herself of her little one's continued well-being.

Otherwise, what may any widow do, but keep all day at her
prayers for the soul of her lord? By diligent prayer, fasting
and privation, she may perhaps win him a higher place in his
next incarnation upon earth.

And if Sita's life, thought by thought, move by move, was
fore-ordained in immemorial law, so also was the thought
and deed of that little Hindu village lying over beyond in the
sun-gilt dust. Landlords, cultivators of the soil, artisans and
outcast slaves, its sluggish human stream ebbed down the
centuries as an echo eternally fainter, eternally dying, eternally one.

Yet, not sixty miles removed, big modern Calcutta, largest
city of India, stewed on the fires of political unrest. For this
was the autumn of 1921. In the very streets of the capital
secret plotters and killers vied with open assassins to terrorise
all who opposed the will of the new-made saint, Gandhi, then
at the zenith of his power. And though the saint himself
continued to preach 'non-violence', his speech, day by day,
was the speech that breeds hatred and destruction and drives
simple folk to the spilling of blood.

Yet, save where young city-bred politicals had run abroad swinging the torch, great India in her hamlets slept the sleep of the ages, aloof and unconcerned.

Unconcerned lay Sita's village, when, this sun-up, two young strangers appeared in haste, demanding audience. Little white rabbit-caps they wore on their heads and their tongues were hot. So the people, wondering, led them before the headman, to recite their tale.

'What is this ye babble!' the headman scoffed through his long grey beard, having heard them through. 'Will ye feed my people thistles? "The British came with the scales in their hand, and sat down with the sword," say ye? And therefore folk like us must rise against them and destroy all the cloth that their ships have brought, and drive them out! Go back speedily to the knaves that sent ye and tell them this:

'It is true that the sahibs came to trade and remained to rule. *But whose is the advantage?* Think ye we here be so thick of skull that we tire of peace and justice and desire you, robbers, set to rule us in the sahibs' place?

'And now begone in haste, lest my *chokidars* break your heads.'

So the young men left, but with wrath in their hearts, having failed in their errand.

And it chanced as they pushed across the fields, seeking the highroad, that they came upon a solitary hut, and a woman in a white sari issuing from the door of the hut.

'Who art thou?' called the strangers.

'I am the widow,' a frightened voice returned.

'Whither goest thou?'

'Even to the market, to buy food.'

'And what is it thou wearest, thou thing of foul omen!' cried one of the strangers, laying hold upon her garment. 'A Manchester-made sari by the gods!'

'What is Manchester?' asked the widow. 'It is my sari, the

only one I have.'

'You must give it up, none the less, and let us burn it. Off with it! Quick!' And he wrenched at the cloth.

But Sita clutched it tight about her, covering her face. 'Who says I must take it off?' she panted.

'Mahatma Gandhi.'

'Who is Mahatma Gandhi?'

'He who can curse. And if you do not instantlȳ give us your sari, cursed you shall be – '

Sita stood dazed. According to the law of widows, she wore but one garment. To remove it were to strip herself naked before these men.

'You will not? Then on your head be it!' cried the stranger. 'Cursed you are, in the name of Mahatma Gandhi whose disciples we be. Cursed you are, with the curse of leprosy. It begins on your forehead, moving slowly, slowly, down your spine, eating, eating all your flesh away in sores. See! See! The marks are there, on your finger-tips, now!'

With a shriek Sita turned and fled into the hut, tore off her sari and threw it from the door into the strangers' hands.

'Take back the curse! Take back the curse!' she screamed. But they, laughing, sped on their way.

Three days passed.

'Where is Sita the widow?' asked the market folk. 'She comes not for food.'

'Where is my mother?' asked Sarat's wife.

And Sarat, the kindly, answered, 'For thy peace I will go to the hut and see.'

But the door of the hut was shut. 'O Mother-in-law, art thou within?' called Sarat.

No reply.

'O Mother-in-law, art thou ill?'

No reply.

'O Mother-in-law, thou art surely ill!' And Sarat opened

the door.

In the far corner, crouched on the floor, a skeleton figure, naked, quaking, staring with great burning eyes at its out-stretched finger-tips. The fever-cracked lips formed words — but to what sense?

'O Great Ones! O Great Ones! Not clean! Not clean!'

'What meaneth this!' cried the man.

'The two young men, disciples of the Gandhi — a saint — who sent them to take my sari — to burn my *sari* in fire — and because I would have kept it they cursed me in the name of their saint — cursed with a filthy curse that consumeth all the body in sores. It beginneth at the finger-tips — here — O Son-in-law, look! Canst see the marks? *Are the Great Ones dead?*' And the dry voice strangled in a gasp.

But Sarat, averting his eyes, tore off his scarf and threw it towards her. 'Cover thyself, O Mother-in-law. I go to fetch thy daughter to comfort thee.' He closed the door and ran.

When he returned, an hour later, with women and cloth-ing and food, that door turned slowly on its hinges because against it, swinging with the empty food-jar from the peg, hung a small limp body — dead — choked with the noose of the scarf.

(1929)

GEORGE ORWELL
A Hanging

It was in Burma, a sodden morning of the rains. A sickly light, like yellow tinfoil, was slanting over the high walls into the jail yard. We were waiting outside the condemned cells, a row of sheds fronted with double bars, like small animal cages. Each cell measured about ten feet by ten and was quite bare within except for a plank bed and a pot for drinking water. In some of them brown silent men were squatting at the inner bars, with their blankets draped round them. These were the condemned men, due to be hanged within the next week or two.

One prisoner had been brought out of his cell. He was a Hindu, a puny wisp of a man, with a shaven head and vague liquid eyes. He had a thick, sprouting moustache, absurdly too big for his body, rather like the moustache of a comic man on the films. Six tall Indian warders were guarding him and getting him ready for the gallows. Two of them stood by with rifles and fixed bayonets, while the others handcuffed him, passed a chain through his handcuffs and fixed it to their belts, and lashed his arms tight to his sides. They crowded very close about him, with their hands always on him in a careful, caressing grip, as though all the while feeling him to make sure he was there. It was like men handling a fish which is still alive and may jump back into the water. But he stood quite unresisting, yielding his arms limply to the ropes, as though he hardly noticed what was happening.

Eight o'clock struck and a bugle call, desolately thin in the wet air, floated from the distant barracks. The superintendent of the jail, who was standing apart from the rest of us, moodily prodding the gravel with his stick, raised his head at the sound. He was an army doctor, with a grey toothbrush moustache and a gruff voice. 'For God's sake hurry up, Francis,' he said irritably. 'The man ought to have been dead by this time. Aren't you ready yet?'

Francis, the head jailer, a fat Dravidian in a white drill suit and gold spectacles, waved his black hand. 'Yes sir, yes sir,' he bubbled. 'All iss satisfactorily prepared. The hangman iss waiting. We shall proceed.'

'Well, quick march, then. The prisoners can't get their breakfast till this job's over.'

We set out for the gallows. Two warders marched on either side of the prisoner, with their rifles at the slope; two others marched close against him, gripping him by arm and shoulder, as though at once pushing and supporting him. The rest of us, magistrates and the like, followed behind. Suddenly, when we had gone ten yards, the procession stopped short without any order or warning. A dreadful thing had happened – a dog, come goodness knows whence, had appeared in the yard. It came bounding among us with a loud volley of barks, and leapt round us wagging its whole body, wild with glee at finding so many human beings together. It was a large woolly dog, half Airedale, half Pariah. For a moment it pranced round us, and then, before anyone could stop it, it had made a dash for the prisoner and, jumping up, tried to lick his face. Everyone stood aghast, too taken aback even to grab at the dog.

'Who let that bloody brute in here?' said the superintendent angrily. 'Catch it, someone!'

A warder, detached from the escort, charged clumsily after the dog, but it danced and gambolled just out of his reach, taking everything as part of the game. A young Eurasian jailer picked up a handful of gravel and tried to stone the dog away, but it dodged the stones and came after us again. Its yaps echoed from the jail walls. The prisoner, in the grasp of the two warders, looked on incuriously, as though this was another formality of the hanging. It was several minutes before someone managed to catch the dog. Then we put my handkerchief through its collar and moved off once more, with the dog still straining and whimpering.

It was about forty yards to the gallows. I watched the bare brown back of the prisoner marching in front of me. He walked clumsily with his bound arms, but quite steadily, with that bobbing gait of the Indian who never straightens his knees. At each step his muscles slid neatly into place, the lock of hair on his scalp danced up and down, his feet printed themselves on the wet gravel. And once, in spite of the men who gripped him by each shoulder, he stepped slightly aside to avoid a puddle on the path.

It is curious, but till that moment I had never realised what it means to destroy a healthy, conscious man. When I saw the prisoner step aside to avoid the puddle I saw the mystery, the unspeakable wrongness, of cutting a life short when it is in full tide. This man was not dying, he was alive just as we are alive. All the organs of his body were working — bowels digesting food, skin renewing itself, nails growing, tissues forming — all toiling away in solemn foolery. His nails would still be growing when he stood on the drop, when he was falling through the air with a tenth of a second to live. His eyes saw the yellow gravel and the grey walls, and his brain still remembered, foresaw, reasoned — reasoned even about puddles. He and we were a party of men walking together, seeing, hearing, feeling, understanding the same world; and in two minutes, with a sudden snap, one of us would be gone — one mind less, one world less.

The gallows stood in a small yard, separate from the main grounds of the prison, and overgrown with tall prickly weeds. It was a brick erection like three sides of a shed, with planking on top, and above that two beams and a crossbar with the rope dangling. The hangman, a grey-haired convict in the white uniform of the prison, was waiting beside his machine. He greeted us with a servile crouch as we entered. At a word from Francis the two warders, gripping the prisoner more closely than ever, half led, half pushed him to the gallows and helped him clumsily up the ladder. Then the hangman climbed up and fixed the rope round the prisoner's neck.

We stood waiting, five yards away. The warders had formed in a rough circle round the gallows. And then, when the noose was fixed, the prisoner began crying out to his god. It was a high, reiterated cry of 'Ram! Ram! Ram! Ram!' not urgent and fearful like a prayer or a cry for help, but steady, rhythmical, almost like the tolling of a bell. The dog answered the sound with a whine. The hangman, still standing on the gallows, produced a small cotton bag like a flour bag and drew it down over the prisoner's face. But the sound, muffled by the cloth, still persisted, over and over again: 'Ram! Ram! Ram! Ram! Ram!'

The hangman climbed down and stood ready, holding the lever. Minutes seemed to pass. The steady, muffled crying from the prisoner went on and on, 'Ram! Ram! Ram!' never faltering for an instant. The superintendent, his head on his chest, was slowly poking the ground with his stick; perhaps he was counting the cries, allowing the prisoner a fixed number — fifty, perhaps, or a hundred. Everyone had changed colour. The Indians had gone grey like bad coffee, and one or two of the bayonets were wavering. We looked at the lashed, hooded man on the drop, and listened to his cries — each cry another second of life; the same thought was in all our minds: oh, kill him quickly, get it over, stop that abominable noise!

Suddenly the superintendent made up his mind. Throwing up his head he made a swift motion with his stick. '*Chalo!*' he shouted almost fiercely.

There was a clanking noise, and then dead silence. The prisoner had vanished, and the rope was twisting on itself. I let go of the dog, and it galloped immediately to the back of the gallows; but when it got there it stopped short, barked, and then retreated into a corner of the yard, where it stood among the weeds looking timorously out at us. We went round the gallows to inspect the prisoner's body. He was dangling with his toes pointed straight downwards, very slowly revolving, as dead as a stone.

The superintendent reached out with his stick and poked the bare brown body; it oscillated slightly. '*He's* all right,' said the superintendent. He backed out from under the gallows, and blew out a deep breath. The moody look had gone out of his face quite suddenly. He glanced at his wrist-watch. 'Eight minutes past eight. Well, that's all for this morning thank God.'

The warders unfixed bayonets and marched away. The dog, sobered and conscious of having misbehaved itself, slipped after them. We walked out of the gallows yard, past the condemned cells with their waiting prisoners, into the big central yard of the prison. The convicts, under the command of warders armed with *lathis* were already receiving their breakfast. They squatted in long rows, each man holding a tin panikin, while two warders with buckets marched round ladling out rice; it seemed quite a homely, jolly scene, after the hanging. An enormous relief had come upon us now that the job was done. One felt an impulse to sing, to break into a run, to snigger. All at once everyone began chattering gaily.

The Eurasian boy walking beside me nodded towards the way we had come, with a knowing smile: 'Do you know, sir, our friend (he meant the dead man) when he heard his appeal had been dismissed, he pissed on the floor of his cell. From fright. Kindly take one of my cigarettes, sir. Do you not admire my new silver case, sir? From the boxwallah, two rupees eight annas. Classy European style.'

Several people laughed — at what, nobody seemed certain.

Francis was walking by the superintendent, talking garrulously: 'Well, sir, all hass passed off with the utmost satisfactoriness. It was all finished — flick! like that. It iss not always so — oah, no! I have known cases where the doctor wass obliged to go beneath the gallows and pull the prissoner's legs to ensure decease. Most disagreeable!'

'Wriggling about, eh? That's bad,' said the superintendent.

'Ach, sir, it iss worse when they become refractory! One man, I recall, clung to the bars of his cage when we went to take him out. You will scarcely credit, sir, that it took six warders to dislodge him, three pulling at each leg. We reasoned with him. "My dear fellow," we said, "think of all the pain and trouble you are causing to us!" But no, he would not listen! Ach, he wass very troublesome!'

I found that I was laughing quite loudly. Everyone was laughing. Even the superintendent grinned in a tolerant way. 'You'd better all come out and have a drink,' he said quite genially. 'I've got a bottle of whisky in the car. We could do with it.'

We went through the big double gates of the prison into the road. 'Pulling at his legs!' exclaimed a Burmese magistrate suddenly, and burst into a loud chuckling. We all began laughing again. At that moment Francis' anecdote seemed extraordinarily funny. We all had a drink together, native and European alike, quite amicably. The dead man was a hundred yards away.

(1931)

GEORGE ORWELL
Shooting an Elephant

In Moulmein, in lower Burma, I was hated by large numbers of people – the only time in my life that I have been important enough for this to happen to me. I was sub-divisional police officer of the town, and in an aimless, petty kind of way anti-European feeling was very bitter. No one had the guts to raise a riot, but if a European woman went through the bazaars alone somebody would probably spit betel juice over her dress. As a police officer I was an obvious target and was baited whenever it seemed safe to do so. When a nimble Burman tripped me up on the football field and the referee (another Burman) looked the other way, the crowd yelled with hideous laughter. This happened more than once. In the end the sneering yellow faces of young men that met me everywhere, the insults hooted after me when I was at a safe distance, got badly on my nerves. The young Buddhist priests were the worst of all. There were several thousands of them in the town and none of them seemed to have anything to do except stand on street corners and jeer at Europeans.

All this was perplexing and upsetting. For at that time I had already made up my mind that imperialism was an evil thing and the sooner I chucked up my job and got out of it the better. Theoretically – and secretly, of course – I was all for the Burmese and all against their oppressors, the British. As for the job I was doing, I hated it more bitterly than I can perhaps make clear. In a job like that you see the dirty work of Empire at close quarters. The wretched prisoners huddling in the stinking cages of the lock-ups, the grey, cowed faces of the long-term convicts, the scarred buttocks of the men who had been flogged with bamboos – all these oppressed me with an intolerable sense of guilt. But I could get nothing into perspective. I was young and ill-educated and I had had to think out my problems in the utter silence that is imposed on every Englishman in the East. I did not even know that the British Empire is dying, still less did I know that it is a great deal better than the younger empires that are going to supplant it. All I knew was that I was stuck between my hatred of the empire I served and my rage against the evil-spirited little beasts who tried to make my job impossible. With one part of my mind I thought of the British Raj as an unbreakable tyranny, as something clamped down, *in saecula saeculorum*, upon the will of prostrate peoples; with another part I thought that the greatest joy in the world would be to drive a bayonet into a Buddhist priest's guts. Feelings like these are the normal by-products of imperialism; ask any Anglo-Indian official, if you can catch him off duty.

One day something happened which in a roundabout way was enlightening. It was a tiny incident in itself, but it gave me a better glimpse than I had had before of the real nature of imperialism — the real motives for which despotic governments act. Early one morning the sub-inspector at a police station the other end of the town rang me up on the 'phone and said that an elephant was ravaging the bazaar. Would I please come and do something about it? I did not know what I could do, but I wanted to see what was happening and I got on to a pony and started out. I took my rifle, an old .44 Winchester and much too small to kill an elephant, but I thought the noise might be useful *in terrorem*. Various Burmans stopped me on the way and told me about the elephant's doings. It was not, of course, a wild elephant, but a tame one which had gone 'must'. It had been chained up, as tame elephants always are when their attack of 'must' is due, but on the previous night it had broken its chain and escaped.

Its mahout, the only person who could manage it when it was in that state, had set out in pursuit, but had taken the wrong direction and was now twelve hours' journey away, and in the morning the elephant had suddenly reappeared in the town. The Burmese population had no weapons and were quite helpless against it. It had already destroyed somebody's bamboo hut, killed a cow and raided some fruit-stalls and devoured the stock; also it had met the municipal rubbish van and, when the driver jumped out and took to his heels, had turned the van over and inflicted violences upon it.

The Burmese sub-inspector and some Indian constables were waiting for me in the quarter where the elephant had been seen. It was a very poor quarter, a labyrinth of squalid bamboo huts, thatched with palm-leaf, winding all over a steep hillside. I remember that it was a cloudy, stuffy morning at the beginning of the rains. We began questioning the people as to where the elephant had gone and, as usual, failed to get any definite information. That is invariably the case in the East; a story always sounds clear enough at a distance, but the nearer you get to the scene of events the vaguer it becomes. Some of the people said that the elephant had gone in one direction, some said that he had gone in another, some professed not even to have heard of any elephant. I had almost made up my mind that the whole story was a pack of lies, when we heard yells a little distance away. There was a loud, scandalised cry of 'Go away, child! Go away this instant!' and an old woman with a switch in her hand came round the corner of a hut, violently shooing away a crowd of naked children. Some more women followed, clicking their tongues and exclaiming; evidently there was something that the children ought not to have seen. I rounded the hut and saw a man's dead body sprawling in the mud. He was an Indian, a black Dravidian coolie, almost naked, and he could not have been dead many minutes. The people said that the elephant had come suddenly upon him round the corner of the hut, caught him with its trunk, put its foot on his back and ground him into the earth. This was the rainy season and the ground was soft, and his face had scored a trench a foot deep and a couple of yards long. He was lying on his belly with arms crucified and head sharply twisted to one side. His face was coated with mud, the eyes wide open, the teeth bared and grinning with an expression of unendurable agony. (Never tell me, by the way, that the dead look peaceful. Most of the corpses I have seen looked devilish.) The friction of the great beast's foot had stripped the skin from his back as neatly as one skins a rabbit. As soon as I saw the dead man I sent an orderly to a friend's house nearby to borrow an elephant rifle. I had already sent back the pony, not wanting it to go mad with fright and throw me if it smelt the elephant.

The orderly came back in a few minutes with a rifle and five cartridges, and meanwhile some Burmans had arrived and told us that the elephant was in the paddy fields below, only a few hundred yards away. As I started forward practically the whole population of the quarter flocked out of the houses and followed me. They had seen the rifle and were all shouting excitedly that I was going to shoot the elephant. They had not shown much interest in the elephant when he was merely ravaging their homes, but it was different now that he was going to be shot. It was a bit of fun to them, as it would be to an English crowd; besides they wanted the meat. It made me vaguely uneasy. I had no intention of shooting the elephant – I had merely sent for the rifle to defend myself if necessary – and it is always unnerving to have a crowd following you. I marched down the hill, looking and feeling a fool, with the rifle over my shoulder and an ever-growing army of people jostling at my heels. At the bottom, when you got away from the huts, there was a metalled road and beyond that a miry waste of paddy fields a thousand yards across, not yet ploughed but soggy from the first rains and dotted with coarse grass. The elephant was standing eight yards from the road, his left side towards us. He took not the slightest notice of the crowd's approach. He was tearing up bunches of grass, beating them against his knees to clean them and stuffing them into his mouth.

I had halted on the road. As soon as I saw the elephant I knew with perfect certainty that I ought not to shoot him. It is a serious matter to shoot a working elephant — it is comparable to destroying a huge and costly piece of machinery — and obviously one ought not to do it if it can possibly be avoided. And at that distance, peacefully eating, the elephant looked no more dangerous than a cow. I thought then and I think now that his attack of 'must' was already passing off; in which case he would merely wander harmlessly about until the mahout came back and caught him. Moreover, I did not in the least want to shoot him. I decided that I would watch him for a little while to make sure that he did not turn savage again, and then go home.

But at that moment I glanced round at the crowd that had followed me. It was an immense crowd, two thousand at the least and growing every minute. It blocked the road for a long distance on either side. I looked at the sea of yellow faces above the garish clothes — faces all happy and excited over this bit of fun, all certain that the elephant was going to be shot. They were watching me as they would watch a conjurer about to perform a trick. They did not like me, but with the magical rifle in my hands I was momentarily worth watching. And suddenly I realised that I should have to shoot the elephant after all. The people expected it of me and I had got to do it; I could feel their two thousand wills pressing me forward, irresistibly. And it was at this moment, as I stood there with the rifle in my hands, that I first grasped the hollowness, the futility of the white man's dominion in the

East. Here was I, the white man with his gun, standing in front of the unarmed native crowd − seemingly the leading actor of the piece; but in reality I was only an absurd puppet pushed to and fro by the will of those yellow faces behind. I perceived in this moment that when the white man turns tyrant it is his own freedom that he destroys. He becomes a sort of hollow, posing dummy, the conventionalised figure of a sahib. For it is the condition of his rule that he shall spend his life in trying to impress the 'native', and so in every crisis he has got to do what the 'natives' expect of him. He wears a mask, and his face grows to fit it. I had got to shoot the elephant. I had committed myself to doing it when I sent for the rifle. A sahib has got to act like a sahib; he has got to appear resolute, to know his own mind and do definite things. To come all that way, rifle in hand, with two thousand people marching at my heels, and then to trail feebly away, having done nothing − no, that was impossible. The crowd would laugh at me. And my whole life, every white man's life in the East, was one long struggle not to be laughed at.

But I did not want to shoot the elephant. I watched him beating his bunch of grass against his knees, with that preoccupied grandmotherly air that elephants have. It seemed to me that it would be murder to shoot him. At that age I was not squeamish about killing animals, but I had never shot an elephant and never wanted to. (Somehow it always seems worse to kill a *large* animal.) Besides, there was the beast's owner to be considered. Alive, the elephant was worth at least a hundred pounds; dead, he would only be worth the value of his tusks, five pounds, possibly. But I had got to act quickly. I turned to some experienced-looking Burmans who had been there when we arrived, and asked them how the elephant had been behaving. They all said the same thing: he took no notice of you if you left him alone, but he might charge if you went too close to him.

It was perfectly clear to me what I ought to do. I ought to walk up to within, say, twenty-five yards of the elephant and test his behaviour. If he charged, I could shoot; if he took no notice of me, it would be safe to leave him until the mahout came back. But also I knew that I was going to do no such thing. I was a poor shot with a rifle and the ground was soft mud into which one would sink at every step. If the elephant charged and I missed him, I should have about as much chance as a toad under a steam-roller. But even then I was not thinking particularly of my own skin, only of the watchful yellow faces behind. For at that moment, with the crowd watching me, I was not afraid in the ordinary sense, as I would have been if I had been alone. A white man mustn't be frightened in front of 'natives'; and so, in general, he isn't frightened. The sole thought in my mind was that if anything went wrong those two thousand Burmans would see me pursued, caught, trampled on and reduced to a grinning corpse like that Indian up the hill. And if that happened it was quite probable that some of them would laugh. That would never do. There was only one alternative. I shoved the cartridges into the magazine and lay down on the road to get a better aim.

The crowd grew very still, and a deep, low, happy sigh, as of people who see the theatre curtain go up at last, breathed from innumerable throats. They were going to have their bit of fun after all. The rifle was a beautiful German thing with cross-hair sights. I did not then know that in shooting an elephant one would shoot to cut an imaginary bar running from ear-hole to ear-hole. I ought, therefore, as the elephant was sideways on, to have aimed straight at his ear-hole; actually I aimed several inches in front of this, thinking the brain would be further forward.

When I pulled the trigger I did not hear the bang or feel the kick – one never does when a shot goes home – but I heard the devilish roar of glee that went up from the crowd. In that instant, in too short a time, one would have thought, even for the bullet to get there, a mysterious, terrible change had come over the elephant. He neither stirred nor fell, but every line of his body had altered. He looked suddenly stricken, shrunken, immensely old, as though the frightful impact of the bullet had paralysed him without knocking him down. At last, after what seemed a long time – it might have been five seconds, I dare say – he sagged flabbily to his knees. His mouth slobbered. An enormous senility seemed to have settled upon him. One could have imagined him thousands of years old. I fired again into the same spot. At the second shot he did not collapse but climbed with desperate slowness to his feet and stood weakly upright, with legs sagging and head drooping. I fired a third time. That was the shot that did for him. You could see the agony of it jolt his whole body and knock the last remnant of strength from his legs. But in falling he seemed for a moment to rise, for as his hind legs collapsed beneath him he seemed to tower upward like a huge rock toppling, his trunk reaching skywards like a tree. He trumpeted, for the first and only time. And then down he came, his belly towards me, with a crash that seemed to shake the ground even where I lay.

I got up. The Burmans were already racing past me across the mud. It was obvious that the elephant would never rise again, but he was not dead. He was breathing very rhythmically with long rattling gasps, his great mound of a side painfully rising and falling. His mouth was wide open – I could see far down into caverns of pale pink throat. I waited a long time for him to die, but his breathing did not weaken. Finally I fired my two remaining shots into the spot where I thought his heart must be. The thick blood welled out of him like red velvet, but still he did not die. His body did not even jerk when the shots hit him, the tortured breathing continued without a pause. He was dying, very slowly and in great agony, but in some world remote from me where not even a bullet could damage him further. I felt that I had got to put an end to that dreadful noise. It seemed dreadful to see the great beast lying there, powerless to move and yet powerless to die, and not even to be able to finish him. I sent back for my small rifle and poured shot after shot into his heart and down his throat. They seemed to make no impression. The tortured gasps continued as steadily as the ticking of a clock.

In the end I could not stand it any longer and went away. I heard later that it took him half an hour to die. Burmans were bringing *dahs* and baskets even before I left, and I was told they had stripped his body almost to the bones by the afternoon.

Afterwards, of course, there were endless discussions about the shooting of the elephant. The owner was furious, but he was only an Indian and could do nothing. Besides, legally I had done the right thing, for a mad elephant has to be killed, like a mad dog, if its owner fails to control it. Among the Europeans opinion was divided. The older men said I was right, the younger men said it was a damn shame to shoot an elephant for killing a coolie, because an elephant was worth more than any damn Coringhee coolie. And afterwards I was very glad that the coolie had been killed; it put me legally in the right and it gave me a sufficient pretext for shooting the elephant. I often wondered whether any of the others grasped that I had done it solely to avoid looking a fool.

(1936)

JOSEPH HITREC

The Fearless
Will Always Have It

The three walked all the way from Kalbadevi to lower
Hornby Road, but because they hid in open doorways and
side-lanes and dodged the police round house-blocks, the
distance seemed double. The greater part of the work was
over and they now skulked under the arcades, away from
street lights, and found the tall, ARP walls in front of buildings a great comfort. Being on the open street after midnight
and having the large, sleepy town to themselves got to be
exciting, and trying to distinguish a pillar-box from a policeman waiting in ambush in the twilight of the arcade, was
more exciting still.

Young and of the same age, they wore short *dhotis* tucked
in for instant emergency and white, short-sleeved shirts that
gave them freedom of movement. They carried only chalk
and talked in whispers, and when one of them wrote something funny on the pavement and read it out aloud, they
laughed and then moved along holding each other's hands. In
both directions, the street petered out in total darkness and
only the overhead lamps lolled in the breeze and their weak
glow flowed across the tram-rails. The houses were dark and
quiet and their fronts seemed endlessly high, as if growing into
the night.

They passed the intersection of Home Street and Outram
Road and came into the shadow of the Kodak arcade. They
stopped and listened for footsteps. The boy called Lakshman
said:

Mine is almost finished. What should I write?

He was the youngest of the three, with a soft voice and an
easy laugh.

Save the chalk, Rade said. This is an American firm.

There's no difference. The walls are only the means and the property does not concern us.

It's a waste of good chalk all the same, Rade said. Much still remains to be written.

Walls are walls, he again said, they have no nationality.

He went to the blast wall and wrote QUIT INDIA on it. He couldn't see the writing but he knew the shape of the letters by heart, and he spaced them instinctively and put an exclamation mark at the end. I will see it in daylight tomorrow morning, he thought. He was proud of his writing.

I am hungry, Raman then said. Let's find a tea-stall.

They slipped out of the enclosure and passed the Lawrence & Mayo shop-front. They wrote on it; the stone here was smoother and the available space larger and they could write more than usual. They stumbled over a sleeping coolie and the man woke up and cursed them.

A great deal of bellowing from a small cause, Raman said to the coolie. Sleep, *baba*, while your country is awakening.

You sound like a thief, the man said. It is the time of thieves.

A thief of your callous sleep, O useless one!

Should I call the police? the man said.

Shut up instead, Raman said. You are even more useless asleep than awake.

They joined hands again and came to the big store on the corner of Hornby and Phirozeshah Mehta roads. Here, the arcades were completely enclosed by a blast wall and they could only see each other as grey apparitions. He thought: These are big windows and they are costly and afterwards I could run into the *maidan* and hide in a tree; what is struggle without daring?

This is a British house, Rade said. One of the biggest.

One of us should watch, Raman added.

But the idea suddenly became so dominant that he didn't hear them. Daring is all, he thought again, whether at the start or the end. They think we are soft because we eat no meat, but there is other strength and being right is one aspect of it, and those who are right dare. He went forward and felt for the glass in the dark, but his fingers touched steel shutters. He moved to the left, passing his hand over it, came to the end and felt the stone again. Tomorrow morning, he thought, with the people passing this way in hundreds, it will be an important example. Writing is a duty, but a broken window would transcend it. Feeling cheated he spat on the shutters.

What have you done? Rade said.

Nothing, I have no chalk. These windows are shuttered.

I wrote QUIT INDIA OR BEWARE. Mine broke and I can't find the other half. We should get charcoal.

We shall. There is no limit to what can be done.

Raman came up and tittered in the dark: If there is no vacancy in the telegraph department, I should like to be a sign painter.

I want to be a minister, Lakshman said.

You talk like one already, Rade said.

My life belongs to my country, he said stubbornly. I don't want to shirk responsibility. It is said that a man without attachment does twice the work.

And he should be twice the fool, Rade said. That's a hackneyed idea. The work of a minister is with the people, not *mantras*. What good is an unnattached man in an epidemic of plague?

It's true nevertheless. Only the impartial should serve the country, and they shall be unattached in order to be impartial.

Do you consider marriage partiality?

In a manner I do. And I am not the only one.

With your leave, O minister, I should like to move on, Raman said.

But you are not married, Rade said.

No.

He blushed and was glad of the darkness. Most of his college friends were married and had already lived with their wives, while the others had put their wayside information to practical tests in various ways. He was a Surti and his father was a widower who believed that young men should make their own decisions, but studying and trying to live on an allowance of thirty rupees a month had made that decision an impracticable one.

I think you should know, Rade said, that some attachment is extremely pleasurable. For my part, I should like to be so attached every night.

Raman laughed out aloud and Rade joined him and after a while he, too, couldn't hold himself.

All the same, he said, impartiality is a considerable virtue

You forget the Muslims, Rade said. They are strongly attached to some things.

They would be reasonable if assured of complete impartiality. That is the main difficulty. We should set an example.

Example! Rade puffed.

Gentlemen, Raman suddenly said in English, I move that this meeting be adjourned.

I think they're suspicious and unreasonable, Rade went on. Examples make them more suspicious and that is truer now than before.

Much has been our own fault no doubt.

Arre, baba, what talk is that for a minister? Rade said. Let us go and finish the work.

I only have chalk for another sign, Raman said.

They cut the crossing, passed the Petit Institute and Cook's Building and then the road broadened out into the shapeless square of Flora Fountain. One or two *gharis* clattered across it and in one of them an English voice sang *Bless Them All*.

Observe the attachment of the ruling classes, Rade said.

Their time is up, Lakshman said.

That does not reduce the empire.

Sailors are underdogs, Raman said. They do not rule, they are ruled like ourselves.

Their attachment for India is one that cannot be removed by impartiality, Rade said. Else we would be home sleeping.

What building is this?

Reuter's, Rade said. Where the movement is written down and filed. We must give them *our* news.

They began feeling for the wall and pillars. He wrote FREEDOM IS HERE and then the chalk was no more than a crumb in his hand and he threw it away in disgust. He undid his *dhoti* and urinated on the front pillar.

So that the freedom of the press may flower thereafter, Rade said. He took the next pillar.

In the quiet hollow of the arcade footsteps rang out suddenly. They stood stiff and listened; the sound of hobnailed Pathan shoes was familiar to all three.

Yellowcap, Raman said.

He can't prove anything. We are returning from the cinema, this is not a curfew area.

When have policemen needed proof? Come on.

The footsteps came nearer, quicker now, and a voice called out.

Apoiio Street, Rade said. Hurry!

As he fumbled with the *dhoti* he saw the policeman's shape loom from the arcade's shadows. I should command my nerves better, he thought. But his heart beat very fast and he saw the other two had started running. He gathered his *dhoti* in his left hand and moved quickly on. Halt there! the policeman said, entering the enclosure. But he ran fast, his chest suddenly shrinking in excitement, and he rubbed his free hand against his shirt to remove the chalk dust. He was barefooted and avoided the uneven parts of the pavement.

Halt, *badmash*! the voice behind his shouted.

He caught up with Raman and Rade and they ran on together. The sound of a whistle pierced the night and they heard the familiar trot, only much louder and thicker than usual.

Observe that we run because we lack the attachment for the police, Rade said. His gasp sounded like derision but there was no time to make sure.

Let us not quibble over finer points, Raman gasped. The mercenary is displaying unexpected energy.

The whistle blew once more and an answer came from the other side of the square and a third came from the shadow of Bruce Street. The sudden commotion gave their flight a sinister meaning. They stopped talking and when they entered the narrow approach to Apollo Street the square behind them sounded completely awake. Why do we run if we are a proud race? he thought resentfully. The *dhoti* had fallen completely loose and he only had time to catch it and gather it hurriedly. At once the cool night air came between his legs and the breeze lifted his shirt high.

They ran into a dark side-lane and slowed down to consult. The street smelled of refuse and horse-dung, and all along the pavement were dark outlines of people sleeping out in the open.

If we separate and hide they can't catch us, Rade said. Three are easier to see than one.

Where shall we meet? Raman asked.

There is no need to meet again tonight. The work is done.

I don't know this locality, Lakshman said.

The whistling caught up with them and there were other

new sounds mixed in it.

See you at the college in the morning, Raman said.

Good luck, Rade said. Parsee Bazaar may be more peaceful. If one of us is caught he was alone, understand?

Yes, Lakshman said.

They reached the bottom of the lane and separated; for a time he tried to keep up with Rade, but he soon tired and the distance between them increased. He wanted to call out and ask him to wait, but he checked himself. Even though I'm a coward I can't show it, he thought briefly and unhappily. He ran at random and paused to ease the stitch in the side. Every lamp-post looked like a canary. He tripped over a garbage-can and over sleeping bodies and once he ran into a *ghariwallah* leaning against a lamp-post. The man fell down backwards, too astonished to curse. He came to the Parsee Bazaar street; several yellowcaps stood in the shadow of the Cotton Exchange and another was joining them from the direction of the Circle.

He went back the way he came, breathing hard now and thinking. He turned into a passage that looked like a blind alley and jumped into an open doorway. He stopped for a moment, lungs tingling with the strain, and listened, and when the sound of whistle and running steps became more distinct he advanced in the dark and found the steps. Feeling the railing with his hands and lifting his feet carefully, he climbed the staircase until the floor became level once more. He went tapping along the corridor and crashed into a wooden wall and groaned loudly. Then a door creaked open and a woman's voice said: This way! An invisible hand caught his shirt and led him inside. The door closed with another weak creak.

You are the clumsiest man, the voice said in Mahratti.

It was a young voice and comforting, like the smell of jasmine that suddenly enveloped him. He stopped in the dark, the hand no longer touching him, and fought for his lost breath. He thought of a thousand things and the thoughts flashed through his head like pictures and when they were no longer there only the brightness of the flash remained. Then the voice was behind him, but it was hesitant and different.

Who are you?

They may be gone now, he thought. The smell of jasmine came on him again and he inhaled it deeply and felt safer.

I had mistaken you for someone, the woman said. Please go now.

Let me stay awhile, he said. The police are chasing me, when they pass I will go.

He waited for her but she was quiet, and he added: I am not a burglar, don't fear me.

They waited in silence and he listened to the street noises and found that they were faint. The dark mellowed into dusk and he saw that the room was big and that she was standing against the wall watching him. She seemed small and when she moved her bangles jingled.

You are a student, she said. Wherefore the hiding?

The writing of slogans. How did you know?

From your speech, she said. Have they seen you enter?

I don't think so, I hope not.

Lie on the bed, she said, and if they come you can climb out of the window and hide in the empty garage in the rear.

She went to the door, locked it and came near him.

What is that in your hand?

He realised then he was holding his *dhoti* and sitting on the bed with only his loose shirt between his legs. He blushed. My coat, he said. They faced each other in the twilight, waiting for each other to speak first. He had never before been so close to a woman and no one had ever smelt quite the same.

You must leave soon. Are you hurt?

The voice was kinder and she seemed not to be afraid any more. The slight draught in the room brought her perfume to his face again and again and he started to tremble without reason.

I am only out of breath, he said.

Lie down, she said, and I will bring you water.

She walked very lightly. Then she stood over him saying: You may be foolish, but you are brave. Take this.

He reached for it and found her hand and the hand was small and hot. He drank the water and wet his chin and returning the glass he felt her hand again and his fingers twitched. Who are you? he said, if I am allowed to ask. His voice had weakened.

You should know better than ask, you are only a temporary guest.

With pounding ears but without fear he again held out his hand and found hers, and then passed his fingers over the bangled wrist and higher up, and all the time he saw himself as another person standing by and wondering.

It is time you go, she said quietly. I am expecting someone.

Whom?

The pleasant tickle of jasmine was now deep in his nostrils and still rising.

Your notion of freedom is a peculiar one, she said. Her voice was teasing.

He pulled her towards him and sat her on the bed. He found her head and stroked it with his shaking hand, and then he explored her face and found that it was smooth and pointed. He removed the hardness of the saree border and burrowed into the folds and went on exploring, fearfully and clumsily, unable to stop or think, and her smell became stronger, sending little shivers down his uncovered back. The dark room turned into a river of rushing red and all that happened was tenseness and compression and travelling very fast, so fast he never noticed her hand under his shirt, and then all was temples and heart and quivering fingers, painful ignorance and needles on his fingertips, the end never to come, but all thought ebbing away in a fainting reach for the seemingly inaccessible.

Afterwards he lay flat on his back, the line of touch of their legs feeling pure and cool, and stared at the dim ceiling, and his outstretched arms felt powerful enough to gather the fullness of the room and crush it to nothing. Their hands met from time to time and their fingers interlocked in hushed secrecy and the purple outline of the window was a private passage into the boundlessness of higher space. When sleep came it caught them twisted and merged, unable to separate, and all it could do was to loosen the strain at the point of contact.

He woke up after dawn. The room was empty but his clothes were there, slung over the chair. He washed from the earthen *chatti* near the door and then dressed. He sat on the bed for half an hour but nobody came and he rose and went out.

On the street, he looked at the house, from window to window, but there were only shutters and sun-shades and above them a yellowing sky and a few dying stars. The air was crisp and cool and it soothed his mouth as though it were coconut milk. He walked to the top of the lane watching the sky and breathing luxuriously and his chest seemed to swell with the expanse of air, with the town waking from sleep and the force of all things unbegun and latent, and he thought of his friends at the college and of the running last night and his hands tightened involuntarily. His mind worked coldly and lucidly and when the thought coalesced there was a vague threat in it:

This is the beginning and the fearless will always have it.

(1946)

CHRISTINE WESTON
A Game of Halma

I remember Vasi. When I was about fourteen and living in India, he was often at our house in Aligarh. He was a tall, slender Mohammedan with grey eyes and a fair moustache. He greatly resembled my French father in temperament as well as in appearance; both men were high-strung and talkative, and both were ardent amateur politicians. Vasi was a *munshi*, which is to say he served as a sort of confidential secretary to some rich man in the neighbourhood. He had somehow or other become involved in a lawsuit, and our acquaintance dated from the time when he engaged my father, who was then practising law, as defending counsel. Their odd resemblance to each other may have had something to do with drawing them together, and for a long time after his case had been won, Vasi would arrive on his bicycle to spend the afternoon talking and playing Halma with my father, who had taught him this rather simple game earlier in their acquaintance. Vasi liked Halma and played it skilfully and with visible and voluble excitement. But he was wanting in tact and quite unable to restrain his delight when he beat my father, who disliked to be beaten in anything and was incapable of accepting defeat gracefully. Whenever my father beat Vasi, the results were reversed. It was then Vasi's turn to glower and chew the ends of his moustache.

My brother and I used to watch the two men as they sat under the pipal tree in the garden with the Halma board between them and a servant standing near, fanning away the mosquitoes with a large palm-leaf fan. Vasi always wore a red fez, a formal black alpaca coat, and white trousers. When they played indoors, he would remove his shoes and leave them outside the drawing-room door. His formal apparel was in marked contrast to that of my father, who in his hours of relaxation discarded coat and necktie and thrust his feet into a pair of ancient morocco-leather slippers. Vasi usually began by being respectful, but by the time they were halfway through their first game the barriers were down and they quarrelled and argued as equals. I remember that my mother thought Vasi inclined to be insolent and disapproved of my father's lenient attitude towards him.

When they had finished several games, they would relax and a servant would bring whisky and cigarettes. My father always took his peg, but Vasi, being a good Moslem, never drank. Both would then launch into a discussion of local affairs, of lawsuits, official intrigue, politics, philosophy, religion. They showed a baffling facility for changing sides in an argument. Thus we frequently heard Vasi, an innate seditionist, actually defending the British raj against my father's critical appraisal, while my father time and again took up the cudgels in defence of some concept which he had excoriated only the day before. They conversed in Urdu, for my father was an accomplished linguist. He was French by birth – French in his marrow, he used to say – though he had been brought up in India as an Englishman. There was, however, a perpetual conflict going on inside him, his Gallic temper at odds with his English phlegm. Whenever Vasi worsted him at Halma or in an argument, my father became very French – rude, sarcastic, brilliant, witty. When he won, he was cool, lordly, and condescending. Either way he infuriated Vasi, who, as a member of the subject race, never quite dared to lose his temper openly.

During the period when Vasi was much at our house we had another frequent caller, an old client of my father and, like Vasi, a Mohammedan. He often came when Vasi was there.

This man was known to us simply as Nawab Sahib. He was aristocratic, a *taluqdar*, or landowner, with large estates and much influence in the district. Nawab Sahib was short and inclined to stoutness, and his features reminded one of a fifteenth-century Persian miniature — the eyes dark, the brown oval of his face partially concealed in a fine, pointed black beard. He possessed immense dignity, and we never saw him hurried, angered, or confused. Nawab Sahib's wardrobe was, to us children, an endless source of fascination, for in this respect he was almost like a woman. Of his many costumes I especially remember two. One, which he wore in winter, was made up of a long moleskin coat cut in Moslem style, worn over a muslin shirt and voluminous Pathan breeches. With this he wore a black astrakhan cap. The other, in which he appeared in hot weather, had a coat of the same cut, made of a rich, cotton brocade, and a cap of the same material. Round his waist he always wore a leather belt fastened by a gold buckle in the form of a serpent with rubies in its eyes.

I have forgotten the details of the case which brought Nawab Sahib into conflict with the law; it had something to do with unpaid debts and the inexplicable death of one of his creditors. Nawab Sahib was reputed to be a great lover of women, and that, as we heard Vasi observe dryly to my father, is an expensive hobby in any society. The fact that he emerged from the trial with reputation unblemished was, I believe, due more to my father's skill as counsel than to the merits of the case itself or to the inherent virtues of the defendant. Notwithstanding all this, Nawab Sahib was a favourite with most English officials. They were soothed by his formality, charmed by his hospitality, and reassured by his undeviating respect for protocol. Since he rarely joined in the political discussions which took place between my father and Vasi, we never discovered just where Nawab Sahib's sympathies lay or, indeed, whether he had any. Toward my father his manner was deferential without being in the least servile, and yet I can remember one very curious thing about him: he never removed his shoes before coming into our house. It is as inevitable for an Indian to remove his shoes before entering a house as it is for a European to remove his hat. Even more curious than Nawab Sahib's little dereliction was the fact that it was allowed to pass without comment from my father, though he knew that had Vasi been guilty of such a lapse he would have been given short shrift. Looking back on it now, I wonder whether this was not Nawab Sahib's subtle little gesture of defiance towards the alien raj, even though that raj was personified in my father, who had befriended him and for whom he had a visible affection.

When the three men were there together, my father and Vasi would settle down to their Halma and Nawab Sahib would sit to one side, watching them gravely as he smoked the cigarettes which a servant always placed beside him. Sometimes he told stories about the exploits of his ancestors who invaded India in the sixth century A.D. At other times he described in detail and with the utmost seriousness the vagaries of a long line of family ghosts. No one dreamed of challenging his veracity, and once he started to talk, in his soft, persuasive voice, he had the field to himself. My brother and I infinitely preferred Nawab Sahib's monologue, with its accounts of rape, loot, battle, and the rest of it, to the endless political and sociological tirades of the two others.

All one summer, while the hot wind beat against closed doors, and all the following winter, under the pipal tree in the garden, the three men sat together, resolving, each in his own fashion, the interminable affairs of the universe. There seemed then, to us children, no reason why those conversations, those daily contests over the Halma board, should not continue forever. But one day, towards the end of that winter, the players played their last game. My father was lying back in his long chair, his legs stretched out on its arms, his red slippers dangling from his toes. Vasi sat opposite, brooding over the Halma board with its array of victorious and defeated men. He had won the final game of the afternoon and there was a jubilant glint in his eye. Nearby sat Nawab Sahib, a neat, erect figure in his moleskin coat, a cigarette between his plump brown fingers.

Vasi laughed suddenly. 'It is like life – your move, my move, my move, your move! Now triumph, now defeat – wah!'

'Visions, visions,' murmured Nawab Sahib with an indulgent smile. 'Life is not in the least like a game. Now, when Ala-ud-din marched on the fortress of Chirot in 1302 – '

'The Rajputs gave him a damn good run for his money,' interrupted my father ill-naturedly. He was still smarting from his own defeat at Vasi's hands.

Vasi laughed again. 'Dogs in the manger, those Rajputs. They committed *jauhar* by immolating their women, then rushing out themselves to perish on the conqueror's sword.'

'A form of chivalry, nevertheless,' said my father acidly.

'Chivalry, pah!' Vasi was carried away by excitement. 'I tell you chivalry has lost its exponents more battles than it ever won for them. Chivalry is the curse of Europe. It nearly lost *you* the last war!'

'It will not, however, lose *you* anything!' snapped my father. Nawab Sahib remained silent as the pair glared at each other.

'Had I been chivalrous,' said Vasi at last and with incredible rashness, 'I would have let you win that game.'

My father's eyes became incandescent. 'You imply that I could have won it by no other means?'

The other smiled, and my father tightened like a spring.

'You . . . !'

Vasi's smile vanished. He jumped up, knocking over the Halma board. 'No names, Sahib!'

'Then get out!'

Vasi turned and marched towards the door. He had not gone three paces before my father, plucking a slipper from his foot, hurled it after the retreating figure. It struck Vasi squarely between the shoulders and for a full minute he stood as though transfixed. Then he returned, picked up the slipper, and carried it back to where my father sat. In silence, and with an indescribable air, he hung the slipper on my father's foot. Then he turned once again and walked across the room and out through the door, never to return.

Nawab Sahib, whose cigarette had gone out, lighted another one, and in his soft, persuasive voice, exactly as if nothing had happened, he took up the thread of his story at the point where it had been interrupted.

(1947)

KHUSHWANT SINGH
Karma

Sir Mohan Lal looked at himself in the mirror of a first-class waiting room at the railway station. The mirror was obviously made in India. The red oxide at its back had come off at several places and long lines of translucent glass cut across its surface. Sir Mohan smiled at the mirror with an air of pity and patronage.

'You are so very much like everything else in this country, inefficient, dirty, indifferent,' he murmured.

The mirror smiled back at Sir Mohan.

'You are a bit of all right, old chap,' it said. 'Distinguished, efficient — even handsome. That neatly trimmed moustache — the suit from Savile Row with the carnation in the buttonhole — the aroma of eau de cologne, talcum powder, and scented soap all about you! Yes, old fellow, you are a bit of all right.'

Sir Mohan threw out his chest, smoothed his Balliol tie for the umpteenth time and waved a goodbye to the mirror.

He glanced at his watch. There was still time for a quick one.

'*Koi hai?*'

A bearer in white livery appeared through a wire gauze door.

'*Ek chota,*' ordered Sir Mohan, and sank into a large cane chair to drink and ruminate.

Outside the waiting room Sir Mohan Lal's luggage lay piled along the wall. On a small grey steel trunk Lachmi, Lady Mohan Lal, sat chewing a betel leaf and fanning herself with a newspaper. She was short and fat and in her middle forties. She wore a dirty white sari with a red border. On one

side of her nose glistened a diamond nose ring, and she had
several gold bangles on her arms. She had been talking to the
bearer until Sir Mohan had summoned him inside. As soon as
he had gone, she hailed a passing railway coolie.

'Where does the *zenana* stop?'

'Right at the end of the platform.'

The coolie flattened his turban to make a cushion, hoisted
the steel trunk on his head, and moved down the platform.
Lady Lal picked up her brass tiffin-carrier and ambled
along behind him. On the way she stopped by a hawker's stall
to replenish her silver betel-leaf case, and then joined the
coolie. She sat down on her steel trunk (which the coolie had
put down) and started talking to him.

'Are the trains very crowded on these lines?'

'These days all trains are crowded, but you'll find room in
the *zenana*.'

'Then I might as well get over the bother of eating.'

Lady Lal opened the brass carrier and took out a bundle of
cramped *chapattis* and some mango pickle. While she ate, the
coolie sat opposite her on his haunches, drawing lines in the
gravel with his finger.

'Are you travelling alone, sister?'

'No, I am with my master, brother. He is in the waiting
room. He travels first class. He is a *vizier* and a barrister, and
meets so many officers and Englishmen in the trains – and I
am only a native woman. I can't understand English and
don't know their ways, so I keep to my *zenana* inter-class.'

Lachmi chatted away merrily. She was fond of a little
gossip and had no one to talk to at home. Her husband never
had any time to spare for her. She lived in the upper storey of
the house and he on the ground floor. He did not like her
poor illiterate relatives hanging about his bungalow, so they
never came. He came up to her once in a while at night and
stayed for a few minutes, He just ordered her about in

anglicised Hindustani, and she obeyed passively. These nocturnal visits had, however, borne no fruit.

The signal came down and the clanging of the bell announced the approaching train. Lady Lal hurriedly finished off her meal. She got up, still licking the stone of the pickled mango. She emitted a long, loud belch as she went to the public tap to rinse her mouth and wash her hands. After washing she dried her mouth and hands with the loose end of her sari, and walked back to her steel trunk, belching and thanking the gods for the favour of a filling meal.

The train steamed in. Lachmi found herself facing an almost empty inter-class *zenana* compartment next to the guard's van, at the tail end of the train. The rest of the train was packed. She heaved her squat, bulky frame through the door and found a seat by the window. She produced a two-anna bit from a knot in her sari and dismissed the coolie. She then opened her betel case and made herself two betel leaves charged with a red and white paste, minced betel nuts and cardamoms. These she thrust into her mouth till her cheeks bulged on both sides. Then she rested her chin on her hands and sat gazing idly at the jostling crowd on the platform.

The arrival of the train did not disturb Sir Mohan Lal's sangfroid. He continued to sip his Scotch and ordered the bearer to tell him when he had moved the luggage to a first-class compartment. Excitement, bustle, and hurry were exhibitions of bad breeding, and Sir Mohan was eminently well bred. He wanted everything 'tickety-boo' and orderly. In his five years abroad, Sir Mohan had acquired the manners and attitudes of the upper classes. He rarely spoke Hindustani. When he did, it was like an Englishman's – only the very necessary words and properly anglicised. But he fancied his English, finished and refined at no less a place than the University of Oxford. He was fond of conversation, and like a cultured Englishman he could talk on almost any subject –

books, politics, people. How frequently had he heard English people say that he spoke like an Englishman!

Sir Mohan wondered if he would be travelling alone. It was a Cantonment and some English officers might be on the train. His heart warmed at the prospect of an impressive conversation. He never showed any sign of eagerness to talk to the English as most Indians did. Nor was he loud, aggressive, and opinionated like them. He went about his business with an expressionless matter-of-factness. He would retire to his corner by the window and get out a copy of *The Times*. He would fold it in a way in which the name of the paper was visible to others while he did the crossword puzzle. *The Times* always attracted attention. Someone would like to borrow it when he put it aside with a gesture signifying 'I've finished with it.' Perhaps someone would recognise his Balliol tie, which he always wore while travelling. That would open a vista leading to a fairyland of Oxford colleges, masters, dons, tutors, boat races, and rugger matches. If both *The Times* and the tie failed, Sir Mohan would '*Koi hai*' his bearer to get the Scotch out. Whisky never failed with Englishmen. Then followed Sir Mohan's handsome gold cigarette case filled with English cigarettes. English cigarettes in India? How on earth did he get them? Sure he didn't mind? And Sir Mohan's understanding smile — of course he didn't. But could he use the Englishman as a medium to commune with his dear old England? Those five years of grey bags and gowns, of sports blazers and mixed doubles, of dinners at the Inns of Court and nights with Piccadilly prostitutes. Five years of a crowded glorious life. Worth far more than the forty-five in India with his dirty, vulgar countrymen, with sordid details of the road to success, of nocturnal visits to the upper storey and all-too-brief sexual acts with obese old Lachmi, smelling of sweat and raw onions.

Sir Mohan's thoughts were disturbed by the bearer an-

nouncing the installation of the Sahib's luggage in a first-class
coupé next to the engine. Sir Mohan walked to his coupé with
a studied gait. He was dismayed. The compartment was
empty. With a sigh he sat down in a corner and opened the
copy of *The Times* he had read several times before.

Sir Mohan looked out of the window down the crowded
platform. His face lit up as he saw two English soldiers
trudging along, looking in all the compartments for room.
They had their haversacks slung behind their backs and
walked unsteadily. Sir Mohan decided to welcome them,
even though they were entitled to travel only second class. He
would speak to the guard.

One of the soldiers came up to the last compartment and
stuck his face through the window. He surveyed the compartment and noticed the unoccupied berth.

' 'Ere, Bill,' he shouted, 'one 'ere.'

His companion came up, also looked in, and looked at Sir
Mohan.

'Get the nigger out,' he muttered to his companion.

They opened the door, and turned to the half-smiling,
half-protesting Sir Mohan.

'Reserved!' yelled Bill.

'*Janta* – Reserved. Army – *Fauj*,' exclaimed Jim, pointing to his khaki shirt.

'*Ek dum jao* – get out!'

'I say, I say, surely,' protested Sir Mohan in his Oxford
accent.

The soldiers paused. It almost sounded like English, but
they knew better than to trust their inebriated ears. The
engine whistled and the guard waved his green flag.

They picked up Sir Mohan's suitcase and flung it into the
platform. Then followed his thermos-flask, suitcase, bedding, and *The Times*. Sir Mohan was livid with rage.

'Preposterous, preposterous,' he shouted, hoarse with

anger. 'I'll have you arrested – guard, guard!'

Bill and Jim paused again. It did sound like English, but it was too much of the King's for them.

'Keep yer ruddy mouth shut!' And Jim struck Sir Mohan flat on the face.

The engine gave another short whistle and the train began to move. The soldiers caught Sir Mohan by the arms and flung him out of the train. He reeled backwards, tripped on his bedding, and landed on the suitcase.

'Toodle-oo!'

Sir Mohan's feet were glued to the earth and he lost his speech. He stared at the lighted windows of the train going past him in quickening tempo. The tail end of the train appeared with a red light and the guard standing in the open doorway with the flags in his hands.

In the inter-class *zenana* compartment was Lachmi, fair and fat, on whose nose the diamond nose ring glistened against the station lights. Her mouth was bloated with betel saliva which she had been storing up to spit as soon as the train had cleared the station. As the train sped past the lighted part of the platform, Lady Lal spat and sent a jet of red dribble flying across like a dart.

(1948)

Biographical Notes

RUDYARD KIPLING (1865-1936): Born in Bombay, at the age of seven he left for England, but owing to poor health did not go to school until he was eleven. After studying at the United Services College, Westward Ho!, he returned to India in 1882 and worked as a journalist for the next seven years. His early works, all dealing with India, come from this period. In 1890 he left India and, except for a brief return two years later, lived the rest of his life first in the United States and then in England. The publication of his first two collections of short stories, *Plain Tales from the Hills* and *Soldiers Three* (both in 1888), made India a major theme in English literature.

FLORA ANNIE STEEL, *née* Webster, (1847-1927): Born at Harrow-on-the-Hill, she married a member of the Indian Civil Service and left for India in 1868. During the next twenty-two years she served India in various capacities and, unlike most of the Anglo-Indian ladies of the time, managed to establish relations with Indians of all classes. She returned to England in 1889 and wrote numerous novels and short stories, including a fine study of the Indian Mutiny, *On the Face of the Waters* (1896). She is equally well-known for her *Tales from the Punjab* (1894), a unique collection of authentic versions of oral legends.

SARA JEANNETTE DUNCAN (1862-1922): Born in Brantford, Ontario, Canada, and educated there and in Toronto, after a spell at teaching she turned to journalism and began writing for the Toronto *Globe* and the Montreal *Star*. In 1891 she married Charles Everard Cotes and went to live in India where her husband was the curator of the Indian Museum at Calcutta. Although she was not primarily interested in portraying the Indians, her novels give a brilliant insight into the lives of the British in India. Among these are *The Simple Adventures of a Memsahib* (1893), *His Honour and a Lady* (1896) and *The Burnt Offering* (1909).

ALICE PERRIN (1867-1934): Born in India, the daughter of General John Innes Robinson of the Bengal Cavalry, she was educated in England. She married a medical officer of the Indian Civil Service and spent some twenty-five years in India. Almost all her work (she

wrote some twenty books) deals with India and the best reveals a
gentle irony and humour rarely found in Anglo-Indian writing. Her
most successful books are her collections of short stories, *East of
Suez* (1901) and *Red Records* (1906). After her return from India she
lived in Switzerland until her death.

OTTO ROTHFELD (1876-1932): Educated at George Watson's
College, Edinburgh, and Merton College, Oxford. He joined the
Indian Civil Service and was for some time president of the An-
thropological Society, Bombay, and also of the Civil and Military
Examination Committee of the province. After retirement he lec-
tured on India in the United States under the auspices of the British
Consular authorities. His two works of fiction are *Indian Dust* (1906)
and *Life and Its Puppets* (1911). He alwo wrote a sociological study,
Women in India.

LIONEL JAMES (1871-1955): Educated at Cranleigh, he was
Reuter's special correspondent during the Chitral campaign (1894-
95) and the Mohmund, Malakand and Tirah campaigns (1897-98).
He joined the staff of *The Times* in 1899 and remained with the
newspaper until 1913. Between 1915-18 he was with the B.E.F. in
France and Italy, and later worked in a variety of jobs until his
retirement from public service in 1946. Of the small portion of his
writing which deals with India, most notable is his collection of
stories, *Side-Tracks and Bridle-Paths* (1909).

EDMUND CANDLER (1874-1926): A graduate of Emmanuel
College, Cambridge, he served as a correspondent to the *Daily Mail*
and *The Times* and travelled widely in the East. After a stint as
Classical Master in a school in Darjeeling, private tutor to a rajah and
journalist of a Bengal newspaper, he became the principal of
Mohimara College in Patiala. In 1920 he was appointed Director of
Publicity to the Punjab Government, a job he held for only two
years, partly because he offended Gandhi. His novel *Siri Ram,
Revolutionist* (1912), which led to a considerable debate in England,
marks the emergence of Indian nationalists as major characters in
English fiction.

LEONARD WOOLF (1880-1969): British historian, novelist and
political essayist, he was born in London and educated at Trinity
College, Cambridge. He joined the Ceylon Civil Service and served

in Ceylon from 1904 to 1911. Returning to England, he married Virginia Stephen (better known by her married name) and became a regular contributor to liberal papers and magazines. With his wife, he founded the Hogarth Press in 1917 and the two published most of their own books themselves. His fictional work includes a novel, *The Village in the Jungle* (1913), and *Stories of the East* (1915).

JOHN EYTON (1890-): A popular writer about the Indian scene in the 1920s. The influence of Kipling is apparent in his novel *Bulbulla* (1928), which follows the general pattern of *Kim*. His best work, however, is his collection *The Dancing Fakir and Other Stories*, first published by Longman, Green, London, in 1922, and reprinted by Books for Library Press, New York, in 1969.

MAUD DIVER *née* Marshall, (1867-1945): Born at Murree, a hill-station in the Himalayas, and sent by her parents to England for schooling, she returned to India at the age of sixteen. She married a subaltern in the Royal Warwickshire Regiment and soon after left for England again. It was in England that she began her writing career with short stories. Her first novel, which was an immediate success, was *Captain Desmond V.C.* (1906). Her Indian novels were slow to catch on, but she eventually won a fair degree of popularity with romantic tales such as *Ships of Youth* (1931).

KATHERINE MAYO (1868-1940): Born of American parents in Ridgeway, Pennsylvania, she was educated at private schools in Boston and Cambridge, Massachusetts. She made her mark in the United States with *Justice to All* (1917), but it was *Mother India* (1927), a sensational study of child marriage in India, with which her name is chiefly associated. Several rebuttals were published by indignant Indians, and *Volume Two* (1931) was Miss Mayo's documented defence of her statements. Her collection of stories *Slaves of the Gods* (1929) was, she claimed, 'not fiction, although cast in fiction form'.

GEORGE ORWELL (1903-1950): Born (real name Eric Blair) in Motihari, Bengal, and educated at Eton, he went to Burma in 1922 and served with the Indian Imperial Police until 1927, an experience which is reflected in his first and only novel on the Empire, *Burmese Days* (1934). On his return to Europe he lived for the first few years in poverty in Paris and London. In 1937 he went to Spain to fight for the Republicans, a brilliant account of which appears in *Homage to Catalonia* (1938). He is best known for his political satires, *Animal Farm* (1945) and *Nineteen Eighty Four* (1949).

JOSEPH HITREC (1912-1972): Born and educated in Zagreb, Yugoslavia, he started working for a British advertising agency in London in 1935. He was later transferred to the agency's branch offices in Calcutta and Bombay and remained in India until 1946. From 1946 he lived in New York, becoming a naturalised citizen of the United States in 1951. Apart from several short stories, he wrote two novels about India, *Son of the Moon* (1948) and *Angel of Gaiety* (1953). The former was awarded the Harper Prize.

CHRISTINE WESTON (1904-): Born in Unao in the United Provinces, the daughter of a naturalised Englishman in the Indian Imperial Police, she was educated at a convent school in the hills, and lived in India until her marriage to an American in 1923. She started publishing in the early forties, and her novel *Indigo* (1944) has been compared to E.M. Forster's *A Passage to India* for its authenticity and understanding of the complexity of the Indian problem.

KHUSHWANT SINGH (1915-): Novelist, historian and editor of the *Hindustan Times*, he was born in Hadali (now in Pakistan). After university education in Delhi and Lahore, he went to London and obtained his Bar-at-Law in 1938. He published his first fictional work, *The Mark of Vishnu and Other Stories*, in 1950, but it was *Train to Pakistan* (1955) which brought him into prominence. His writing includes some authoritative studies of Sikh history and religion. He has held visiting academic appointments at Oxford, Princeton and Syracuse.

Glossary of Indian Words and Phrases

Angrez: Englishman

Anna: coin, one-sixteenth of a rupee

Ari, Arre: oh!

Arrack: native spirituous liquor

Ayah: nanny; lady's maid

Azan: Muslim call to prayer

Baba: respectful address for an old man or a father

Babu: learned man; also used derogatively for an Indian clerk who wrote in English

Backsheesh: tip; present

Badmash: rogue

Baipari: agent; tradesman

Baisakh: Bengali name for the month corresponding to the period April 14 – May 14

Bayt Allah: house of God; mosque

Behosh: delirious

Bigah: land measure, usually more than an acre

Boxwallah: door-to-door salesman

Brahman: highest caste among Hindus

Bunnia: shopkeeper; member of the merchant class

Chalo: let's go; move

Chapatti: Indian pancake; unleavened bread

Charpoy: light wooden string bed

Chatti: round earthenware storage vessel

Chirag: oil lamp

Chokidar: watchman

Chupkan: native Indian frock-coat

Chur: sandbank or sandy spit of land

Dah: heavy knife

Dhoolie: covered litter

Dhoti: loin-cloth worn by Indian men

Dohai Sahheb-ka: I beseech your Honour

Dongi: canoe made of sheaths of plantain leaves

Durbar: royal court, levée

Ek chota: small tot of whisky

Ekka: two-wheeled pony cart

Fakeer, Fakir: Muslim religious mendicant

Ferash: medium-sized tree found in Northern India

Feringhee: European; literally foreigner

Gani: saintly Muslim

Ghari: cart; generally a horse-cart

Ghariwallah: driver of a *ghari*

Gol-patta: small palm tree

Haj: pilgrimage, especially to Mecca

Haji: Muslim who has been, or is, on a pilgrimage

Hauli: kind of fruit drink

Hental: large palm tree

Huzoor: Sire; also, abstractly, the Government

Jai Kali: victory to the goddess Kali

Jauhar: courting of death by wives of Hindu warriors to prevent themselves falling into enemy hands

Jehannum: Hell

Jubba: long outer coat worn by Muslims

Kaabah: the central shrine in Mecca, object of the pilgrimage

Kafila: caravan

Khal: creek or channel connecting rivers

Khansamah: cook

Khutbah: prayer or discourse pronounced in a mosque during Friday service

Koi hai: is anyone there?

Lakh: a hundred thousand

Lathi: bamboo pole; any strong stick

Log: people

Lungi: head-cloth; more commonly a coloured check worn by Muslims as a *dhoti*

Mahadev: the Great God; a name of Shiva

Mahajan: money-lender

Mai: mother; often prefixed to a name to denote respect

Maidan: open meadow or plain

Malik: headman

Mallah: boatman

Manjhi: captain of a boat

Mantra: sacred text; prayer or incantation

Mela: fair

Mem-sahib: wife of a Sahib; lady

Moulvie: Muslim religious teacher

Mullah: Muslim title of one learned in sacred law

Nullah: river-bed

Pandit: learned man

Pasi: a lawless, semi-Hinduised tribe

Pesh-bundi: Advance consideration; a euphemism for bribe

Pie: coin of the lowest denomination

Pipa: earthenware jar

Pir: Muslim saint

Puggaree: turban

Punkah: fan, usually suspended from ceiling and pulled by hand

Purdah: curtain screening women's quarters

Pushtu: language of the Afghans

Ram!: invocation of the Hindu god Rama

Ryot: peasant; cultivating tenant

Şadhu: Hindu who has renounced worldly possessions

Safa (and *Marwah*): hills near Mecca, sacred to pilgrims

Salaam: Indian salutation with bow of head and right palm raised to forehead

Sarishtidar: clerk who administers oaths, records, depositions, etc

Sarkar, Sircar, Sirkar: The Government; high government officials

Serai: lodgings for travellers

Shab-i-barat: the night of record, a festival held on the 14th Shaban, when the fates of the unborn souls are supposed to be registered

Shulas: air-shoots projecting from the roots in a forest

Siringhi: stringed musical instrument

Sirus: large, flowering, thick-foliaged tree

Soubadar-Major: chief Indian officer of company of sepoys

Sraddha: ceremony of propitiatory prayers and offerings to the spirits of departed ancestors

Surti: one from Surat, a city of Gujarat State

Syce: groom

Takbir: the expression '*Allahu Akbar*' — God is very great

Tamasha: spectacle; entertainment

Tarka Devi: the daughter of the demon Sunda, who was herself turned into a demon and avenged herself by ravaging the countryside

Tehsil: district; administrative unit of a district

Thana: police station

Topi: sun-hat

Tonga: light two-wheeled carriage

Ulank: type of small cargo boat

Vakil: agent, man of business

Vizier: high state official

Wahabeeism: Muslim reformist movement, noted for its strictness

Yunani: system of Indian medicine of Islamic origin

Zemzem: sacred well near the *Kaabah* at Mecca

Zemindar: well-to-do landowner

Zenana, Zenan-khana: secluded female quarters of residence; carriage reserved for women

Zilla: district; adminstrative division of territory